shattered dreams

THE SHATTERED HALO SERIES
BOOK 1

PATRICE ASHLEY

Cover Art: Love Lee Creative

Editing: Owl Eyes Proofs and Edits

❋ Created with Vellum

For everyone trying to find themselves. I believe in you.

contents

prologue

BELLE

FIVE YEARS AGO

"I DON'T KNOW ABOUT THIS," I mutter to myself in the mirror. The dress I'm wearing hugs all my curves and leaves little to the imagination.

"You look hot, babe! Kai's pants are going to fall right off!"

"Jesus hell, Willa! Have you ever heard of knocking?" I exclaim while pressing my hand to my rapidly beating heart.

"You mean like the way you want to knock boots with Kai?" Willa says, snickering to herself.

"I have no idea what you're talking about," I say, turning back to the mirror just in time to see my entire face turn red. I've been in love with Malikai Irons for as long as I can remember. He's two years older than me and one of our best friends. So he's off limits, no matter how much I want him. That doesn't stop Willa from teasing me about it.

"Yes, I do. You marry Kai, and I'll marry Ezra. Best

friends married to super-hot twins. I see no flaw in this plan," Willa says with her signature smirk.

"Except the part where neither of them is interested in us, and Cal would kill both me and Kai. Possibly you just for fun," I say, returning her smirk.

Willa rolls her eyes before plopping herself down on my bed. "Callahan can try, but he'd never succeed. I can take his prickly ass any day."

I scoff while fixing my hair. It's usually curly, but I straightened it for tonight. The dark brown of my hair, mixed with the black of my dress and the paleness of my skin, makes me look like a witch, and I kind of love it. I add a smokey eye to make my dark blue eyes pop and some deep red lipstick to finish the look.

"You and my brother fight more than anyone I know. He's not even prickly," I say, turning to look at Willa. I frown when I notice what she's wearing. "We match."

"No. I'm blonde, Bellamy," she says in complete seriousness.

"Willa! We're wearing the same dress!" I complain. It's not the first time this has happened. We have similar taste in clothes, but I told her what I was planning to wear to the party tonight ahead of time.

"No, we aren't. Mine has a slit in the leg and yours doesn't," she says, gesturing to the slit in her dress.

I sigh, not willing to continue this argument. "At least tell me you brought different shoes."

"Nope. Fuck-me-heels or nothing," she says, shimmying her shoulders as she heads for my bedroom door.

"Willa, we're going to a party in the woods. Heels are a bad idea," I try.

"Maybe I can get Ezra to carry me," she says with a wink. I roll my eyes again. She doesn't have a thing for Ezra. The five of us — Willa, Cal, Kai, Ezra, and me — have been friends since we were kids. We grew up in the same neighborhood and our parents are all close. Willa is just trying to be a good friend by pretending so that my crush on Kai isn't as awkward. Sometimes I love her for it, right now it's annoying me.

"You two are going to be late for your own graduation party," Cal says from the couch where he's been waiting for us. My brother is tall, with hair just as dark as mine, but his eyes are dark brown like our dad's.

"It's not our graduation party, Cal. You of all people know that." I argue. Cal, along with Kai and Ezra, graduated from high school two years ago. Willa and I just graduated yesterday. Every year, the returning college kids throw a party for the graduating seniors. It's always in the woods and usually broken up by the police after a few hours, but it's fun while it lasts.

"It's for graduating seniors. That's you. Hence, your party." Cal stands and walks to the front door, gesturing for us to follow him.

"Where are the hot twins?" Willa asks Cal.

"Probably there already," Cal grumbles before getting into the driver's seat of his beat-up truck. I slide into the middle seat between Willa and Cal.

We formed a band a few years ago called Shattered Halo. It was just for fun, and we still play together when the guys are home from college. Willa plays the drums, and Cal is the lead singer. They disagree on almost everything, causing the once fun band practice to be more of a nightmare. Kai plays the guitar while Ezra plays bass. I play anything with keys. Piano, keyboard, synthesizer. Things like that.

"Ezra remembered my keyboard, right?" I ask Cal. We practice in the Irons' garage, so I needed Ezra to bring it for me. We're playing at the party tonight, and I'm nervous. We've never played in front of anyone other than our parents before. But Cal thought it would be a good opportunity and open more doors for us. His passion is music. Same goes for the twins. Willa loves music, but she loves attention more. I love writing music and singing. My voice isn't as good as Cal's or even Kai's, but I enjoy adding what I can for vocals.

"Yes, Belle. For the thousandth time, Ezra has your keyboard. He probably already set it up too," Cal says with a sigh. He's nervous too. I can tell because he didn't comment on how tight and short my dress is. Usually he would try to make me go change into something that covered me from neck to ankles.

The moment we pull into the clearing and park next to the other cars, I'm pushing Willa out the door so I can get to our instruments. The need to go over the sheet music and check the set list is overwhelming any excitement I had about being here tonight.

I don't even register any of the people I pass as I make my way to the instruments under a canopy of trees. My keyboard is off to the left side, already set up with my sheet music, like my brother suggested would be the case. Willa's drums are at the back and Kai's guitar along with Ezra's bass are to the right of Cal's mic.

"Does Cal know you're wearing that?"

I spin from where I was standing in front of my keyboard

to see Ezra smirking at me. His black hair is cut short, and his blue eyes are bright, even in the dimness of the trees. Ezra and I have always been extremely close. Even though him and Kai are identical twins, I've never had a crush on him the way I do on Kai.

"He drove me here, but I think his nerves blinded him because he didn't say anything," I tell him. "Watch out for Willa. She's on the prowl," I tell him jokingly.

Ezra gives me a half smile, and I know something's up. Those two make jokes about dating each other all the time. They always have.

"What's wrong, Ez?" I ask. He looks at me and seems to assess something. "You know you can tell me anything."

"Come with me," he says, holding out his hand. I take it, and he leads me through the trees. I wave and say hello to classmates and my brother's friends on the way, but Ezra ignores them all.

Summer Bay, Maine, is a small town, and everyone knows everyone. I'm a little surprised Ezra is acting the way he is because I know his mom is going to hear about it tomorrow. Adira Irons is strict and no nonsense. The twins never get away with anything, especially being rude.

Ezra leads me into a thick copse of trees and looks around quickly. The hand holding mine is suddenly sweaty, and it's making me worry. The smell of a decade's worth of decaying leaves with the crunch of sticks under our feet overwhelms my senses. It's so quiet this far into the woods, and my brain is running wild trying to figure out what Ezra would need to talk to me about.

"I need to tell someone before I explode," Ezra says in a small voice.

"You're my best friend, Ez. You can tell me. Whatever it is, we can figure it out together," I say to him, squeezing the hand I'm holding and reaching for the other one. He gives it to me and takes a deep breath.

"I'm seeing someone," he lets out quickly.

"That's great!" I say, genuinely happy for him. "Who is she?"

"He. I'm gay, Belle," he whispers while looking at his feet.

I'm shocked for a split second and only because I know some of Ezra's old flings and they're definitely of the female variety. Once the shock wears off, I throw my arms around my friend and hug him as tightly as I can.

"I love you, and I'm sorry if this is a part of you that you feel you need to whisper quietly in the woods instead of shouting from the rooftops," I say into his chest, since that's where my head is resting, and I don't want to let him go yet.

"You're the first person I've told," he says as he squeezes me back just as tight. I feel his shoulders relax and the stiffness leave his body.

"Our group will love and support you, no matter what. We'll fight anyone who doesn't," I say confidently, knowing how much we all love him. I'm surprised he told me before Kai, but I decide to let that go for now. I'm sure he has his reasons, and we don't need to get into that in the middle of the woods before we perform in front of a crowd for the first time.

"I know that. I'm not worried about them. I'll tell everyone tonight. I just really needed to tell someone now, and you were the first person I wanted to know."

I smile and look up at him. "Who is he? Do I know him?"

Ezra smiles the first genuine smile I've seen from him in years, and it takes seeing it just now for me to realize that.

"You know him. It's Maverick Wolfe," he says, still smiling.

"Shut up! Mav's gay?" I almost shout before catching myself and turning it into a whisper. Ezra just laughs. Maverick is a year younger than Ezra and a year older than me. He graduated last year, which means he's probably here tonight. I don't know him well, but he always seemed nice. His father has a reputation around town for being a prick. He's also a state judge and is running for some political thing. I can't imagine how hard it was to grow up with someone like that.

"He's bi. But Belle, I love him," Ezra says, and I can see the truth of it in his face. He's a man in love, and I'm so happy for him I start to tear up.

"Please don't cry. I know you had baby names picked out for our future children. There are so many fish in the sea. You'll find one that likes your lady bits someday," Ezra says while laughing.

I smack his arm. "You're so funny, Ez. You know these are happy tears. I'm an ugly crier when I'm sad."

"You're not wrong. You look like the evil witch from *Snow White* when she turns up with that apple," he jokes.

"I hate you," I say, crossing my arms.

"You don't," he says before kissing me on the top of my head and throwing his arm around my shoulders. "We should get back. We're playing soon."

I nod and let him lead me back to our instruments.

"Tell me about him," I say as we walk.

"He's amazing Belle. He's better than I am on the bass,"

he chuckles and shakes his head. "Mav is kind and funny. He's loyal to a fault. He's just…" Ezra sighs, and I can see the hearts in his eyes. "He's my person."

"I'm so happy that you're happy," I tell him, and he squeezes me tight.

All the happiness I'm feeling vanishes, and anxiety takes its place the moment we return to the clearing. My anxiety increases when I see the amount of people standing in front of our setup. Kai is tuning his guitar while Willa twirls her drumsticks. Cal is talking to a group of girls that are shamelessly flirting with him. Ezra pulls me to my keyboard and gives my shoulders one more squeeze before he heads to tune his bass.

I walk over to Kai, wanting the hug he always gives me when he sees me. He looks up, but instead of the warmth I usually feel coming from him, his blue eyes are as cold as ice. My steps falter, and I stop in front of him.

"Hey," he says before turning away from me and continuing to tune his guitar.

I hold back the tears that instantly want to fall at the indifferent tone in his voice. I saw him yesterday, and he was the same warm and friendly Kai he always is. I don't know what happened between then and now for him to act this way. Maybe this is just how he's handling being nervous about playing tonight.

"I, uh — I just came for a hug," I mutter, almost embarrassed. I've never had to ask for or explain a hug to him before.

He looks at me again, the same cold expression still plastered on his handsome face. His shaggy black hair is falling in his eyes and making him look like a model. An angry model. Kai nods and quickly gives me a stiff, one-arm hug. He always gives me hugs I melt into. Hugs that take away every anxiety and sadness. I don't understand what's different.

My body has run through a gauntlet of emotions in such a short amount of time that it panics. My breathing gets heavy and difficult, my tongue feels like it weighs more than an elephant, and my palms are sweating. Kai doesn't notice since he's back to tuning his guitar again, but I see the moment Willa does.

She drops her drumsticks and quickly walks over to me, pulling me away from Kai and behind a tree.

"Breathe, Bellamy," she says as she breathes deeply in front of me, gesturing for me to copy her. I do as she says and as my breathing calms back down, I cry. "What happened?" she asks quietly.

"I'm really nervous about playing in front of people," I say between sobs.

"What did Kai do?" she asks, not fooled by my excuse.

"Nothing," I mutter.

"What did he do, Belle?" she asks again, glaring over my shoulder at where I'm assuming Kai is standing.

"Nothing, Willa. I went to hug him, and he looked angry with me and then gave me a hug he gives to people he doesn't actually want to hug. It was weird and with my nerves being all over the place because we're playing tonight, I just panicked," I tell her honestly.

Willa keeps glaring for a few more seconds before she turns her eyes on me. "He better apologize later, or my heel is meeting his ass."

I laugh at how serious she is before hugging her. "Thank you for calming me down."

"Always, babe. Now let's go play so hard everyone's panties drop!" she yells before grabbing my hand and pulling me back towards the crowd.

My hands are shaking as we wait for Willa to knock her drumsticks together to start the set. We're playing a set of ten covers tonight. Nothing original and nothing we haven't played hundreds of times before.

Once the crowd hears Willa count, a deafening silence falls over the woods. I hear the last smack of her sticks and play the first note. The moment the music leaves my fingertips, I'm in the zone. The crowd fades away behind the notes and the sound of Cal's smooth voice.

Before I know it, we've played all ten songs. I'm sweaty and a little shaky from the adrenaline. The crowd is screaming and clapping, and a group of girls are throwing bras at the guys.

"Classy," I mutter under my breath.

"You guys sounded great."

I look away from Kai, who's smiling while holding a bright pink bra he caught, to find Maverick in front of me.

"Thanks, Mav," I tell him. He's looking between me and an uncomfortable-looking Ezra who was just hit in the face with the biggest bra I've ever seen. I snicker as I watch him try to hide the look of disgust on his face.

"Ladies really love musicians, huh?" he asks, his hands in the pockets of his jeans. I tilt my head and get a good look at him. Maverick is tall, not as tall as my guys, but he still towers over me. His hair is short and a light brown color that complements his honey eyes. He's attractive and seems really sweet. I can see why Ezra fell for him.

I hug him. I can feel the surprise in the jolt his body gives before he wraps his arms around me. "Treat him well. He deserves it," I whisper.

Maverick pulls back and looks at me, definitely not aware Ezra told anyone about them. He smiles and nods before hugging me again. "I will, I promise."

Ezra comes over to us and sweeps me up into his arms. I giggle and hug his neck. "I told you we'd be great," he says.

"You were right. As always," I say.

"Did you hear that, Mav? I want it in writing and notarized," Ezra jokes. I can see the twinkle in his eyes as he looks at Maverick.

Maverick's phone vibrates in his hand. He looks at it as his face falls and all the color leaves his cheeks. "I have to go," he says, looking at Ezra.

"Are you serious? You can't. You're bailing on our plan?" Ezra asks him angrily.

"I have to. I'm sorry. I'll explain later. I just . . . I have to go," Maverick says before rushing away.

"Fuck!" Ezra yells before stomping off. I quickly follow him, grabbing his arm to stop him.

"Ez, talk to me. What was that?" I ask, looking around to make sure no one else followed us.

"We were supposed to come out tonight. Together. We were going to tell all our friends we're together. And he just left me," Ezra says as he looks up into the night sky.

"Maybe he had a good reason," I say.

Ezra looks at me like I betrayed him. "You're on his side?" he asks in a voice so still that it scares me. "His dad caught us making out and was disgusted. He probably decided I wasn't worth it."

"No, I'm on your side. Always. I just think you should talk first. I saw how you looked at each other. I don't think he just left you or even cares if his backwards thinking father is disgusted by you," I try to tell him, but he just scoffs and walks away from me.

Ezra is the most emotional out of our group, and I know better than to keep trying when he's like this. So instead of following him, I walk back to find Willa and have a good time. He'll calm down and we'll talk about it later.

"Have you seen Ezra?"

I look up from the rock I'm sitting on and nursing a warm beer in my hands.

"Not recently," I tell Kai. I mingled with Willa for an hour and then made my way to this rock so I could look out over the river. I can only take so much social interaction before my battery drains.

"Are you going to help me find him? Or are you planning on sitting here by yourself until Cal drags you home?" he asks with more anger than I've ever heard from him.

"What is your problem, Kai?" I yell as I jump up to my feet. "You've been angry with me all night, and I don't understand what I did to earn it."

Kai takes a deep breath and stares at me. Then he sighs. "You didn't do anything. I'm just in my head. I'm sorry,

Belle," he says, pulling me into one of his warm hugs. The kind I was looking for earlier, and he denied me. I melt right into him like I always do. His smell of mint and sweat surrounds me and calms me like it always does. Damn him, I wanted to be mad at him.

"I forgive you," I say as he pulls away and runs his fingers through his messy hair.

"Always and forever?" he asks. I'm annoyed with him, but that makes me smile. We've been saying it to each other since we were kids. It's been our easy way of saying we'll always be there for each other, no matter what.

"Always and forever," I agree.

"Can you help me find Ezra? I haven't seen him in hours, and he isn't answering his phone."

I frown and look around. Ezra was angry and upset when I saw him earlier, but he usually gets over things quickly. Now I'm worried I let him go off and get lost in the woods. I tell Kai where I saw his brother last, leaving out the part about him arguing with Maverick. As far as I know, I'm still the only one that knows about them.

"Which way did he go?" Kai asks. I lead him to where we were, seeing Cal and Willa looking for him along the way and signaling them to follow us.

We pull out our phones and use the flashlights on them to look around as we call his name. Kai keeps trying him on his cell with no luck.

"Where is he?" I ask anyone and no one.

We keep searching, and as the minutes pass, the worry increases. Cal runs back to find more people to help and before I know it, we have an entire search party looking.

"Do you have Maverick's number?" I whisper to Willa.

"Maverick Wolfe?" she asks, confused. I don't have it, but she might. Willa talks to significantly more people than I do.

She nods and hands me her phone. I type his number into mine and call.

"Hello?" he answers on the second ring.

"Mav, it's Bellamy. Is Ezra with you?" I whisper into the phone. Willa is still staring at me, confused and now suspicious, but thankfully she keeps her mouth shut.

"No. I haven't seen him since I had to leave," he says, and I can hear the concern in his voice.

"Mav, we can't find him. We've been looking for over an hour. He was upset after you left and stormed off. He won't answer his phone."

"Fuck! I'll look everywhere I can think of. Keep me updated," he pleads.

"I will. I promise," I tell him before hanging up.

"Tell me later?" Willa asks as we continue searching and yelling Ezra's name. I nod to show her I will.

We search until the sun rises. The police were called, and they've started searching the woods with us. Our parents are driving around town and calling local hospitals.

I'm a mess. I feel guilty for not going after him when he was upset. He needed me, and I let him walk away from us. Now he's missing.

Maverick has checked in with me every hour. He has had no luck either. Kai's worry has turned into rage, with everyone keeping their distance. His voice is hoarse from screaming his brother's name for hours on end, but it hasn't stopped him. Cal, Willa, and I are right by his side, throats equally sore. We all have blisters that formed and then burst and are now bleeding, but we don't stop. We can't stop. Ezra is one of us, part of our family, and we need to find him.

Ezra has been missing for three months. We're all supposed to be leaving for college next week but none of us wants to. The police called off the search after twenty-four hours, claiming that Ezra was a runaway. The officer who spoke to his family told them that since Ezra was over eighteen and there was no evidence of foul play, they just need to accept that he went off on his own. Our group still goes out to look. We've asked around every bus station, airport, train station, and hospital in fifty miles. He wouldn't just run away like this.

I'm sitting on my bed, looking around my room. The floor is old and worn, the varnish having come off the wood a long time ago. The pink paint on the walls is dull and all my furniture has chips or stains from nail polish. My parents aren't wealthy, and the used furniture and decaying house are evidence of that. I used to sit here, excited about new adventures. Now I feel like I'm sitting on the edge of a knife and no matter what direction I go in; I'm going to fall.

"Belle? Where are you?" Cal yells. I get up and head down the creaky stairs to see what he wants.

"I'm here. What's up?" I ask him when I find him in the kitchen.

"We got offered a record deal," he says. I watch as his emotions flicker from intense excitement to utter devastation and back again.

"What? How?" I ask, utterly confused. We only ever played the one time in the woods.

"I submitted a tape of us when we did that song you wrote," Cal says sheepishly. We record ourselves at practice so we can watch it back and tweak what we need to. Or at least I thought that was the only reason.

I wrote a song and showed it to them. Ezra wrote the chords. Kai and I sang it together. Then we practiced it until it sounded perfect. I wrote that song about my feelings for Kai. No one else was ever supposed to hear it. I feel betrayed but stop myself from voicing that. Cal has no idea that's who my song is about. I told everyone I wrote it after reading a romance novel that didn't have a happy ending.

"You submitted a tape of us performing 'Shattered Dreams?'" I ask again, dumbfounded.

"Yeah. I didn't think anything would come of it, but they want to sign us," Cal says, looking almost hopeful for a split second.

"But Ezra..." I say.

"I know."

"Does anyone else know?" I ask.

"Not yet. Kai and Willa are on their way over to talk about it," he says.

I sit on the old saggy couch in the living room feeling numb. I barely hear my brother tell our friends about the record label wanting to sign the band. Numbers are thrown out, but I don't register them.

I look at Kai to see him staring at me. His gaze burns, and I look away. Things have been strange between us. Every time I try to ask him about it, he just says he's stressed. Which I'm sure he is, but it started before Ezra disappeared.

"I'm out," I announce, standing up.

"What? What do you mean? We can't miss the opportunity!" Cal exclaims, looking at me like I've lost my mind. And maybe I have.

"Then don't. You don't need me to do this," I tell him.

"You wrote the song they want!" he yells.

"Keep the song, Callahan! I'm not taking that from you! This isn't what I want. I can't do this without Ezra," I plead with him to understand. "I just. . . I can't, Cal."

"Let her go, Cal. She said she doesn't want to be with us anymore. Just leave it," Kai says without a hint of remorse. Like it's not his brother that's missing and should be here signing this deal too.

I look at him, the man I've loved my whole life, and see a stranger looking back at me. He's looking at me like I betrayed him, but I can't help feeling like he's the one betraying his brother.

"What about Ezra? You're just going to do this without him?" I ask, wanting Kai to hurt as much as he's hurting me. I watch as his spine stiffens, and his eyes grow impossibly colder.

"Ezra is gone. You heard the cops. He ran. Just like you're doing."

"What the fuck, Kai!" Willa yells, leaping to her feet from where she was sitting next to me. I never told anyone that Ezra was angry when he stormed off. I couldn't answer why he was if I did. Ezra wanted to tell them about his sexuality and the man he fell for himself, and that wasn't something I was going to take from him. But part of me wonders if Kai knows or suspects something. It's the only thing I can think of to justify his behavior towards me.

Kai ignores her, keeping his eyes trained on me. He's never looked at me with anger before and now that's all I see.

"So much for always and forever," he says through clenched teeth.

"No. Always and forever means exactly that. You know how to get in touch with me when you're done being an asshole."

I don't know who he is anymore, and I'm not sure I know who I am on my own. But I'm about to find out.

I turn on my heel and head to my room to finish packing. They can go off and become famous rock stars if they want. I'm going to college like I planned, and I'll keep looking for Ezra even if they've all given up.

one

BELLE

NOW

MY HANDS GRIP the steering wheel harder, trying to stop the shaking. I glance at the rearview mirror for the millionth time in the last four hours.

"He's not following me. He doesn't know I left," I tell myself over and over again.

I glance at the clock on the dashboard of my car. It reads 4:45 PM. He may not know now, but he's about to find out.

Brad was so mad this morning. I forgot to set my alarm, so I didn't wake up in time to make him his breakfast.

My eyes fly open when I feel a sharp pain in my skull.

"Wake up, you lazy fucking cunt!" Brad screams as he pulls me from our bed by my hair. I cry out as he tosses me to the floor and leers over me.

"I'm sorry!" I don't even know what I'm apologizing for, but I've learned it's better to grovel. Questioning him makes him angrier.

"You're a useless piece of shit! You think you can sleep all day

while I work and pay for everything?" Spit flies in my face as he screams.

I stand with my hands out in front of me, trying to placate him. "I'm sorry. I must have forgotten to set my alarm. I'll make your breakfast right now."

I move towards the kitchen, but I'm stopped by Brad's fist connecting with my cheek. He hit me so hard that my head ricochet off the bedroom wall, and I collapse back down to the cold floor.

Brad keeps yelling about my worthlessness as his foot connects with my ribs again and again until I black out.

I turn the radio up, hoping music can drown out the terror of the memories overtaking my heart.

"We are lucky enough to sit down with the members of Shattered Halo, Callahan Griffin, Willa Prince, Maverick Wolfe, and Malikai Irons to talk about their upcoming European Tour," the radio DJ says.

"Of course, they're the first thing I hear," I grumble to myself.

Mav took Ezra's place as the band's bassist. From what Cal told me, he was reluctant about it, but eventually agreed when Kai spoke to him.

"Thank you for having us! We're so excited to meet all our sexy fans across the pond!" Willa's voice comes through. Her tone is playful and flirty. I miss her the most. We still talk, but I haven't seen her in months. Brad didn't like her. He always said she was a bad influence on me and forced us apart. Unfortunately, it took me too long to realize what he was doing.

My phone rings over the Bluetooth in my car, and I jump so aggressively it causes me to swerve onto the dirt embankment. I right the car before pulling over. My brother's name flashes across the console screen. I take a deep breath before I answer.

"Hey big brother," I say, trying to sound normal.

It doesn't work.

"Belle? What's wrong?" Cal asks immediately. Our relationship is in a weird place and has been since I decided not to be a part of Shattered Halo. But Cal is still my brother, and he'll worry about me no matter what.

"Nothing, I —"

"Bellamy. Don't lie," Cal demands in a low voice that brokers no argument.

I sigh and gather what little strength I have. "I left," I whisper.

Cal is quiet for a long time before he speaks again. "Where are you?" he asks in a much gentler tone.

I look around for a road sign or mile marker of any variety and only see trees. "I don't know. I got in the car and drove."

I hear his loud sigh on the other end, and I close my eyes, preparing for a lecture about safety. I'm pleasantly surprised instead.

"Put my address into your phone. I'm home for another week before we go on tour. Come stay with me." It's not a request.

I look at myself in the mirror and see the black eye Brad left on my face and feel the probably broken rib every time I inhale. I want to tell Cal no, that I can handle myself. But looking and feeling the damage done to my body while trying to hide the weakness I feel in my soul, I decide to let

Cal take care of me. I don't have anyone else. I can't go home to my mom looking like this.

"Ok," I say quietly.

"Ok?" Cal asks, surprised by my easy acceptance.

"Yeah. Ok," I say again. I can tell he wants to ask more questions. Agreeing isn't like me. Especially when it comes to letting my brother take care of me.

"I love you, Belle," he says.

"I love you too," I tell him before hanging up the phone.

I cry silently as I punch in his address and head back to the small town I used to call home.

Two hours later, I'm pulling into the circular driveway of Cal's cliff-side mansion. The place is massive. It was white when he bought it, but he had it painted black almost immediately. I thought he was crazy when he told me what he was doing, but I have to admit, it looks really cool.

"Cal?" I yell as I open the red front door with the key he gave me when he bought the place years ago.

"In here!"

I follow the sound of my brother's voice, finding him propped on a barstool in his massive kitchen. I stop in my tracks when I notice the large man sitting next to him.

"Kai," I whisper. His head whips around and his eyes land on mine. The always messy black hair on his head is now longer and curly. I've seen him a few times over the years, but we never got back to the place we were when we were younger. A wedge came between us the night Ezra disappeared and has only increased in size.

I watch Kai's eyes go from surprise to anger the moment he notices the bruising under my eye. He stands quickly and marches over to me. When he lifts his hands, I flinch back on instinct. I register the shock and hurt in Kai's expression before he schools his features.

"Who did this to you?" he asks, his voice a mask of deathly calm.

"I'm just clumsy," I say, my voice weak even to my ears. "I fell down the stairs on my way out of the house this morning."

Kai lifts his hand slowly and gently takes my face in his warm hand. His touch is gentle and sweet. Just like the old Kai that exists only in my memories. A tear falls from my eye, even as I will it to stop. Kai catches it with his thumb, his expression pained.

"Who did this to you?" he growls through clenched teeth.

Cal, who until now was doing something on his phone, comes charging over.

"I'm going to fucking kill him!" he screams the moment he sees my face, causing me to cower and then whimper from the pain in my ribs.

"Dude. Stop," Kai says to Cal, his hand still gently holding my face.

Cal turns to me, anger blazing in his eyes. They soften the moment he sees how distressed I am. He walks over and pulls me into his arms, causing me to yelp.

Cal lets me go immediately, and I watch as his expression mirrors the one of Kai's. Angry and calm. It's terrifying.

"Let me see," Cal says, his voice low.

"Cal, it's fine —" I start.

"Let. Me. See."

I gulp and slowly lift my shirt. I'm not afraid of my brother. He would never harm me. But he would hurt anyone else who did. And I know the moment he sees the bruises covering my torso, that's all he's going to want to do.

"Fuck!" Cal yells, and I flinch again.

"Mo chridhe," Kai whispers, his voice low and eyes pained as his hand falls from my face, and he fists it at his side. I have no idea what that means, and I'm honestly surprised by Kai's reaction to me. He's been little more than indifferent towards me. Which was an improvement on the anger he used to bring with him whenever he saw me over school breaks before the band hit it big.

"Where is he? I'm going to fucking kill him!" Cal exclaims while pacing back and forth in front of me.

"Please, Cal. Stop. I just want this to all be over," I plead with him. I wasn't going to tell him about Brad hurting me. I planned to stick to the falling story, but neither of these men will believe me. I can see in their faces that they know the truth.

"He can't get away with this, Belle," he says with forced calm.

"Who?" Kai asks Cal when it's clear I wasn't going to tell him.

"Brad Foley. Her boyfriend," Cal snarls out his name.

"Ex. I left him," I say softly.

"Not soon enough," Cal says, and I immediately start crying.

"I know I'm weak. I know I let Brad hurt me. For years he's hurt me, and no one knew. I finally got the courage to leave him, and that was only because I knew the next time would be the last. I wouldn't survive. And I'm not ready to die," I sob. I didn't mean to let all that out either, but my brother has a way of making me feel safe. Just his presence has me spilling all my secrets. Kai used to make me feel that way too.

I watch Cal's shoulders deflate as he gently takes me into his embrace, careful not to hurt my ribs. Kai's eyes are molten with rage, his hands are in fists, and the muscle in his jaw is ticking from how tightly he's clenching it.

"You're not weak, Belle," Cal whispers in my ear. "You're one of the strongest people I know. It takes a weak man to beat a woman. He just needs to control the uncontrollable and used his fists to do it. You're safe now. He'll never hurt you again. I promise."

I snuggle into my brother's embrace, letting the safety and security of being near him wash away some of the pain. I chance a glance at Kai to see his angry eyes are still on me. But for the first time in years, it's not me he's angry with. He's angry *for* me, and I take comfort in knowing that maybe I haven't lost him completely. Maybe my Kai is still in there somewhere. If he is, I'm going to find him.

two

KAI

I'M STILL PACING the length of the kitchen when Cal returns from getting Belle settled into his guest room.

I'm such a fucking idiot. I called her mo chridhe, *my heart*. The name I've always called her in my head, never out loud. I don't think she understood it. Very few people understand Scottish Gaelic in the states. Me included. But my dad was born in Scotland and knows curses and terms of endearment. Which he passed onto his sons. Curses first.

"She's coming with us," Cal says.

"Coming with us, where?" I ask, wondering if he said something else while I was mentally chastising myself.

"On tour," he says while looking at me like I'm an idiot.

"No," I say before I can stop myself. I've kept my distance from Belle for years and for good reason. It'll be impossible on nights spent on the bus with her.

"I wasn't asking," Cal says to me, his eyes filled with fury.

"This band is just as much mine as it is yours. I don't want her in my space!" I yell.

"This band is hers too! She may not perform with us, but "Shattered Dreams" is still our number one single and the song we're known for. It's still the song we're asked to perform the most, and we haven't been able to release anything as good since. You and I both know it," Cal says, stepping into my space and daring me to argue with him.

I groan and roll my eyes, trying to walk away, but Cal grabs my arm, stopping me.

"Look, I don't know what happened between you two, but it's been years. You need to get past it," he says. "You saw and heard her, Kai. She needs to come with us. I can't go anywhere with her like that. I can't risk him getting to her while we're gone."

I sigh and drop my head. "Ok," I say before jerking my arm out of his grasp and leaving the house.

I get into my car and slam my fists on the steering wheel. "Fuck!"

I've tried to forget her. Forget every smile and laugh. Forget the way she felt in my arms every time she hugged me. Forget her sweet smell. I tried to fuck her out of my system with groupies. When that didn't work, I gave them up too. Bellamy Griffin is an addiction I can't shake, even though I've never had her.

The day I got the call from my parents saying the police found Ezra's phone and a rock with blood matching his next to the river was the worst day of my life. They ruled it an accidental drowning even though they never found his body. The first person I wanted to run to was Belle. I wanted her to hold me while I mourned the loss of my twin, my brother, the other part of my soul. But instead, I drank until I couldn't feel anymore. Then I kept drinking every time that pain resurfaced. Cal put me in rehab and told me I had to get my shit together or I was out of the band.

I almost didn't care.

Almost.

But that song. The one I know she wrote about Ezra no matter what she tells people. That song is forever in my head and heart, keeping me tied to her, to him. Pulling me from the brink again and again.

I owe Belle my life in more ways than she knows. The least I can do is suck it up and let her come with us.

I take a deep breath and put my car in gear, ready to head home and finish packing. The European tour is six weeks long. Six weeks of having to watch the once fiery girl I grew up with walk around as a shell. Every minute of those six weeks is going to hurt, but I can't tell if it's me or her who is going to feel it the most.

Cal is right about the band. Belle and Ezra were the heart and soul of Shattered Halo. Belle had a way with words and Ezra felt music in his soul in a way I wish I did. We hit it big because of her words and his music. We're barely hanging on, still riding the high they deserved. The upcoming tour is just to fulfill the rest of our contract. I honestly doubt we'll be resigned.

Once I'm home, I throw my keys on the table by the door and look around. My house isn't as big or ostentatious as Cal's, but it's still huge. Huge and empty. The flooring throughout is black wood and the walls are white and gray. I was at the height of my anger and depression when I bought this place and it still reeks of it. Nothing about it is warm and inviting. Though, nothing about me is warm and inviting either.

My parents divorced after Ezra was declared dead. I haven't seen or heard from my dad since, and my mother is drowning her sorrows in pills and rum. The only people I have in my life are the band.

I walk over to the fireplace in the main room. I painted it black and stained the mantel a dark brown. It stands out against the white walls. Grabbing the picture in the middle of the mantle, I take it over to my couch and sit.

It was taken on the beach when we were in high school. Ezra has his arm slung over my shoulder. My arm is over Cal's. Belle and Willa have their arms locked around each other's waists, where they stand in front of us. We were all happy and smiling, tan from spending our summer in the sand.

Ezra and I looked so much alike that the only way people who didn't know us well could tell us apart was from how I kept my hair longer. Ezra liked his cut shorter, so he didn't have to deal with the curls. I've always embraced them.

My eyes keep going back to Belle, like they always do. The happy, smiling girl in this picture looks nothing like the sad woman I just left in her brother's kitchen.

Tossing the picture onto the cushion next to me, I lean back and sigh. "What the fuck is my problem?"

I keep letting my anger get the better of me. Anger about my brother, anger about my parents. But mostly the anger and resentment that comes from feeling like one of the most important people in my life abandoned me. I know that's not fair to put on Belle, but I keep doing it. I keep blaming her for the band's lack of success without her. Blaming her for leaving us. The worst of all is how much I blame her for not choosing me. *Like I was ever an option.*

I need to get my fucking shit together and my head on straight. I can't spend the entire tour avoiding her, and I can't continue to be angry.

Pulling up my phone, I open a new message thread with her and just stare at the blank screen.

Hey

Nope. Delete.

Can we talk?

Do I even want to talk? No. Delete.

Your ex is a piece of shit.

That's super fucking helpful, Kai. Delete.

Why?

Yeah, why? Why what? Delete.

Why did you leave? Why didn't you choose us? Why didn't you choose me? Why Ezra?

The same sense of betrayal and defeat that's been my companion for the last five years settles over me as I delete my last attempt at texting Belle.

BELLE

MY PHONE VIBRATES again in my hand as I watch text after text come in.

> BRAD
>
> Where are you? My dinner should be ready and waiting for me, but instead I come home to an empty house.
>
> Answer your fucking phone!
>
> You do not want to mess with me, Belle.
>
> You stupid cunt!
>
> I'll find you. You can't run from me!
>
> You're nothing without me!

I turn my phone off and throw it across the room, where it smashes against the wall before falling to the floor.

The door to my room flies open and a very concerned looking Cal is staring at me.

"Are you ok? What was that loud bang?" he asks, looking around.

"My phone," I say, pointing to the dent it left in the drywall.

Cal sees the damage and frowns. "Was he texting you?" he asks.

"Yeah, and I was over it," I mutter. I should apologize for ruining his house, but I don't have the energy.

"I'll get you a new phone with a new number," he says. "Do you have your car keys? I'll get your bags from your car for you."

"I left quickly. I only have my purse." I pull my knees up to my chest and rest my head on them.

"Well, that makes packing to go on tour easier," he chuckles uneasily.

My head pops up at that comment, and I glare at him.

"Don't look at me like that. I'm not leaving you here without me. You're coming with me, and I don't want to discuss it," Cal says firmly.

"I can't, Cal. I need to find a job and get on with my life."

"You can find a job when we get back. Plus, you still get residuals from your song, so it's not like you need one immediately," he says as he leans against the doorway. He looks calmer than I know he feels. He's expecting me to fight him, but there's no fight left in me.

"I don't have any money. Brad takes it. The residuals all go into his account," I say sadly, looking down at the blue comforter under me.

"What?" Cal barks.

"You don't understand, Cal. It's ok. We both made choices in our lives and unfortunately, that kept us apart."

"What does that even mean?" he asks, frustration coming off him in waves.

"Brad isolated me. He slowly took over my finances and removed my friends and family from my life. It took me too long to realize what he was doing and by the time I did, he was…" I swallow the lump in my throat. "He was trying to beat that last of my resistance out of me with his fists."

"Belle, if I had known —" Cal starts, but I hold my hand up to stop him.

"You didn't. No one did. I was embarrassed and hid it. Plus, with your schedule, we wouldn't have seen much of each other, anyway."

"I'm so sorry —"

"Stop. This isn't your fault," I say with as much finality as I can muster.

Cal looks at me for a long time before he sighs. "Fine, but we're going to the hospital and then filing a police report. I'll take you to get clothes on the way home."

"Cal…" I start to argue.

"No, Belle. This needs to be on file. You need a restraining order against him," Cal says, eyes hard. They soften a fraction before he says, "Please let me help you."

I sigh and stand, letting my brother take my hand and lead me out of the room.

It's amazing how quickly you can get in and out of hospitals and police stations when people of all genders want to sleep with your rockstar brother.

We went to the hospital, police station, phone store, and Target all in under three hours. I'd be impressed if I wasn't so grossed out.

I let Cal carry in all my bags since he insisted on buying me everything I looked at or even accidentally touched. Instead of helping, I fiddle with my new phone as I walk in the door behind him.

"Belle!"

That's all I hear before I'm plowed into, a tuft of lilac hair in my face and sniffling coming from who it's attached to.

"Willa," I say with a groan. My ribs aren't broken, but they are bruised, and her aggressive hugging isn't helping. She steps back quickly, looking horrified.

"I'm so sorry! Kai told me about your ribs, and I forgot the moment I saw you!"

"It's Kai's fault you're in my house right now?" Cal asks, only half joking.

Willa completely ignores him and hugs me again, more gently. "I hate the reason you're here, but I'm so happy you are. I missed you so much," she cries into my shoulder.

"I missed you too," I tell her, tears falling from my own eyes too. For the first time in years, I feel safe and loved.

"It's getting late, and she needs to sleep. You can visit her tomorrow," Cal says to Willa. She shoots him a glare that would have most people peeing themselves.

"She's not a zoo exhibit or a child. I don't need to set up visiting hours with her," Willa chastises. I just laugh. I missed how much they bicker.

"Willa, will you sleep with me tonight?" I ask shyly. I don't want to be alone, but I felt weird about asking my brother to sleep in my room with me.

I haven't seen Willa in a long time, and we've barely talked. Brad hated her. So instead of facing his anger, I just stopped talking to her. I'm worried she'll be upset or think it's strange that I want her with me.

"I'm not leaving your side, babe," she tells me, placing a kiss on my cheek. Then she turns and sticks her tongue out at Cal before taking my hand and leading me back to my room. I laugh as I hear Cal grumble something under his breath.

"So, what's with this outfit?" Willa asks, gesturing from my shoulders to my feet. I'm wearing khaki slacks and a powder blue blouse. "It's giving snobby soccer mom in her forties."

I'd laugh if I didn't want to cry. Willa is wearing black leggings and an oversized shirt that hangs off her shoulder. It's simple and comfy, and I wish I was wearing it. Brad would never let me dress like a "slob."

"Uh, Brad. He didn't like the way I dressed. His mom picked out my clothes," I say quietly. I'm embarrassed, my cheeks are heating, and I want to hide.

"Oh, Belle. I'm sorry. I was just teasing you."

I look at Willa and see pity there, but more strongly, I see her fire. She wants to hurt Brad just as much as Cal does. Possibly Kai too, but who knows what he feels? I know I should be appreciative that I have people in my life that love me this much, but I'm so tired. I just want to be done with everything that was my life for the last five years and figure out how to move on from it.

All the clothes and shoes I picked out today are closer to what I used to wear before I met Brad. Ripped jeans and bright shirts. Oversized hoodies that I can hide my hands in when they get cold. Funky socks and combat boots. I don't know if that style is me anymore, but it's closer than what I have been wearing.

"It's ok," I say as we enter my room and get comfortable on the bed. "Tell me what's been going on. How's the band? Any new guys in your life?"

"You're terrible at deflecting, but I'll allow it," she says as she shakes her head. That's her way of telling me she's waiting until I'm ready to talk, but I will have to talk about it. "Honestly, we're not great. The last album we put out isn't doing as well as the label hoped it would. This tour might be the end of the road for us."

"What? You're kidding. I hear your music on the radio all the time!" I'm so shocked, I just stare at Willa, catching flies with my mouth.

"You hear "Shattered Dreams." Have you heard any other songs from us?"

"I'm sure I have," I say immediately, but I don't think that's true.

"You haven't. We're just not the same without you and Ezra. The magic of us together is gone, and the label knows it. Honestly, I think they know they made a mistake agreeing to sign us without you two." Willa stares down at her hands and shakes her head.

"I don't know what to say." Cal never told me any of this when I talked to him on the phone over the years.

"To answer your question about my dating life, no. No new guys in my life. I've been enjoying myself," she says with a small smile. *Talk about deflecting.* "What about you? What's your job like?"

"Oh. Um. Brad made me quit my job." I avoid looking at

her. The embarrassment that comes with this situation keeps hitting me, and I hate it.

"Hey. Look at me, Belle," Willa insists. I chance a look and see the fire back in my friend's eyes. "He was a manipulative piece of garbage. Stop feeling embarrassed about what he did to you. He should be embarrassed that he's still breathing."

"I know you're right. I'm just having a hard time convincing myself. It feels like my fault. Like I let him do this to me," I admit.

"Well, what were you doing before?"

"You know how my plan was to become a teacher?" She nods. "Well, after Ezra, I changed my major to Forensic Science. I wanted to, I don't know, join the FBI or something. I initially thought about becoming a detective, but I didn't think I could stomach the field work."

"I'm guessing you're not with the FBI?"

"No. I met Brad in college. We started dating senior year, and he convinced me to work for his mother's financial firm. Well, until they both talked me into staying home and taking care of him instead."

"That sounds like the most boring job in the world. I hate numbers. Math is the devil's way of fucking with us," Willa says so adamantly that I laugh.

We spend the rest of the night talking about the multiple boyfriends Willa has had and all the places she's been. It helps me relax, not talking about myself or my past, and soon I'm drifting off to sleep.

I'm running and no matter how fast I go, he's still on my heels. The sand from the beach is chilly against my feet. The roughness usually bothers me, but the cold has made me numb. I look over my shoulder, the freezing wind whips my hair across my face. It's dark, but I can see him gaining on me.

He's so close I can feel his hot breath on my neck. It sends chills down my spine.

"You think you can run from me?"

"Please!" I plead, but it falls on deaf ears.

He grabs my hair and throws me to the sand.

"You're mine!" he yells in my face while straddling my waist. I try to fight him off, but he grabs my hands and holds them above my head.

"Brad, please!"

"Shut the fuck up! I'm going to kill you and anyone who helped keep you from me, you stupid waste of space!" His blue eyes are manic, and I know he means it. This time he's going to do what I always knew he would. He's going to kill me.

I scream. I scream with every last molecule of oxygen I have left in my lungs, hoping that someone will hear me and save me, but knowing in my heart they won't. No one can save me. I'm all alone. I danced with the devil and now I'm going to pay.

"Belle! Wake up!"

My eyes fly open, and I see Willa leaning over me, her eyes wide with panic as she shakes my shoulders.

"What the fuck is going on in here?" Cal asks as he bursts through my door and turns on the light. He's in blue plaid pajama pants and a black t-shirt with the Shattered Halo logo on it. Which is predictably an image of a golden halo shattered into five pieces. His hair is sticking up all over the place.

I take a minute to calm down and take in my surroundings.

I'm at Cal's house.

Willa is here with me.

Brad can't get to me here.

I'm safe.

"Nightmare," I manage to say, eventually.

"That was one hell of a nightmare, babe. You scared the shit out of me. I couldn't get you to wake up," Willa says, her eyes still showing her panic.

"I'm sorry," I whisper, wringing my hands in my lap.

"Don't, Belle," Cal says as he comes to my side and grabs my hand, stopping me from fidgeting. "We're here for you. You just scared us. That's all."

"What time is it?" I ask to change the subject. I don't want them asking what I was dreaming about, although I'm sure they can guess.

"It's around three in the morning," Willa says, then turns to Cal. "Do you have stuff to make Midnight Macaroni?"

I burst of excitement shoots through my body, and I almost don't recognize the feeling. "Do you?" I ask Cal eagerly.

"Of course I do. What kind of question is that?"

Willa and I squeal like we used to when we were kids and Cal would make us mac and cheese during a sleepover. It's just boxed stuff that he adds bacon and extra cheese to, but we all love it. We started calling it Midnight Macaroni after Willa and I watched *Practical Magic*. We were too young for Midnight Margaritas.

We all head down to Cal's kitchen in our pjs. Which

takes a lot longer than it should. This man does not need this amount of house. It's ridiculous.

Willa and I sit at the island while Cal gets started on our mac and cheese. I look at the empty stools next to me and blow out a heavy breath.

"We can invite Kai. He's probably awake," Willa offers.

"I doubt he'll come. He hates me." I look at her to see her turn to Cal. He just shrugs.

"What do you mean? Why do you think that?" Willa asks in a gentle voice, like she's afraid she'll spook me.

I tap my fingers on the marble countertop anxiously before sighing. "I don't know. I honestly don't. He was weird to me that night in the woods, and our relationship hasn't been the same since."

"You haven't really been around. Are you sure? Maybe he's just—"

"Stop, Willa. Don't speak to me like I'm a child who doesn't understand life yet. Something caused Kai to act like a dick to me before we played that night. Then Ezra vanished, and I attributed his shitty behavior to that after. Which I'm sure was the cause of most of it." I shake my head in frustration. "But the day Cal told us about the record deal, and I chose school over the band, he never forgave me and has treated me like he can't stand to be around me since."

Willa, to her credit, doesn't argue with me, but the way her brow furrows and the clear confusion across her face makes me question everything. I look over at Cal, who's watching the water boil instead of looking at me.

"What? You both clearly don't agree. What is it?" I demand.

Willa looks at Cal and when it's clear he's leaving this up

to her, she glares at him. Turning to me, she takes my hand and sighs.

"I want to make sure you understand that I'm not denying anything you just said or trying to invalidate your feelings in any way. I just have been around Kai a lot. . . obviously, and that's not how I see it. He looks hurt when your name is brought up. He looks hurt when Cal takes your phone calls. Hell, he even looks hurt every time we perform 'Shattered Dreams.'"

"What?" That's all I manage.

"He's hurting Belle. He doesn't let it show, but I see it. Cal sees it too, even if this conversation is making him so uncomfortable, he's trying to make the water boil with his pea brain."

"I just don't want to be in the middle! They're adults. They know how to speak. Let them do it," Cal exclaims while whipping his arms around dramatically.

"Well, that's obviously not going to happen if Kai keeps acting like a giant butthole when he's around Belle. Maybe tell him to use his words like a big boy," Willa taunts.

Cal glares at her. Willa glares right back.

"That man that stood in my kitchen earlier?" Cal turns to look at me. "The one who looked like he was about to go to war with whoever would dare to harm you? That's not a man that hates you, Belle." He turns back to his pot of water like he didn't just drop a bomb on me.

"You two are annoying," I grumble before getting up and heading to the couch. I need a minute to figure out the thoughts racing through my head.

Kai is hurting? Just the thought of that kills me. I knew Ezra's disappearance hurt him, but Willa is making it seem like I'm the cause, and I can't figure out why. What could I have done to cause him pain? Yes, I went to school and didn't live the life of a rockstar, but that didn't need to hurt him. I tried to keep in touch initially, but he would never respond to my texts or answer my calls. If anyone should hurt in this situation, it should be me. It is me. Kai's anger and silence hurts.

I don't know how long I sit there, trying to solve a puzzle with missing pieces. Long enough for Cal to have finished making the food and for Willa to be standing in front of me, holding out a bowl like it's a peace offering.

"I'm sorry. It's just. . . you and Kai are my best friends and you're both clearly hurting. I wish I knew how to fix it. To go back to how we were," she says as she takes the spot next to me.

"We can't. Ezra was part of how we were," I say softly.

She nods before digging into her mac and cheese.

Cal joins us quietly, turning on the tv and picking a movie. We eat in silence, none of us willing to risk bringing the atmosphere down any further. At some point, the sun rises, and we all go our separate ways.

BRAD

"THAT FUCKING CUNT!" I scream at the door to my house.

I pace the length of the hallway, which is maybe five steps, before turning around and doing it again. She really fucked up this time. My steps falter when I feel my phone vibrating in the pocket of my jeans. *Shit.*

"This is Brad," I say as I answer.

"I'm well aware of that. Now please enlighten me on why I heard from my wife that your girlfriend was spotted in town when she should be with you," my bosses cold and angry voice comes through the speaker.

"She has family there —"

"You are supposed to inform me of any trips ahead of time!" he screams before I can finish my sentence. I cower, even though he can't do anything over the phone. It's an involuntary reaction my traitorous body makes.

"I'm sorry, sir. I'll handle Belle," I say with as much apology in my voice as I can muster.

"You better or I will."

He ends the call there.

"Fuck!"

She has no idea what she's done by running off like this, but she's about to find out.

I look around my apartment, every inch of it reminds me of why I'm doing this. So I pick up my phone and make a call.

"Maine Medical, this is Deidra speaking. How may I direct your call?"

"Patch me through to Regina Foley's nurse. She's in the long-term care ward," I snipe at the woman on the line.

"One moment."

"Hello again, Mr. Foley," the voice comes through on the line quickly.

"Martha, is my mother showing any signs today?" I ask the nurse. I call every day and ask her the same question. The stroke that almost took my mother's life is also preventing her from speaking to me. She's the person I tell everything to. I don't know how I'm supposed to be making decisions without her input.

"I'm sorry, but your funding stopped. Until her bill is paid, she won't be able to attend any therapies."

"What!" I shout, knowing full well who is responsible. The bastard already stopped paying for her care. "When?"

I hear typing coming through the phone and then, "It looks like it happened last night."

The fucking prick! He had no faith I'd get Belle back and already took steps to ensure my compliance. Like he didn't already have it. I've been fucking the boring pussy for years under his direction.

"Get her back in therapy. I'll handle the billing."

"I can't —"

"I said get it done!" I shout into the phone. "Don't make me come down there!"

"I'll see what I can do," Martha says before hanging up on me.

Fucking bitch. All of them.

Belle is going to pay for this.

five

KAI

"EZRA! IS THAT YOU?"

I sigh, scrubbing my hands over my face and prepare myself. "No, mom. Ezra's gone," I say as gently as possible.

"Oh. Right. How are you, Malikai?" My mom is sitting on her worn black leather couch, drink in hand. She has on an oversized blue t-shirt I recognize as Ezra's. When she finally turns her head to look at me, I see how glassy her eyes are, pupils the size of pinholes. Great. It's fucking nine in the morning and she's already halfway to blacking out.

"Already?" I mutter under my breath. She hears me though.

"Fuck off. I lost my son and my husband. I can do whatever the fuck I want." She turns her angry gaze away from me and stares out the window instead.

I take the moment to look around my childhood home. I don't even recognize it. The once vibrant turquoise walls are faded and scratched. The wood floors are scuffed. My mom removed my dad from all the family pictures but left the rest

46

of the torn photos in their frames. It's like even the house is suffering. I hate it here. I hate coming here.

"I'm still here, you know. You still have me," I say, trying to keep the emotions in my voice level.

My mother just scoffs and continues staring, but not really looking.

Not enough not enough not enough. The phrase rears its ugly head like it does every time I visit her. It attacks me and breaks me down like the monster that it is. I can't push it away when it's so obviously what she wants to say to me.

"Mrs. Henry will check on you while I'm gone. We fly out in the morning, and I just wanted to come and say goodbye before I leave." I don't know why I fucking bother. I hate coming here just as much as she hates me coming. My face is the same as her lost son's and she can't stand to even look at me. It's why she's still staring out the window. It's only out of some twisted sense of obligation that I'm here, and we both know it. Ezra would want me to check on her, *so here I fucking am.*

She wasn't always like this, my mother. Yeah, she could be strict and had a no-nonsense attitude, but she was also loving and fun. Ezra and I were lucky to have grown up in the home she created for us. But that person, the loving mother of my childhood, she died with Ezra.

"I'm not a fucking child, Malikai! I don't need a sitter!" She yells without looking at me.

"Go to rehab like I keep asking you to, and I won't hire one anymore." We've had this discussion a million times. And I'll have it a million more if there's even a small chance she'll go.

"Fuck off."

"I'll see you when I get home. Love you, Mom," I whisper, emotion clogging my throat. She waves me off, still keeping her gaze locked on the window.

I leave my mother's house, slamming the door behind me, and go to the place I always go before leaving town.

The rock I'm sitting on is making my ass numb. February in Maine is brutal, but I need to come here. I need to sit in the last place my brother had been. When he was declared dead, my parents had a headstone placed in the town cemetery for him. Going there seems wrong. He's not there. He's not here either, but at least he was.

"I don't know what to do about Mom, Ez," I tell the river rushing in front of me. "She can't even look at me anymore. I —" I have to stop as I choke up. A single hot tear traces a path down my icy cheek. "I leave for six weeks in the morning. The band is shit without you." *I'm* shit without you.

"Do you remember when we were little, and Dad would take us to this river to go fishing? He got the line caught in the tree almost every time he went to cast and touching the worms made him gag." I laugh at the memory. "He had no idea what he was doing but wanted to do something with his sons. I'll never know why he picked fishing."

My smile drops. "Dad still hasn't come back. So I guess I really will never know."

The wind picks up and I shiver, tucking myself deeper into my wool jacket.

"Belle is back. She's coming with us on tour." I shake my head and look down at my feet. "Someone hurt her, Ez. He put his hands on her and all I see when I think about it is red. I want to fucking kill him."

There's so much more I want to say to him. I want to tell him about Mom, about my own shit. I keep it in, feeling like if I say it, he'll somehow hear it. He'll know I failed him, our parents. Hell, I feel like I failed Belle in some way too.

So instead of voicing everything, I stand and shove my freezing hands into my jacket pockets.

"I miss you, Ez. *God*, do I miss you."

"Open up, Mav!" I yell as I bang on the door. "I'm not leaving until you let me in!"

"I'm fucking coming, Kai! Chill."

Maverick's door swings open to reveal him dressed neatly in a blue long-sleeve shirt and jeans. Not what I was expecting. He moves to the side so I can enter his house. His hair is messy and curls around his ears, but it's clean. His brown eyes have that haunted look they always do when he has too much alone time.

"Cal beat you to it this time," he says, answering my unasked question.

Maverick has a hard time being home. I think if he had his way, we would always be on the road, and he would never have to set foot in this town again. He was close friends with Ezra and took his loss really hard. His relationship with his parents isn't great either, but I've never been able to get him to open up about it. I know enough from town gossip to guess.

I always check on him while we're home. Usually, it

consists of forcing him to shower and throwing away all his takeout containers. I've tried to get him to move in with me. It's not like I don't have the room, and I like the idea of having someone that was close to my brother around while we're home. He always refuses, though. Says he doesn't want to be a burden.

"Are you all packed? The flight leaves early tomorrow."

Mav rolls his eyes. "Yes, Mom. I packed my bag for the sleepover."

I chuckle as I walk by him and into the living room. Where my house has black floors and white walls, Mav did the opposite. His walls are black, and his floors are white. I'm expecting a mess, but everything is clean. Someone even folded the throw blanket he keeps on his couch.

"He brought Belle," Mav says, answering my thoughts yet again.

"Ah," is all that comes out.

"Are you ever going to tell me what happened between the two of you? She already quit the band before you came begging at my door to get me to join."

I look over at him to see him smirking. I did pretty much beg him. He only agreed when I told him Ezra really wanted him to join and was even showing us videos of the two of them playing together in their dorm. Mav is amazing on the bass and deserved to be a part of our band. He just felt like he was taking Ezra's place and had a hard time coming to terms with that.

"There isn't much to say. She bailed on us and that's it."

"Ezra would hate the way you've treated her." His words are like a punch to the gut.

"I know. It's complicated." Complicated doesn't even

begin to explain my feelings towards Belle, towards the entire situation, but it's the most I'm willing to give him right now. The love and resentment I feel towards Belle is almost identical to the love and resentment I feel towards Ezra. It's so beyond complicated, and I don't have the strength to unpack it.

Mav arches an eyebrow, clearly not convinced, but doesn't push me on it. It's an unspoken rule we have in our friendship. We've become really close over the years and talk all the time. But if a subject comes up that we don't want to talk about, the other doesn't push.

"Cal asked me to stay with them tonight, but I told him I was staying at yours."

I nod and shove my hands in my pockets. I want to tell him he can go over to Cal's, but I like the tradition of him spending the night before we go on tour with me. We always watch Ezra's favorite movie (*Monty Python and the Holy Grail*) and eat his favorite food (chicken broccoli alfredo) while talking about our happy memories with him.

"Come on. Let's load my bag into your stupid car, and I'll order the food on the way," he says, grabbing his leather jacket.

"My car is not stupid," I grumble. It's a two-seater that goes way too fast and isn't great in the snow. Was it a stupid purchase for someone living in Maine? Probably, but I love it.

"We barely fit into the damn thing. You didn't need to be a stereotype and buy a sports car. Cars that fit tall people are just as nice."

I just shake my head and leave him to his teasing. Our tour manager made the rounds this morning and picked up our luggage and instruments. Lucky for me, otherwise we wouldn't have been able to fit it all in my car, and I would never hear the end of it.

"Hey, did I tell you about that time Ezra and I got caught walking back to our dorms drunk by campus police?"

I smile at his question. This is exactly what I need; a night listening to my brother's best friend talk about him, so that I can feel close to him again.

six

BELLE

"OK. WE HAVE ten shows in the UK, four in Ireland, four in Germany, and then back to the UK for our last show in Glasgow," Cal announces in the limo on the way to the airport. We all already know that. Even I know that. He handed out folders with the schedule and all the hotel information for the entire tour.

"No bus?" Willa asks him.

"We have one for part of the UK leg and all of Ireland. We couldn't get one big enough to block out the sound of your random hook ups in Germany," Cal says to her.

"Pot meet kettle," Willa retorts while shoving her middle finger in his face.

I ignore their squabbling and chance a look at Kai. He's been quiet the entire ride so far, just staring out the window. My brother's words have been running through my head the past week... *that's not a man who hates you, Belle.* He may not hate me, but he certainly doesn't like me. Being in such close proximity to him is making it hurt so much more. I was used to ignoring that hollow feeling in my heart where he used to be. Now it's becoming impossible.

Kai must sense me watching him because his head suddenly turns, and his icy blue eyes lock on mine. I don't know what I was expecting. Maybe a snarl? But what I get is a small smile before he returns his gaze to the window.

What the fuck? Is he messing with me?

I must have imagined that smile. Malikai Irons does not smile at me. Not anymore.

Or maybe he's remembering how close we were as kids? How much we meant to each other?

Maybe he misses me just as much as I miss him.

"Belle?"

"Huh?" I snap out of my discussion with myself to see Mav staring at me.

"I asked if you saw your mom while you were in town," he repeats.

"Oh, um. No. I didn't want to answer questions about..." I trail off and just gesture to the yellowing bruise on my face. I didn't even tell her I was home and begged Cal to keep it from her.

My mom loves Brad. Or she loves that his mom has money that he would inherit one day. I think part of her was hoping I had found someone to take care of me. At least that's what I'm trying to make myself believe. Deep down, I know how much appearances matter to my mom. Way more than feelings ever will. A rich son-in-law would look good for her, and she could brag about it to her friends. Who cares what her daughter is suffering to get that for her? Not Paula Griffin, that's for sure.

My dad left her a few years ago, and she hasn't really

moved past it. It seems to be a trend in our friend group from what I heard from Cal about Gavin Irons, Kai's dad.

It shocked me when he told me. Gavin was the fun and loving type of dad. Leaving Adira and Kai without keeping in touch seemed so unlike him. My dad, at least, still calls us to check in. But my dad also hasn't lost a child.

Mav nods in understanding. I'm looking forward to spending more time with him. Ezra loved him, and I loved Ezra.

I haven't brought it up, not since that day in the living room of my parent's house. I don't even know how to bring up the topic without upsetting Maverick, but I want to know if he thinks Ezra is dead. There's also the question of why he left so suddenly that night.

But I can't bring any of that up right now. When Cal took me to Mav's house yesterday, he warned me that it would be a mess. I still wasn't prepared for the state Maverick was in. His hair was greasy, there were food stains on his shirt, and the number of takeout containers scattered around his house could fill a construction dumpster. Cal said he always gets like that when they're home for too long.

Everyone assumes it has something to do with the relationship with his parents that he won't talk to them about. And I guess that could be part of it, but I know that look I saw in his eyes. The despair and longing that was haunting him. It's too hard for Mav to be in the place he lost the man he loved. I'm the only one who knows, and I wish they had made me aware, so I could've been there for him sooner.

The moment I have the thought, I realize it wouldn't have mattered. Brad would have found a way to pull me away from Maverick too. Just like he did with everyone else I ever cared about. The sadness that realization brought is now bringing anger. I'm angrier with myself than I am with Brad. I can't believe I let him do this to me. Let him take everyone from me. The distance made it easier for him, but my lack of fight is really what enabled him to take over my life so easily.

"Finally. Let's go. The sooner we board the plane, the sooner I can go back to sleep," Willa says as she jumps out of the limo that had barely stopped moving.

I follow everyone through the security lines and out onto the private tarmac to board the plane. As we ascend the stairs, I pause and turn around. I intend to ask Kai if we can talk once we land, but the words get caught in my throat when I see a figure standing in the distance.

"Why are you just standing there? Let's go," Kai says. "Belle!"

My gaze snaps to his, and I know there are tears in my eyes.

"Shit. Sorry. I didn't mean to yell," he says apologetically, but I'm too scared to register that. "It's just fucking freezing, and you're blocking the stairs."

"I thought I saw Brad," I whisper as more tears fall. I bring my shaking hand up to wipe them away.

"What? Where?" he asks, his head whips around, searching the area. "Belle, where did you see him?" His tone is pleading and that snaps me out of my momentary panic. I point with a shaky finger to the area near the entrance to the airport. It looks like one that would be used by staff and is partially covered in shadows.

"It's ok, Kai. I'm probably just seeing things. Let's get on the plane." I say as I grab his arm and stop him from marching off in the direction I pointed.

He watches me, his eyes penetrating mine and searching. Eventually, he gives me a stiff nod and places his hand gently on the small of my back, helping to guide my trembling body up the stairs.

I plop down in a window seat, and I'm shocked when Kai plops down next to me.

"You don't need to sit next to me."

Kai looks at me and frowns. "I want to."

I sigh. I'm tired and beyond frustrated. I just had a mini heart attack thinking I saw the man who abused me seconds ago. Now Kai is being nice to me. Maybe this is just a dream.

"I'm fucked up, Belle. I'm so fucked up, and I don't want you to be dragged into it. But Maverick pointed out that Ezra would hate how I'm treating you. And he was right." Kai looks at me, and I can see the pain Willa mentioned. It's as clear as day in his eyes.

"You're being nice to me for Ezra?" I ask, not sure how I feel about that.

"Yes. No. . . I don't know. There's no excuse for how I've treated you. I'm genuinely sorry for my behavior." Kai looks at me, and all I see is pain and regret in his eyes. My instinct is to forgive him. I'm so desperate for him to be back in my life that I think I would forgive anything he asked of me. But I stop myself. If I've learned anything in the past few days, it's respecting myself first. And he hasn't shown me any respect.

"You don't want to be my friend because of whatever is going on with you, but you're fine staying friends with everyone else?" I ask him, my words deliberately slow.

"You're the best of us," he whispers.

"What does that even mean?" I ask, my voice hardening.

"I just. . . I can't. I can't," he says, his voice turning into a whimper.

"Sit somewhere else, Kai. I think you need to figure out what you want. I'd like to be friends again, but I won't force it on you. I don't need pity friendship."

"Belle, I —"

I watch him struggle to find words for a few seconds before putting on my headphones and turning away from him. I feel him get up from his seat, and then I let the tears fall.

seven

BRAD

I'M SO FUCKED. I just watched Belle board a plane with the sorry excuse of a band her brother is in. She has no talent and is nothing but an inconvenience, but her brother must have wanted her with him.

Callahan hasn't let Belle out of his sight since the moment she arrived at his house. I've been following them and there hasn't been a single opportunity for me to get her alone and get her back home.

Now she's on a fucking plane that's leaving the damn country. What the fuck am I supposed to do about that? I chance a peek around the corner of the building and watch as the plane starts down the runway.

My phone starts ringing, and I already know who it is without looking. Maybe I should book myself a plane and get the fuck out of here.

No.

He'll find me no matter where I go.

"Hi sir, I can explain —"

"Can you? You can explain how that meek girl has

evaded you and is now on a flight across the ocean? Please. Explain." His voice has that calmness that is more dangerous than anything.

"Callahan hasn't left her side, and you told me he's too in the public eye to mess with. I had no choice but to not get involved."

"That girl has information that could ruin me. You understand that, right? If I go down, so do you. And now you've let her get on a flight with my son."

"Sir, if I may? I don't think she knows anything, or she would have used that information already," I argue.

He pauses before answering, no doubt to make me think he's considering my words when I know he isn't.

"Is that a risk you're willing to take?" he asks menacingly.

"No, sir. What should I do?"

"Figure it out!"

"Yes, sir."

I put my phone back in my pocket and head back to my car. I feel defeated, but I can't let that last.

I know what I have to do.

KAI

"STOP LOOKING AT ME LIKE THAT," I grumble, taking the seat next to Willa. We landed over an hour ago and are just now getting into the cars taking us to the hotel. Customs is a bitch when you have to bring in the amount of equipment we do.

"Bellamy is my best friend."

"I'm aware," I say on a sigh, not liking where this conversation is going and regretting not fighting Mav to get in the other car.

"She was your best friend too, once."

I can feel her gaze burning a hole in the side of my head, but I don't look at her. "She was so much more than that," I whisper.

"Then what the fuck are you doing? It's not like we all weren't aware of how you two felt about each other. Probably still feel for each other. You should grovel at her feet!" Willa yells, startling the driver.

I finally turn and look at her. She's furious, and I don't blame her. I was the only one who saw Ezra and Belle that night. I don't know if Belle never told Willa because she didn't get the chance before Ezra disappeared or if the plan all along was to keep their relationship a secret. But whatever the reason, Willa can't understand where my anger stems from, and I don't want to explain it to her. It just rips at the barely healed scab on my heart. I do a good enough job ripping that particular wound open by myself, no help needed.

"Why? She just got out of a relationship that could have killed her, Willa. What would you have me do? Come sweeping in as her knight in shining armor?" I ask as anger creeps in, and I want to slam my fist into something.

"Well, yeah," Willa admits.

"I'm not the hero, Willa. My armor isn't shiny. It's dented and rusted, with holes the size of softballs." I stare down at my hands and push back the emotions bubbling to the surface. "How can I save her when I can't even save myself?"

"Belle is well on her way to saving herself. I'm not asking you to. I'm not asking you to marry her or fuck her, Kai. She just wants her friend back."

I turn my head to see Willa's gaze has softened.

"I think you need her too." She turns and looks out the window, clearly finished with this conversation.

I watch the rain travel down the window of the car. I don't know what to do. I've felt lost for a while. Even before Ezra. I was going to school, majoring in business, just because I had to choose something. I had no plans for the future because all I wanted was to play music, but it seemed so out of reach.

Now I have my dream, but I don't have my brother, and I

didn't get the girl. My family fell apart, and my mother can't even look at me. Maverick is drowning and the best I can manage is a movie night to help him. For a long time, it felt like we all paid a price to get what we wanted. The price was too high and if I could trade it all to get Ezra back, I would.

But now, even that dream is failing us, and we paid the price for nothing.

I sit on my hotel bed, strumming away absentmindedly on my guitar. It's the middle of the night here, but because of the time difference, it still feels like late evening to me. My phone vibrates next to me, and I roll my eyes. It's probably Cal complaining that he's bored.

CAL

All the bars are closed.

ME

We're in London. All the pubs are closed.

CAL

Whatever. Either way. I'm bored.

MAV

I had 2am! You guys owe me $50!

WILLA

Dammit! Couldn't have waited another
hour, Callahan?

ME

I had 1am. I thought he was going to break
sooner.

CAL

...wow.

So...?

Who wants to hangout?

ME

No one. Go to sleep.

WILLA

I'd rather stub every single one of my toes.

CAL

Stop acting like you don't love me, Willa.
You said you always wanted a big brother.
Here I am. Basically a gift. You're welcome.

WILLA

For fuck's sake.

CAL

Mav?

You know you want to get your ass kicked
in Mario Kart.

MAV

Fine. You can come hang with me. But for
the record, you've only won once.

CAL

Pretty sure we've only played once.

ME

You played on the plane and lost every
time, Cal.

CAL

Weird. I don't remember that.

MAV

You have two minutes before I change my
mind and don't let you in.

CAL

On my way!

WILLA

$50 says he loses the first race.

ME

I'm not dumb enough to take that bet.

CAL

Fuck you guys.

I snicker and toss my phone on the nightstand.

I'm just about to turn the lights out and try to get some sleep when I hear a blood-curdling scream coming from the room next to me. *Belle.*

I'm instantly on my feet and banging on the door that connects our rooms.

"Belle!" I scream as my fist pound on the door. "Belle! Open the door!"

She screams again, and I feel it hit me like a knife. I back up and run at the door, shoulder first. Pain flairs when I connect with the wood and I can hear it splinter, but it's still closed. So I back up again and run at it with everything I have. *I'm coming mo chridhe.*

This time the door gives, and I stumble into the dark room. There's a sliver of moonlight that illuminates the room enough for me to see Belle on her bed. I rush to her. Her limbs are tangled in the sheets, and she's covered in sweat. Tears fall down her face as she screams again.

"Belle," I whisper as I gently shake her shoulders, trying to wake her.

"No!" she screams as she thrashes. My heart breaks seeing her like this. So broken by a man that he can still get to her in her sleep.

"Belle, it's Kai. Wake up," I say as gently as I can.

"Kai. . ." she mumbles but doesn't wake. Her grip on the sheets relaxes, and I can see her body visibly calm.

I push the sweaty hair out of her face and look at her. Her face is no longer contorted in fear and pain, making her look peaceful. She's wearing a baggy t-shirt with our band's logo on it and pink sleep shorts. Everything is covered in sweat and she's getting goose bumps.

Before I can think more about it, I scoop her up in my arms and take her to my room. She buries her face in my chest, and I hold her tighter. Walking carefully around the ruined door, I put her down on my bed as gently as I can.

Grabbing my phone, I quickly call Willa.

"I swear, if you tell me you're bored now too —"

"Willa. I need you to come to my room. Belle was having a nightmare," I tell her quickly.

"Fuck. Alright. Two seconds," she says and hangs up.

I watch Belle sleep. She's so beautiful, it's physically painful to look at her, but I can't stop. All the pain she carries throughout her day is more obvious when she's sleeping peacefully. The minute that realization hits, so does the rage.

I stomp over to my door and swing it open to see Willa standing there, fist raised like she was about to knock. She's in the same t-shirt as Belle, and her lilac hair is in a messy bun on the top of her head.

"Her sheets are soaked from sweat. So are her clothes. I couldn't wake her up, so I moved her in here. I don't think I should be the one to change her."

Willa nods. The look on her face is indecipherable.

"I'll be right back," I say as I brush past her, not waiting for a response.

It only takes a few seconds before I'm standing in front of Maverick's door, fist pounding on the wood. He swings the door open with a smile on his face. It immediately falls when he sees me.

"Dude, what's wrong?"

"Where's Cal?" I ask, teeth clenched.

Mav just moves aside and lets me in. Cal is standing, heading towards the door. I stop him with my fist to his face.

"What the fuck!" he screams, clutching his bleeding nose.

"How could you let that happen to her?" I roar in his face, fists clenched at my sides so I don't hit him again. Hot rage is burning in my veins, turning my vision white.

"What are you talking about?" Mav asks from where he's standing. I can tell he wants to get in the middle, but he's the type that likes to get all the information before he does anything.

I ignore him and step closer to Cal, who, to his credit, doesn't move. "How could you let him hurt Belle? She's your sister. You're supposed to protect her!" Cal flinches at my words, and I know he must be asking himself the same questions, but I can't stop. "Two years! He hurt her for two years and you let him!"

"I didn't know!" he screams, dropping his hands and

letting the blood flow down his face. "I didn't know," he says softly before collapsing on the end of the bed.

Maverick hands him a towel and moves to sit on the couch by the window. It's not a huge room, so he's only a couple of feet away from us.

"How could you not know?" I ask him, surprised by how much calmer my voice sounds. The burning rage from a moment ago is boiling down to a simmer.

"I was so busy with the band. We packed our schedules so tightly that I barely had time for anything else. I should've tried harder to be in her life. She still called me, but I could tell she was distant. I just thought that was my fault. I never thought..." Cal's words trail off as he gasps and starts crying into the towel. "I never thought she was being hurt, Kai. I swear. I would've killed him myself if I had known."

I watch my best friend break, but I'm still too angry to comfort him. Especially when I'm to blame too. I pushed her away. I ignored all her calls and texts. But Cal didn't. He took every call and returned every text. He saw her on holidays. I can't get past blaming him, even if I know that isn't fair.

I spin on my heel and leave Cal to sit in his blood and tears. I may not have protected Belle then, but I will now. Whether she wants me to or not.

Pushing my door open slowly, I see Willa sitting on my bed next to Belle, looking worried.

"She's getting worked up again. She's not screaming, so I haven't tried to wake her up."

"Belle was always a heavy sleeper. Do you remember when she passed out in the car on the way to Boston and Cal carried her over his shoulder for like forty minutes before she woke up? People thought he was dragging a drunk lady around."

Willa chuckles softly. "Yeah. I wish she grew out of that, though. This is horrible to watch."

I walk over to Belle and gently stroke her cheek with my knuckles. She instantly calms. I look at Willa, surprise written all over my face, but she just smirks.

"I told you she needs you, Kai," she says before hopping off my bed and leaving the room.

I think about sleeping on the couch, but the moment I pull my hand away, she whimpers, and her breathing speeds up.

"It's ok, mo chridhe. I'm here. I won't leave you."

Belle relaxes the moment she hears my voice. So before I can overthink it anymore, I strip out of my jeans and t-shirt, then crawl into the bed next to her. I watch her for a moment, unsure where the line is in this situation and afraid to cross it. Her face scrunches up, and she takes in a jagged breath, like she's about to cry.

I grab her waist on instinct and pull her into me, resting her head on my chest and running my fingers up and down her back. Belle melts into me, snuggling even closer. I wait until her breathing is even, and I'm sure she's free of her nightmare, before I close my eyes and let sleep take me too.

nine

BELLE

"THE NEW PEOPLE *are moving into the house across the street!" Callahan yells, half running, half stumbling down the stairs.*

I'm already staring out the window, watching them. I hope they have more kids for me to play with. I only have Willa and she has to stay home a lot. Her mommy is sick, and my Dad says she's going to heaven soon.

"Mom? Can I go say hi to the new neighbors? I think they have boys!" Callahan screams the moment his feet slam into the floor.

"Take your sister!" comes the response from the kitchen.

Callahan grumbles something under his breath before walking over to me, taking my hand, and dragging me out the door. Mom always makes Callahan take me with him. Sometimes, I want to stay home and watch cartoons, but she always says no.

There's a big truck in the driveway of Mrs. Lawson's house. Dad says she moved to a new home and doesn't need this house anymore. I watch as different people move around, lifting big things and bringing them into the house. I don't see anyone my size yet, but Callahan keeps walking, so I follow.

"There!" he shouts, pointing at something near a tree. I follow where he's looking and see two boys sitting under the tree. Callahan runs in their direction, and I do my best to keep up, but my legs are smaller, and I fall.

"Cal!" I cry, the stinging pain in my knees causing tears to form in my eyes.

"Don't cry, Belle! Mom's going to be so mad at me. I'm not supposed to let you get hurt," Callahan pleads. I can't stop crying. My knees hurt, and it makes me sad.

"Are you ok?"

I blink through my tears to see a boy standing in front of me, holding out his hand. His eyes are the color of the sky, and his hair is brown like mine. I take his hand and let him pull me up.

"I'm ok," I sniffle, embarrassed that I cried in front of new friends.

"I'm Malikai, but everyone calls me Kai," the new boy says after helping me up.

"I'm Bellamy, but everyone calls me Belle."

"I'm Callahan, but everyone calls me Cal."

"No, they don't," I argue. I've never heard anyone call him that.

"Shut up. Yes, they do," he mutters under his breath.

"Belle, like the girl in Beauty and the Beast?" I hear someone yell. I look around Kai and see... Kai? I look back at him, confused.

Kai laughs. "That's my twin brother, Ezra."

"Why is he over there?" Cal asks.

Kai points to my knees. "Blood makes him throw up."

"I'm going to be in so much trouble," my brother complains.

Kai takes my hand and starts leading me towards his house. "My mom is a nurse. She can help."

I smile up at him. "Thank you."

"I get hurt all the time," he tells me.

"How old are you?" Callahan asks.

"We're seven."

"Me too! Belle is only five," Cal says excitedly. He seems to completely forget that he's supposed to be watching me and runs over to where Ezra is still standing by the tree.

"Don't worry. I'll take care of you. I promise," Kai tells me and smiles. His smile makes me happy, so I believe him.

<hr>

I groan and the light from the morning sun shines on my closed eyes. My bed is cozy and warm. I swear I can smell Kai like he's still holding my hand and taking me to get my knees bandaged by his mom. I've had that dream a lot since Ezra's been gone. That first day meeting them. I always wake up before I actually meet Ezra, though. Maybe my brain just finds the memory too painful.

My eyes fly open and my entire body freezes. There's warm breath on my neck and a strong arm gripping my waist. I immediately start to panic. Brad's here and he found me.

"Belle," a groggy voice murmurs into my hair.

I fly out of the bed, tripping when the sheets tangle around my feet and go crashing to the floor.

"What happened? What is it?" Kai asks, jumping out of the bed far more gracefully than I did. He puts himself between me and the door to the room, looking around for the threat.

I stand up slowly, pulling my shirt down. What the fuck? This isn't the shirt I went to sleep in last night. I look around to realize this isn't the room I went to sleep in, either.

"Kai... what? How? What?" I stammer.

He turns around and looks me over in a way that's almost clinical. "You're ok?" he asks.

"No! I'm in clothes I didn't go to sleep in, this isn't my room, and you were half naked next to me!" I exclaim while gesturing to his mostly naked body. He's only wearing black boxer briefs, tattoos and muscles on full display. It takes everything in me not to focus on the bulge in his boxers. I keep my eyes trained on his to prevent them from wandering. I doubt me blatantly checking him out will help our strained relationship.

"Oh. That," he says, looking relieved. "You had a nightmare. I heard you screaming and couldn't get you to open the door. I broke through and brought you in here. Your sheets were soaked. Willa changed you. We couldn't get you to wake up."

Looking at the door he pointed to, I can see the split wood and the broken door frame. He literally broke in to get to me. My heart beat faster knowing he did that for me.

"Why isn't Willa here?"

"She was. You were still restless with her," he says, rubbing the back of his neck and looking uncomfortable.

"But not with you?" I ask, knowing the answer. Kai has always made me feel safe. Even now, when I don't know how he feels about me, I know I'm safe with him.

"Not with me," he says, his eyes locking with mine.

There's always something behind them when he looks at me now. Something I can't identify and want so badly to.

"Um, thanks. Sorry I worried you."

Kai's expression turns stern, and he nods. "I have to get ready for sound check." He moves swiftly to the bathroom and slams the door.

I have so many questions I want to ask him. So many things that I think need to be said in order to close this gap between us. But I can't be the only one who wants to close it.

Stepping over the broken wood, I find my suitcase and get dressed for the day. My phone is still on the charger, so I grab that, checking for any new messages.

> WILLA
>
> You coming with us today?

> ME
>
> Can I?

We never discussed what my role would be. I don't want to just tag along and not have a job. I need to talk to Cal about that later.

> WILLA
>
> Of course you can! Meet me downstairs in ten?

> ME
>
> Sounds good.

Willa is already waiting for me in the hotel's lobby when I get there.

"You left me with Kai," I blurt out.

"Good morning to you too, sunshine."

"Willa. You left me with Kai. I woke up and panicked because I didn't know who was next to me!" I whisper-shout at her.

"It's Kai. Stop acting like I left you with a stranger," she scoffs.

"He may as well be," I counter. Saying it out loud hurts, but it's the truth.

Willa stops walking once we get outside and turns to me with her hands on her hips. "Was he mean to you this morning?"

"No."

"The Kai you knew, and this Kai, are completely different and exactly the same."

"What?" I mutter, wondering if she hit her head at some point and I missed it.

Willa sighs and runs her fingers through her hair. "Kai has lost a lot. He's still coming to terms with a lot of shit that's happened to him. I'm not defending his shitty attitude, but I think you guys need to talk about it."

"He won't talk to me!" I yell, no longer trying not to make a scene.

"I know, babe. He'll come around. Just pay attention. He loosens up and is more like the old Kai when we're on tour."

I think that over as I follow her to the taxi she's climbing into.

"Being home. Is that what gets to him? I saw what it did to Mav," I ask quietly once I'm in the car next to her.

"Yeah. It gets to all of us. But it's the worst for those two."

I nod, understanding. I avoided going home as much as I could for that exact reason. It doesn't change anything, but now I know to be on the lookout for the boy I used to love.

"You're not working, Belle."

"Why not? I can't just sit around for six weeks!" I yell as I chase my brother around the backstage area of tonight's venue, trying not to trip over the cords that seem to be scattered everywhere. I have to dodge people he seems to easily weave around. Between all the staff the band hires for the tour and the staff that runs everything backstage, this place is a zoo.

"Let her do something, Cal," Mav says, coming up next to me.

"No."

"Why?" I plead.

Cal sighs and turns to look at me. I gasp when I see his face. His right cheek and under his eye are black and blue. "What happened?"

"It was a misunderstanding. Don't worry about it," he says, looking down at his feet. Is he embarrassed? Maybe some guy caught him with his girlfriend. Wouldn't be the first time.

"Cal, I need to do something. I don't care what it is. I'll collect the trash for all I care. Please," I beg him.

Cal studies me for what feels like hours. It feels like he's reading every emotion I've ever had on my face. Mav is next to me, quietly offering me his support. I appreciate it, and I make a mental note to thank him with a coffee or something later.

"Fine. You can play with us," Cal says before walking away.

"What?" I shout, running after him, grabbing his arm to stop him. "I can't play with you! I don't know your songs. Most of them don't even have a keyboard part in them."

"Learn them. I know you, and I know how quickly you learn music. We also need female vocals for at least the background."

"What?" I say again, the disbelief rendering me almost mute.

"I actually think that's a good idea. Our songs need those elements, but Cal and Kai refuse to let anyone else play them. So we just leave them out," Mav says.

I turn to look at him and glare, letting him know I feel betrayed.

"I mean. If you want to. If you're even comfortable, that is. I just think it would help. You know. The band. But also your work thing," he stutters, running his hands through his hair and turning a vibrant shade of red.

"I haven't played in years. The only place I sing is in the shower. I don't have a keyboard..." I list off all the reasons it's a bad idea but stop there.

Do I actually want to do this?

I've never performed in front of a crowd this size. Hell, the only time I performed at all was in the woods in front of drunk classmates.

I used to dream of what being a musician would be like. I never regretted leaving the band. At the time, I made the choice I thought was best for me. But now? With the opportunity presenting itself again, can I refuse?

"We can get you a keyboard," Cal says, one side of his

mouth curling up into a half smirk. He knows I'm close to saying yes.

"Shouldn't you . . . I don't know . . . vote?" I ask.

"Kai! Willa! Can you come here for a second?" Cal yells over my shoulder. I turn to see them both walking towards us.

"We haven't even started sound check yet. What could you possibly have to complain about?" Willa asks, and I snort. I love my brother, but he can be a real diva.

"I want Belle back in the band. She wants us to vote," he explains.

"Wait! You didn't even let me decide yet," I try to protest, but he ignores me.

"Hell yeah! My vote is yes!" Willa yells and then throws her arms around me.

"I vote yes," Mav says quietly.

"Obviously, I'm a yes. Kai?" Cal turns to Kai, waiting for his answer. His features are frozen and a muscle in his jaw is ticking. His eyes find mine, and I can see the conflict warring behind them.

"You all voted yes. My vote doesn't matter." Kai turns and walks away.

Willa watches him go, looking like a disappointed parent.

My first instinct is to decline the offer because of Kai's reaction. He was part of this band from the beginning and if he doesn't want me to be a part of it with him, I won't be.

But the submissive Belle, the one I was beaten down into being, she's slowly leaving.

Defiant Belle has arrived, and she's here to stay.

"I'll do it."

ten

BELLE

WATCHING them on stage is surreal. Cal offered me tickets to their Boston shows during their first ever tour, but I made up some excuse about why I couldn't go. I don't remember what it was at this point. Then I met Brad, who said that punk rock wasn't a real genre of music. Now that I've been able to distance myself from him, I think my brother's success threatened him. Or possibly that three of the members have penises.

Shattered Halo brought down the house. It may have not been a sold-out show, but the audience more than made up for it. They ended with the song I wrote. I've heard it played on the radio a ton but seeing it in person and not being involved in that was strange.

I was second guessing agreeing to play with them again right until the first slap of Willa's sticks. The crowd aspect still scares me, but the thrill of playing outweighs it. Plus, Maverick wasn't wrong. The songs are missing something. They might need keyboards and female vocals. At least I can offer that.

"What did you think? We're good right? We're going to be amazing with you!" Cal asks excitedly the moment he finds me backstage. He's sweaty and the excited bouncing he's doing is sending the sweat everywhere.

"Gross, Cal!" I complain, trying to get away from the sweat shower.

"You're coming to the pub with us, right?" Willa asks, coming to stand next to Cal. She looks like a total badass. She drummed in a lacy red bralette and high-waisted black jeans. I don't know how she kept everything in.

"Yeah, I'll meet you in your dressing room," I assure her with a smile.

"Belle! Come on. You have to tell me what you think!" Cal whines. There are people all around us, backstage passes hanging from their necks, trying to get his attention. The security team is keeping them away, but I can't figure out how he's so unbothered by them.

"She thinks you're an idiot and is probably wondering why your nipples are always showing," Mav remarks as he walks past us and winks.

Cal looks down at himself with a frown. He's wearing a black shirt he cut the arms and half the sides off of, so the sides of his chest are on display. Nipples too, depending on how he's moving.

"Women love this look!" he shouts at Mav's back. There are quite a few shouts of agreement coming from the women near us.

"I'm going to go meet up with Willa."

"You hated it," Cal says sadly.

"I didn't. I promise. I took notes so I can figure out where to add my parts to your songs," I say, waving the notebook in my hand around so he sees it. "I wasn't really watching from a fan's perspective tonight. I'll do that tomorrow."

Clapping suddenly comes from behind Cal. He turns and Kai is there, clapping sarcastically. I take him in. He's wearing black jeans with rips in the knees and a silk short-sleeved button down that's ivory with small red flowers. He only buttoned half of it, so his sweaty, muscular chest is on full display. His arms and chest are covered in tattoos that I can't read from where I'm standing. He's been in long-sleeve Henleys since I've been back, well other than this morning. Kai is the most attractive man I've ever seen, and I'm busy salivating over him until I see his eyes.

His icy blues chill me to the bone and burn me at the same time. He's both fire and ice. So hot and cold that my head is always spinning when he's near, and I don't know which way is up.

"Good show, Kai," I mutter. He's still clapping and staring at me like I've insulted him.

"Just good, right Belle? You took notes in that little book of yours to figure out how to fix us. Swooping in to save the day and then leaving again once we're not enough for you anymore? That's what this is, right? Agreeing to play with us. You're not going to stay."

"That's enough, Kai," Cal says, the playfulness from earlier having been completely erased.

"No. I asked her a question, and I would like an answer. Are you going to stay?" Kai's standing directly in front of me now. I can smell mint and cedarwood and sweat.

"I — I don't know," I stutter. His proximity throws me. I can smell him and feel the heat of his body. I'm annoyed with myself for the way my body reacts to him. It still wants him, even with the way he's treating me. My mind is a mess, and Kai is standing there with a spoon stirring it.

"That's what I thought," he responds, his voice angry, but his eyes show disappointment. He tries to walk away, but I grab his arm to stop him.

"No. You don't get to be an asshole here. I don't know what's going on with my life at all. Where am I going to live when we get home? I don't know. What am I going to do for work? I don't know. Can I get my belongings without getting murdered? No idea." I watch Kai blanch at my words, but it doesn't stop me. My mind finally overrode my hormones, and I'm fucking pissed. I'm sick of his attitude. "I'm trying to figure out who I am and what I want all over again. You don't get to be angry with me for that. Let me play at least one show with you before you turn me into the antichrist."

I turn and walk away from him.

"Belle…"

"Fuck you, Kai!" I yell over my shoulder.

"You deserved that, dude," I hear Cal say before I turn the corner towards the dressing rooms.

I find Willa's and barge in, not bothering to knock. I find her standing next to Mav. Both of them staring at a vase of flowers, looking nervous. Willa is chewing on the side of her lip and Mav looks pale.

"Did the flowers insult you?" I ask jokingly, trying to lighten the weird mood in here.

"They're addressed to you," Willa says. Her eyes meet mine, and I see concern there.

"That's weird. Who are they from?" I ask, moving to get a better look.

The flowers are red chrysanthemums. I recognize them easily since my mom used to grow them in her garden every summer. I've never seen them in a vase like this before, though. I grab the note sitting in front of the flowers and read it.

It's me and you,
Just us two.
Come back to me, my dove,
You're my one and only love.

My hands shake so badly that I drop the paper. It's not threatening from the outside. I'm sure that's on purpose. I know it's a threat, though.

Willa wraps her arms around me. "It's him, isn't it?" she whispers.

"I think so. How did he find out I was here?"

"Maybe he has someone following you," Mav says.

"Fantastic. Love that for me. Can't even escape him in another damn country." I went from scared to angry so fast that I'm giving myself whiplash.

"What do you want to do?" Willa asks.

"Can you figure out what that flower means? It's a chrysanthemum. Brad only gave me flowers if there was a meaning to them. Everything was a fucking puzzle."

"Says they mean I love you," Mav says, looking up from his phone.

"We should just go back to the hotel and skip going out tonight," Willa says, squeezing me in a way that's supposed to be supportive, but my ribs are still a little sore. I groan instead and she jumps back. "Fuck. Sorry."

"It's fine. We're going out. I'm not hiding."

"Are you sure?" Mav asks, but he doesn't look as against it as Willa does.

"Brad is a coward. He's hiding behind notes and flowers that someone else probably set up for him. He's probably not even here. Plus, if he is, he won't approach me when I'm with you guys. I couldn't even get him to Christmas at my parent's house because he hated how my dad always confronted him about his attitude." Hindsight is a real bitch.

"I don't know…"

"Willa, please. I need to live again. I can't be his victim anymore," I beg.

"I'm going to take pictures of these," Mav says, gesturing to the note and flowers. "Then we can change and head out."

I smile at him appreciatively. "Can you send them to Cal? He's been handling all this through his lawyer."

"You got it," he says, snapping the pictures and sending them before he leaves the room.

"I'll leave with you or one of the guys if I start to feel uncomfortable. I'll alert security if I see Brad," I tell her the moment she opens her mouth to protest again.

She sighs and pinches the bridge of her nose. "Fine. I'm staying glued to your side the whole night, and I don't want to hear any arguments."

I laugh but agree. Willa is tiny, but I would bet on her in most fights. "A night out with my best friend? How terrible for me."

"Shut up," she laughs. "Let's go before I try to drag you to the safety of the hotel instead."

I'm crammed into a booth in a pub that was built before America was founded. The bar is original, as the flirty server has mentioned to Willa several times over. She giggles every time he tells her, though, so I guess that's working for him. The floor and tables are sticky, and it smells like beer and fry oil, but I'm having a great time.

Except for the fact that I'm squished in between Willa and Mav, with Cal and Kai sitting in a booth directly next to us. Cal paid the security team extra to come with us and stand guard so no one can approach. Any time anyone other than our server attempts to approach the table, Cal practically growls at them, so I'm not sure the security was necessary. Kai glares at strangers for so much as entering the pub. Apparently, he can hurt me, but no one else can. *Fucking men.*

"Someone needs to move before I pee myself," I announce.

"I'll go with you," Willa says, sliding out of the booth.

"Stay. I can pee by myself."

"But —" she tries to argue, but I hold my hand up, stopping her.

"It'll take me two minutes. I'll be right back."

"Fine, but I'm timing you," she says, making me chuckle.

The bathroom is around a corner and down a dim hallway. Shit. Maybe I should have let her come with me. I feel someone behind me and whip around, my hands up in front of me.

Kai laughs. "What are you going to do? Karate chop me?"

"Maybe? I don't fucking know. Why are you creeping up on me like that?"

"I wanted to make sure no one else followed you back here. It's dark," he explains.

I pull my hair in frustration. I'm tired, both physically and emotionally. I can't take his hot and cold personality right now.

"Do you hate me, Kai?" I ask him, taking him by surprise. His eyes go wide before he schools his features.

"I don't know," he says softly.

"What did I do to you?" I ask, on the verge of tears.

"Nothing. Everything. It's complicated."

"So uncomplicate it. Just hate me. That's what you really want to do, isn't it? Hate me and push me away so I'm out of your life for good? Do it!" I taunt, tears streaming down my face. I wipe them away angrily.

I expect him to yell at me. Tell me he hates me and wishes he never has to see me ever again, but that's not what he does. What he does is grab the back of my neck and bring his lips to mine. His kiss isn't gentle, it's rough and possessive. Like he's trying to claim me. When his tongue brushes the seam of my lips, I open for him without hesitation. His tongue tangles with mine in a dance of dominance and passion. He tastes like peppermint and desire wrapped in a muscular package.

Too soon he's pulling away, chest heaving and eyes blazing. Without a word, he turns around and leaves me in the dark hallway.

"It's been two minutes!" Willa says, running up to me like she actually thought I would die if I went past the two-minute mark. "Why are you touching your lips like that?"

I didn't realize I was, so I put my hand down and try to act like my whole world wasn't just rocked. "I'm ready to head back to the hotel if you are," I say, trying to deflect.

The lighting in here may not be great, but Willa's glare is clear as can be. She waits for me to say something, but I'm not sure what to tell her, so I remain mute.

"Fine. I'll get it out of you eventually," she says before looping her arm through mine. She walks us out to the main part of the pub and signals Cal and Mav. Kai isn't sitting with them, and Willa didn't mention seeing him in the hallway. I guess he bolted back to the hotel too.

I've wanted Malikai Irons to kiss me for most of my life. I always pictured something more romantic. Not. . . whatever that was. But for some reason, I want more.

eleven

KAI

"I KISSED HER!"

"Ok. And that's a problem because...?" Mav asks, sitting on the couch in his room and watching me pace back and forth. "Oh shit. Is it Cal? Did he forbid it?"

"You need to stop reading so many romance novels," I grumble.

"If anything, you need to read more. They're great. This is a classic best friend's little sister. Don't worry. It always works out."

I know he's joking, but it's annoying. He must sense my mood because he sighs and leans forward, resting his elbows on his knees.

"Why are you so angry with her?" he asks.

"She left," I whisper, stopping my pacing to sit at the end of his bed.

"She left to go to college. She didn't leave you, Kai."

"Feels like she did," I confess.

"Were you ever anything? Did you ever date?" he asks,

trying to get to the bottom of all my bullshit. Unfortunately for him, it's a bottomless black pit.

"No. She wasn't mine. She was someone else's."

"That's cryptic, but whatever," he mumbles under his breath. "Look, I get it. Ezra left, your dad left, and your mom has pretty much checked out, even if she's physically around. A lot of people have abandoned you. Stop putting her in the same category." I can feel his gaze on me as he speaks, but I keep my eyes focused on the ugly zigzag pattern of the carpet.

"Ezra died. He didn't choose to leave. Everyone else did. Belle included," I say, fighting the truth in his words. I hate saying my brother is dead. It feels like poison dripping from my tongue. But saying he's alive hurts just as much.

"Ezra isn't dead!" Maverick yells, standing up from the couch and glaring down at me. We've had this argument before. Mav won't let the idea of Ezra being alive and happy somewhere, go. It's a beautiful fantasy, but it's not the reality. Ezra wouldn't have left willingly. I know it, and deep down, so does Mav.

"Then he left too."

Mav rolls his eyes and stares up at the ceiling. "I think you're trying to find a reason to hate her, and you can't. So you're manufacturing one. Figure your shit out and stop hurting her. She's had enough of that from men to last a lifetime."

He has a way of humbling me that no one else does. I need it as much as I fucking hate it.

"Get the fuck out of my room," he says, gesturing to the door. I nod, knowing that arguing about Ezra has put him in a foul mood for the rest of the night. I shouldn't have said anything. I should have left it and let him believe whatever he wants. But as painful as it is for him to think Ezra is dead, it's just as painful for me to think he's alive.

The moment I exit his room, I hear a scream.

"Fuck!" I run down the hall to my room, fumbling with the key to get in. Once I do, I plow through the still broken door and into Belle's room. She's curled into a tight ball, muttering something. I get closer to hear what she's saying.

"I'm sorry, I'm sorry, I'm sorry."

My heart breaks with every word she mutters. Then suddenly she's screaming again, and I'm hopping on the bed next to her.

"Shh. It's ok. It's me, mo chridhe," I whisper, stroking her face gently with my knuckles. "It's ok. I'm here and no one will hurt you."

Belle instantly relaxes at the sound of my voice. Her hand snakes up and grabs my shirt, holding onto me and making sure I stay. I slide down next to her, not bothering to remove my clothes, but I'm able to kick my shoes off.

I know this is a bad idea. My feelings are already muddled when it comes to her. But even so, I can't watch her in pain like this. If sleeping next to her allows her some peace, then I'll gladly give her that.

BELLE

I WOKE up to an empty bed and the smell of mint and cedarwood on my pillow. I slept like the dead last night, and if I've learned anything since leaving Brad, it means Kai slept next to me. I didn't even need the lingering scent of him on my pillow to know that. Just the peaceful sleep was enough.

My phone is vibrating nonstop on the nightstand next to me, so I grab it. I groan when I see how many messages I have from a group chat titled *'Band of Badasses and Kai.'* I snort, knowing Willa named it. I ended up telling her about the kiss on the walk back to the hotel. It takes less than five minutes to walk from the pub to the hotel, but her glare forced it out of me. Well, her glare and the fact that I couldn't hold it in even if I wanted to.

WILLA

Are you ready to play with us tonight, Belle?

MAV

She's playing tonight?

CAL

How the fuck does she learn music that fast? I've watched her do it and I still can't believe it.

WILLA

The better question is why you take so long.

MAV

It doesn't when he's paying attention.

CAL

Exactly! Super speedy!

WILLA

I feel bad for every woman you've slept with.

CAL

You know that's not what I meant! I'm a very patient and giving lover.

ME

Never say lover again. I just puked in my mouth.

I'm also not playing tonight. I haven't practiced a single thing. I don't even have an instrument.

CAL

I bought you a keyboard!

ME

You literally never told me. You just said you were going to.

CAL

And I did! Did you doubt me?

ME

You forgot to pick me up at school before.

CAL

That was one time!

WILLA

It was traumatic. You were supposed to
pick me up too!

CAL

That explains why I avoided the place.

MAV

Can we get back on track here?

KAI

I hate everything about this. Stop adding
me to group chats.

ME

I'm not playing tonight. I took notes, but
that's about it.

MAV

Can we go early and practice? Help you
iron out whatever it is you're planning
to do.

ME

I have no idea. Can we?

KAI

No.

CAL

Yes, we can. Stop being a dick nugget.

KAI

What the fuck is a dick nugget?

CAL

A nugget made of dicks. Idiot.

WILLA

Can we actually go early?

KAI

No.

CAL

Stop saying no! We can. I called the venue and booked two extra hours before sound check. I did it yesterday after I ordered Belle's keyboard.

MAV

And you decided to tell no one about this because?

CAL

Honestly, I thought I did. I told someone.

WILLA

Was it the blonde that was rubbing her tits on your arm backstage?

CAL

Fuck. Yeah, I think it was.

WILLA

So. . . Belle's playing tonight?

ME

No!

KAI

No.

MAV

Does she want to?

CAL

Yes!

I flop back on the bed with a sigh. There are so many

conflicting emotions running through my system this morning. I'm equally excited and scared at the thought of playing with the band again. Especially in front of so many people.

Then there's the whole thing with Kai. I can't even begin to process that right now. I thought he just turned into an asshole, but I might be wrong. There's something else going on with him. Something more than Ezra. Trying to talk to him isn't working, but I'll get it out of him eventually. I owe it to our years of friendship to at least try to help him.

The kiss. God, the kiss. I've never been kissed like that before. Like he wanted me more than he wanted oxygen. But then he walked away like he couldn't handle looking at me afterward. Just to sleep in the bed next to me so I wouldn't be terrified all night. I think Kai is more confused than I'll ever be. So, I'll give him his space. For now.

I get dressed and pack my bag quickly. We're dropping our luggage off in Cal's room. Then Nate, the tour manager, will pick it all up and load the tour bus for us while we're at sound check. There's something bothering me though, and I need to talk to Willa about it.

ME

Are you in your room still?

WILLA

Yeah. You coming over to help me pack?

ME

Pack and chat?

WILLA

Obvs.

I grab my luggage, stopping at Cal's door and banging obnoxiously.

"Hold on! For fuck's sake!" Cal yells before swinging the door open.

"Here," I say as I shove my bag at my brother.

"You're not going to hang out with me?"

I snort and shake my head. Cal gets lonely easily. Even as kids, we'd be fighting one minute and then the next he would knock on my bedroom door, asking me to watch *Supernatural* with him.

"I need to help Willa pack if you actually want to get to sound check early."

Cal rolls his eyes, fully aware that Willa's luggage somehow explodes around the entire room the moment she opens it. She's always been a chaotic mess and still is.

"Fine. Hurry up. We need to get you ready for the show tonight."

"Not playing tonight!" I yell over my shoulder as I make my way to Willa's room.

I hear him murmur something that sounds like "we'll see" before shutting his door.

Willa has her door propped open with a chair, so I don't bother to knock.

"Jesus, Willa."

"I know! I can't find half of my makeup," she complains. I was talking about the clothes and shoes scattered over every surface, but sure.

"How about we pack up everything else and save the makeup for last? That way, we have to look under fewer things," I suggest.

"Yeah, that makes sense," she nods, looking around. "So, what did you want to talk about?"

I bite the inside of my cheek, nervous about asking her, but knowing the curiosity is going to kill me if I don't.

"Does Kai think Ezra is dead?"

Willa pauses her mindless stuffing of clothes into an oversized bag. She turns to me, brows furrowed. "Why do you ask?"

"He's the only one that refers to him in the past tense." It's something I picked up on after being around him again. I haven't given up believing that Ezra is out there somewhere. Mav and I haven't talked about it, but I doubt he believes he's dead.

Willa blows out a breath and sits on her bed. "I don't know if he believes it, exactly. More like it's easier for him to cope by telling himself that Ezra died."

I open my mouth to voice my outrage, but snap it shut. It kind of makes sense in a fucked-up way. Kai is the protector of our group. He must feel like he failed his brother and the thought of Ezra alive somewhere without him may be more painful than him being dead.

This would be easier if Kai would just talk to me.

"He looked for him for years, you know."

I turn around and see Maverick leaning against the doorframe.

"He hired a PI and everything. It was a mess of look-a-likes and people looking for their fifteen minutes. It was incredibly painful for him. We eventually forced him to stop," Mav says, hands in his pockets and looking at his feet. I know if I could see his eyes, all I would see is pain.

"It's cruel, the way the world keeps spinning. It doesn't

care if you're hurting or hoping. It just keeps going and the best we can do is move with it," Willa says, before returning to her packing.

I glance over to Maverick and see the torment in his eyes. I each out and squeeze his hand. Then we silently help Willa pack up her room and make our way over to the venue.

KAI

IT'S like she never left and my stupid heart loves that. The warmth in my chest as I watch her play right along with us is unwelcome. I don't want to feel like this. Keeping her at a distance was supposed to be how I survived this tour. So far, I've fucked that up more than I ever thought possible. I need to protect myself from her, or I won't survive when she leaves again.

But deep down, I know I can't protect my heart from her. It was never mine to protect. It was hers. From the moment we met, my heart was hers.

Unfortunately, her heart was never mine. So I walk around a shell of myself. My heart in the hands of another, and my brain held together with bubblegum and duct tape.

"What do you think?" Belle asks after the notes of our final song fade away. I have to admit, she's just as good as she ever was. The notes she took last night were more detailed than I expected, and she fit her parts in each song seamlessly. I never doubted her talent, but I thought she would have some cobwebs to work out.

"That was so good! You're going to kill it tonight!" Cal yells directly into the microphone, causing the workers milling about the stadium to flinch. "Oops. My bad. Sorry, guys!"

"I'm not playing tonight, Cal. I'm nowhere near ready for that," Belle says, blushing slightly. And what that blush does to my fucking emotions... fuck.

Cal pouts. He's been so happy having her with us. You'd think he was suddenly a puppy that was given a special treat.

"Can we do one more go through of *Purple Pleasure* before we're done?" Willa asks. That's not only the worst song, but it's also the one Belle added the most complicated part to. Mav wrote it while drunk a few years ago. It's about a giant purple dildo he said a hookup tried to use on him.

Willa claps her sticks together and starts the song before anyone even answers. We play it through with no mistakes. Nothing new there. I look over and see Willa grinning like an idiot, and I suddenly feel like I'm being left out of the joke.

"What?" Cal and Mav ask her at the same time. I look over and see Belle roll her eyes.

"I get it, Willa. I still don't think it's a good idea."

"Get what? Care to share with the class?" I ask, but I realize what's happening right after I ask. "You had her play the most complicated song that happens to be in the middle of the set, that she's only played once with us."

"Correct," Will says smugly.

"And she nailed it," I state.

"Correct. You get an A plus, Kai!" Willa says sarcastically.

"Honestly, unless you fuck up "Shattered Dreams," no one will even know. That's the only song with keyboards that people have heard from us," Maverick adds. I look over at Cal and see him practically vibrating.

"I guess I —"

She doesn't even get to finish her sentence before Cal is hugging her.

I bow my head and walk offstage. I don't want to ruin their sibling moment, and I'm genuinely happy that Cal gets this. But I'm jealous that I never will and terrified it won't last.

"You know, she might stay if you stop acting like a fuck hole."

I turn around to see Willa staring at me with that look that makes my brain itch. I swear she's walking around in there, reading my every thought.

"I don't know what you mean," I tell her, trying to walk away, but she gets in front of me.

"I've been stuck with your broody ass for literal years. I know how hurt you were when she left the band. Now she's back and you're worried she'll leave again."

"I know she'll leave. She never wanted this."

"You're wrong, Kai. She loves music. I even saw her writing songs again while we were waiting in the dressing room. She left because she was still raw over Ezra. If she leaves again... well that will be on you," Willa gives me one last glare before leaving me standing alone and questioning everything.

Will pushing her away and making her leave for good be more or less painful than if I let her close again, and she stays? I don't fucking know.

"Why is Lindsey calling me?"

Cal looks up from the pair of tits he was staring at. There's some busty redhead sitting in his lap in our dressing room. Mav has a blonde that might be her sister. I refused to let anyone back here, but those two don't care.

"Probably because I'm not answering her," he says before shoving his face into the groupie's chest.

I roll my eyes and brace myself for the phone call with our agent.

"Hi, Lindsey. We're going on stage soon."

"I don't give a fuck! Why isn't Callahan answering me? He sends me an email stating his sister is joining the band. What the fuck is that? This isn't some garage band that plays at a local dive bar once a month! You can't just add people!" she screams into the phone. I hold it out so I maintain hearing in my ear. "And who is the bitch the tabloids keep reporting you with?"

"Stop screaming for two fucking seconds," I tell her sternly. "Cal is busy. Belle is already in the band. Check the fucking contract before you scream at people. You make yourself sound like an idiot."

"Don't you fucking speak to me —"

I hang up my phone, not allowing her to finish. Sleeping with your agent, who is also the daughter of the CEO of the record label you signed with, is a terrible idea. Hanging up on her might have been worse, but I don't care.

"What did you mean about the contract?" Mav asks.

"We made sure there was a clause stating that if Belle or Ezra wanted to rejoin the band, they could do so at any time," Cal says without taking his attention from the redhead.

"And the tabloids?" Mav asks. He seems to just be tolerating the woman on his lap.

"No idea. You know I don't follow those." I shrug, but pull up the browser on my phone anyway, ignoring all the angry texts coming in from Lindsey.

The moment the results come up from searching my name, I immediately tense.

Malikai Irons and His New Beau

Can Irons Keep This One?

The Playboy and the Beauty

The only pictures they have is one someone took of my hand on Belle's back at the airport and another of all of us leaving the hotel earlier today. I opened the door of the car for Belle, and they cut everyone else out. There's nothing negative about Belle here, so I don't see any issues with it. Her face also isn't visible in any of the pictures, but it wouldn't be difficult to figure out who she was if anyone tried.

"Uhh. Kai, did you see the one that was just posted?"

I look over at Mav to see him looking horrified. The moment I refresh my browser, I immediately see what he's talking about. I grip my phone so tightly as I read, I'm surprised the screen doesn't crack. I vaguely hear Mav telling Cal to get our PR team on the phone.

Stolen Love? Malikai Irons Spotted with Dead Brother's Love! His Mother Tells All!

Right under the title is a picture of my mother holding a silver frame that has the word 'Love' etched into it. Instead of the picture of her and my dad that used to be in it, now there's a picture of Belle and Ezra as teenagers. Belle's hair is shorter and a tangled mess of curls around her face. She's smiling at the camera, silver braces on full display. Ezra is next to her, arm around her shoulder, smiling down at her like her smile solves all his problems. I know because it used to do that for me. Back when she used to smile at me. Now all she does it glare, not that I haven't earned it.

My chest feels like it's caving in, and my face might be on fire with the way it's burning up. I suck in as much air as I can before moving on to read the article.

Ezra Irons had the entire world in his hands. He had his twin brother, his best friends, a band that was about to make it big, but most importantly, he had the love of his life. Bellamy Griffin and Ezra grew up together. They were friends from a young age and grew into more as the years progressed.

"They were made for each other. Everyone knew it." Adira Irons told us when we sat down with her. As the mother of Malikai and Ezra, she knew him best.

Malikai and Belle have been spotted together quite a few times in London. Questions have begun to swirl around the pair.

"I'm not surprised." Adira says when asked about her son's relationship. "Malikai was always jealous of Ezra. He wanted everything Ezra had. I'm surprised it took him this long to go after Bellamy."

When asked about Bellamy, Adira smiled warmly. "Oh, she is such a lovely young lady! My Ezra was so happy when he was with her. They'd be married by now, you know? With babies for me to spoil."

When asked if she would be happy if Malikai and Bellamy married, her answer was straightforward. "No. He can't have her. She is Ezra's."

When asked about Ezra's passing, Adira became so worked

up that the interview ended here. But I think we have all the information we need. Malikai Irons is stealing his brother's girl.

"Fuck!" I throw my phone on the couch and start pacing the room.

"Our PR team is working on burying the story," Cal says. I look up to see the two women have left, and it's just us.

I nod to acknowledge I heard him, but it doesn't matter. However fucked up my mother's motivation for giving this interview was, she was right. I can't have Belle. She's Ezra's.

BELLE

"I THINK I'm going to throw up. Or pass out. Maybe have a heart attack and die."

"Your level of drama is rivaling Cal's," Willa says, as she touches up her makeup in our shared dressing room. The guys have their own right next to us. Willa says she always requests her own, so she doesn't have to deal with the groupies they bring backstage. I didn't love hearing that and then was immediately angry at myself. Kai isn't anything to me. He kissed me and has ignored me since.

"Never say that to me ever again."

Willa just laughs me off before turning around to hug me. "You're going to be amazing. If you hate it, we won't make you do it again."

A knock sounds on the door and Willa calls to whoever it is to come in.

Nate sticks his shiny, bald head through the door. The man is all of five foot three inches, but he gets everyone in their places like a trained prairie dog.

"Five minutes, girls," he says before immediately disappearing.

I check myself over in the full-length mirror. Willa helped me get some stage appropriate outfits sent over. I'm in a tight-fitting body suit that covers my entire body. I have it zipped halfway down the middle to show off some cleavage. I don't know what material it is, but it's black and surprisingly breathable. When I saw it on the hanger, it looked like something I would sweat in immediately.

Willa is in a similar bodysuit, but hers is all black lace and entirely see through. You can see her black thong and the matching black pasties she put over her nipples. I admire how risky she's willing to dress, but I'd be so paranoid about my nipples accidentally showing that I would miss notes.

The opening act is playing right now, and we can hear them in here. They're a local band. Mav told me that Kai always has local bands open for them when they tour. I hate having things endear me to Kai even more when I'm trying to be mad at him.

"I think someone needs to tell Nate what five minutes is," I murmur under my breath as I follow Willa out to the stage.

"It's been five minutes, babe. Just don't forget to breathe," she tells me before sitting behind her drums. I barely heard her over the roar of the crowd.

"This is a terrible idea. Why the hell did I agree with it? I'm an idiot," I tell myself as I fiddle with the settings on my keyboard. Anything to distract me from the crowd and their probably confused faces. I've never played with Shattered

Halo in public, and Cal has kept me out of the press. I doubt anyone here knows who I am.

Oh God, what if they think I fucked my way in? The clashing of Willa's sticks interrupts my self-deprecating thoughts.

Cal's velvety smooth voice joins notes from Kai's guitar and Mav's bass. The moment my fingers touch the keys and the music I added to their songs joins in, everything fades away.

"It's a special night tonight, London!" Cal shouts into the mic after the first song ends. The crowd roars and Cal smiles. He's in his element. "My baby sister, Belle, is joining us tonight and for the rest of the tour!" The roar of the crowd is noticeably less, but I'm happy they cared at all.

I wave sheepishly in the general direction of the crowd.

"Belle is a founding member of Shattered Halo and the genius who wrote 'Shattered Dreams!'" Cal shouts. That gets a significantly better reaction.

"How about we play so they can see how amazing she is for themselves?" Willa asks the crowd, knowing how uncomfortable I am right now. I shoot her a grateful look, and she winks before clapping her sticks together to start the next song.

We play through the entire set with only a few interruptions of Cal working the audience. The last song is "Shattered Dreams." Mav told me they always end with it. When I wrote it and we practiced it in the garage as teenagers, Kai sang it with me. Now he just sings it alone, which somehow makes the sad song even sadder.

I play the notes as I watch him. His raspy tone cutting through the blood pumping in my ears. My fingers dance along the keys without much thought. I know this song as well as I know anything. I don't need sheet music to play it.

As Kai sings the last line, he turns his head to look at me. If I had any more notes to play, I would've stumbled. The pure agony in his eyes cuts right through me. The moment the last word leaves his lips, he takes off his guitar and leaves the stage.

"Thank you, London!" Cal calls, ending the show quicker than he did last night.

I hustle off the stage as quickly as I can, searching for Kai. There are reporters and groupies in my way. I see Nate's shiny head thanks to some overhead lights and make a beeline for him.

"Where did Kai go?" I ask him.

"Dressing room," he states, trying to help me through the crowd. He motions for security to make a path for me, and I quickly thank him.

"Kai!" I yell, banging on the door of the guy's dressing room.

"Not now, Belle." His voice is shaky and there's no way I'm taking that as an answer.

I barge in to find him sitting on the couch, elbows propped up on his knees and his face in his hands. His blue and white silk shirt is stuck to his body from sweat. I can see his knees through the rips in the back jeans that seem to be his go-to for stage outfits.

"Kai, what's going on?" I ask, sitting down on the seat next to him.

He doesn't answer me, he just shakes his head. I put my hand on his bicep and squeeze gently. I know what it's like, not being able to verbalize your pain. I wish he would talk to me. He used to tell me everything. Pushing him is my first instinct, but I don't. I just sit with him and hope that it's comfort enough.

"We've got him, Belle. Willa said to send you two over."

My brother and Mav are standing at the door. I nod and walk towards them. Mav immediately takes my seat next to Kai and Cal gives me a quick hug. I want to ask questions, but I know now isn't the time. So I make my way to my dressing room instead.

"Can you tell me what the fuck just happened? Kai is nonverbal and the guys are acting like they're not surprised by it," I demand the moment I enter the room and see Willa waiting for me.

She hands me her phone without saying anything. The look on her face is a mixture of hurt and anger. I look at the screen and immediately realize why.

"What the fuck?" I murmur as I read. This can't be real. Kai's mom gave an interview to a tabloid? Not only that, but she's also making up lies and hurting Kai in the process.

"Cal said Kai read this about twenty minutes before we went on," Willa supplies.

"Why would she make up lies to hurt the only son she has left?"

"They probably paid her," Willa says angrily.

"Ezra and I were never together. Never even close. Kai…"

"I know, Belle. It doesn't matter though. They weren't looking for the truth, they were looking for a story and Adira gave it to them."

"What can we do? There has to be something I can do to help. I'll give a statement or something. Whatever it takes," I plead with Willa, like she has the magic answer to this.

"This isn't the first time something like this has happened. Our team is working on it. It'll blow over. Kai might take a couple of days, but he'll be alright."

"What do you mean? This has happened before?" Who else could they have accused Kai of stealing?

"Not this exactly. There was a strange conspiracy theory that caught traction when we released our second album. People kept claiming they had 'proof' that Kai was actually Ezra. It was bizarre and honestly didn't make much sense, but people ran with it and called him Ezra for months."

"For fuck's sake," I exclaim. "That's horrible! No wonder Kai is so angry all the time."

I'm about to go on a rant about how I plan on confronting Kai's mom when we get back home, but the words get caught in my throat when I see the flowers over Willa's shoulder.

"More flowers?" I ask, my voice sounding weak.

Willa sighs and turns around. "Yeah. They were here when I got back. Nate said they were delivered right as the set started."

"Tulips," I say unnecessarily. They're probably one of the most easily recognizable flowers out there.

"It says red means a declaration of love," Willa offers.

"Great," I mutter as I pick up the note in front of the vase.

Tulips are red,
My balls are blue.
My heart is lonely,
All because of you.

"I'm so stressed about that article that this shitty poem isn't bothering me. It should bother me, right?"

"It's creepy and kind of gross. Our tour schedule is public, so it's less stalkerish than it could be," Willa offers, unhelpfully.

I take pictures and send them to Cal to forward to the lawyer. The high from playing tonight comes crashing down immediately and my body is feeling it. I'm exhausted and my head is pounding.

"We need to be on the bus in twenty!" Nate yells as he walks by our door. Willa gives him a thumbs up.

"So, how was playing with us? You know, before every-thing," she asks, biting her lip nervously.

"Honestly, it was amazing. It was what I was always too scared to dream."

Willa smiles and claps her hands. "My girl is back!"

Both our phones go off and we roll our eyes together. We know it's Cal in the group chat.

CAL

I need to change my number immediately.

ME

What did you do?

"Ten bucks says he gave it to a groupie," Willa says, reading along with me.

MAV

He gave it to the hot redhead, and she posted it on her Instagram.

"Told you," Willa says with a snort.

CAL

Did you see her? Of course I gave it to her.
In more ways than one.

ME

Take me off this group chat.

MAV

If we suffer, you suffer.

CAL

My phone won't stop ringing!

ME

Sounds like a you problem.

"Ready?" I ask Willa, who is shaking her head at her phone.

"This is the fourth time this has happened. He never learns."

I just laugh. Leave it to my brother to break the tension in a room he isn't even in.

"I've never seen them drunk before."

"It happens. Not as often as it used to, thankfully."

Willa and I are sitting on a couch on the tour bus. Kai didn't speak the entire time we were walking to the bus and already went to bed in one of the bunks. Cal and Mav took way too many shots and were now both sprawled on the floor, giggling.

We're traveling to the next, and last, city overnight because the band has an interview with a local morning show first thing. I'm glad I don't have to do interviews. The idea of being asked questions live on television is terrifying. Wait...

"Willa? Am I expected to be on the morning show tomorrow?" I ask her.

She tilts her head and thinks about it. "It's possible. I'm sure they're going to ask about you after tonight's show. But we also submit topics that are off limits ahead of time, which obviously hasn't happened with you." The more she thinks out loud, the more I panic. "Our manager hasn't said anything as far as I know. She usually goes through Cal or Kai. But Lindsey has also been sucking at her job. I guess the answer is, I don't know."

"Why don't you fire her if she sucks?"

"Lindsey Sparks is the daughter of Alder Sparks. AKA, the owner of Sparks Records. The company we're signed with."

"Ah. So if you fire her, daddy will not be pleased," I say, not realizing they were in a tough situation.

"Pretty much. I don't think it matters, since he's not pleased, anyway."

I think about that for a minute, grateful to no longer be stuck imagining myself saying idiotic things on tv. "Would you want to resign if they were happy with you? Cal made it seem like you guys weren't happy with them, either."

"No, I don't think we would. They treat us like machines and not people. We're barely able to be home, and when we are, we're expected to pump out an album and get back on the road in a few months' time. It's exhausting and unsustainable," Willa shrugs and curls her purple hair around her finger. "We were too young and excited when we signed. We know better now."

"Do you think you'll sign with someone else?" I ask what's been on my mind recently. Kai thinks I'm going to leave the band after this tour, but will there be a band after?

"We'd like to, and I'm sure someone will want us. The problem is, because of how quickly we had to push albums out, they're not great. So what the labels see is mediocre and it won't get us a good deal. We don't want to be trapped like we are now."

I nod in understanding. No one understands feeling trapped more than I do.

My brother and Mav are both passed out on the floor, foot to chin. I take a quick picture and stand.

"I'm going to sleep. Please don't wake me up and bring me with you in the morning."

Willa laughs. "No promises, babe. You might be the thing that saves us."

"No pressure," I mumble.

The curtains on Kai's bunk are closed. He's slept with me two nights in a row to keep me from being stuck in my nightmares. But whatever happened on stage today shut him down and no matter how much I want to ask him to take the nightmares away again, I can't.

KAI

SCREAMING WAKES me from a dead sleep. *Fuck.* I meant to stay awake and slip into her bunk after she fell asleep. I slip out of my bunk and see a sleepy Willa pop her head out of hers. She sees me and raises her chin before going back to sleep.

Slowly crawling in next to Belle, I pull her to my chest and whisper to her like I have the past couple of nights. She calms for a minute before she starts sobbing. Well, that's new. I hold her closer, letting her tears soak through my shirt as she clings to me.

"He can't get you here. You're safe, Belle," I whisper into her hair.

"I wasn't dreaming about Brad."

I stiffen, my hand freezing on her back where it was stroking. She's never woken up before, not even when we tried really hard to wake her.

"What were you dreaming about?" I ask her, keeping my voice low.

"That night when Ezra went missing. I dream about it

sometimes, but it's..." she trails off for a moment. I resume stroking her back with my fingers, encouraging her to continue. "I'm a horrible person," she says before sobbing into my shirt again.

"No, you're not, Belle. You're one of the best people I know. I'm sorry if I've made you feel differently."

"You don't understand. In my dream, you're the one who goes missing and Ezra is still here. Then I wake up, and I'm fucking relieved that's not true. Relieved! What is wrong with me?" she asks, her wet eyes filled with utter devastation as she looks at me. That look alone is enough to shatter what's left of my heart into tiny pieces.

"You already suffered Ezra's loss. Your brain is trying to make you suffer another. There's nothing wrong with waking up and realizing you've still only lost the one person," I tell her, wiping the tears from her cheeks. I don't know what else to tell her that will help her.

She snuggles into me and is quiet for so long; I think she's fallen back asleep.

"I'm sorry about the article. I didn't know being seen with you would cause that."

"Shh. It's ok. Get some sleep and we can talk tomorrow." I'm gutted that she thinks my mother giving a bullshit interview is in any way her fault.

"Ok... Kai?"

"Yeah?"

"Thank you."

I think she's dozed off, but then I hear her whisper. "Always and forever?"

Her question causes all the muscles in my body to

stiffen. I want to ignore her and hope she falls asleep before realizing I haven't answered.

But that's the asshole thing to do, and I'm trying to be better.

"Yeah, Belle. Always and forever."

I try to sleep, but I'm up most of the night trying to analyze a dream that was probably just a trauma response. She dreams of the last day she was with Ezra. But instead it was me. If she didn't wake up so upset, I think it would make more sense. She was not only upset; she was nearing hysterical with the number of tears she shed onto my shirt. She said she was relieved I was still alive.

In my darker moments, I've wondered if she ever wished it was me instead. If she wished the twin she loved the most was the one still with her. It would make sense if she did, and I wouldn't even blame her for it. I loved him the most too.

My thoughts went around in circles for hours until the bus parked, and I knew it was almost time to start all the bullshit over again.

The morning show was luckily just an interview and not a performance as well. Our PR team made sure the producers were aware they weren't allowed to ask about the article or mention Belle in relation to me. I could tell they were angry about it, but I didn't give a shit. I won't hurt her like that.

One producer tried approaching her, saying it was an opportunity to put rumors to rest, but Willa shot that down before I even got the chance. We all know better.

"I have to tell you guys, that interview was boring," Belle says as we exit the stage.

"They only wanted to talk about you, but when we vetoed that, I think they asked bland questions on purpose," Willa tells her.

"I'm sorry. I should have gone with you guys. If I'm in the band, I probably should." Belle wrings her hands as she speaks. I've noticed she curls into herself and becomes nervous when we're around a lot of strangers. She's herself when it's just our group.

"We'll work up to that," Cal assures her, patting her on the back.

"What's the plan for the rest of the day?" Mav asks.

"I think I want to write," Belle says. The look on her face says she surprised herself.

"Write? Like songs? Belle! Are you still writing? This could be big for us!" Cal exclaims. He practically runs over a pedestrian on our way out of the building.

"I mean, a little. I don't think I've written anything to get excited about," she says, a blush creeping up her neck. "I wrote in college, but that journal is at Brad's."

"We're getting that and everything else you own the moment we get home from this tour!" Cal yells. Willa shushes him when she sees Belle's face.

I grab her hand on instinct and give it a squeeze. She looked panicked when Cal mentioned going to Brad's, and he was too excited to notice. She looks at me, eyes scared and face pale.

"Ignore him. You don't have to do anything," I whisper.

She nods but keeps my hand in hers. The street the television studio is on is too narrow for the tour bus, so Nate had to park a couple of streets over. Being out in the open, holding her hand like this, is something I want more than anything. It's also something I can't risk right now after the article yesterday. I drop her hand and immediately miss it.

"In case someone with a camera is watching," I explain, even though she didn't ask. She looks around and nods in understanding.

"Kai, that article…"

I stop her with a shake of my head. "I really don't want to talk about it. I'm trying to move past it."

Belle looks at me, trying to read me like she always used to. "Fine." Her tone is firm, letting me know it is, in fact, not fine. I can't bring myself to discuss it with her, so I don't stop her when she quickly walks away from me to get to Willa instead.

sixteen

BELLE

I'VE FALLEN into a steady routine with the band. We've played twelve shows together so far, and I've loved every moment of being on stage. I could genuinely picture myself doing this for as long as I can. Cal asks me constantly, and I see the way Kai flinches every time he does. I thought giving it time would help me figure out if he's flinching because he doesn't want me to stay or if it's because he's worried I won't.

It would be helpful if he would just talk to me, but he doesn't. We're amicable. No more random fights, and he still sleeps next to me if I have a nightmare, but those have become less frequent. I still get flowers and notes from Brad after every show, but they've become easy to ignore.

Our last show in Ireland is tonight and then we're going to Germany, where we have four shows. Our last stop is Glasgow and then home. Time is quickly slipping by and there are so many decisions we have to make. I have to make.

"Can I ask a probably stupid question?"

Cal looks up from the poker game he's playing against Willa and Kai. Mav is watching a movie with me.

"Go for it."

"What's the difference between the band's manager and your agent, and why isn't the manager with us?" I ask. I've been confused about this pretty much the entire tour, but I tried to figure it out myself. "All the opening bands have had their managers with them."

"Because Lindsey sucks. That's what we get for hiring her," Cal says before tossing chips into the growing pile in the middle of the small table. They crammed the three of them into the kitchen booth on the tour bus. "Nate is doing her job. We hired him ourselves. Lindsey schedules tours and interviews. Mostly because it's easy to do without having to leave her house."

"Lindsey used to come on tour for a few stops to fuck Kai," Willa says. I watch him shoot her a glare, but he doesn't deny it. I know he's been with other women, but hearing it makes me want to fight someone. Even if we're barely friends, I think a part of me will always want more from him.

"Lindsey likes to say that she manages us so well she can do it from home," Mav says with a roll of his eyes.

"Please tell me we aren't planning to resign with her. There has to be someone else," I ask, my tone pleading. If I do this with them, I'd like to have people supporting us, not just collecting money. Or fucking Kai.

Cal squirms out of the booth and runs over to me. "What are you doing?" I ask him nervously. He scoops me up and spins me around.

"You said we!" He yells, still spinning me around.

"What are you talking about? Put me down, idiot!" I yell, slapping him on the back. He listens, but just so he can squeeze me into a crushing hug instead.

"You said we, babe. *We* will sign with a better company as long as someone is interested." Willa answers, since Cal is apparently too excited. I look over at the table to see her smiling at me. I chance a look at Kai to see him staring at me.

I lift my eyebrow in question, silently asking for his input. One side of his mouth quirks up into a half smile and that's all I need. I'm staying with this band and my people.

"Hi Mrs. Griffin."

Cal drops me and we both turn to look at Willa. She's on the phone, apparently with my mother.

"Yes, they're both here with me."

I look at Cal and he shrugs.

"Of course you can."

Willa holds the phone out. Cal looks at me and quickly puts his finger on his nose.

"Cheater!" I whisper yell at him before taking the phone from Willa.

"Hi, Mom."

"Bellamy! What are you doing with your brother and that band? Is Brad with you?" My mother's shrill voice comes through the phone, and I wince. I haven't spoken to her in months, even before I left Brad. We're not exactly close.

"No. I left Brad. I actually just decided to join Cal and Shattered Halo permanently."

Kai is fully smiling now, and I briefly return it before my mother ruins any good mood I even thought about having.

"You have got to be kidding me! You need to fly home and make things right with Brad."

"No. Brad abused me, Mom. I'm not going back to him," I choke out, keeping the lump in my throat down.

"I'm sure he didn't mean any harm."

Cal is stiff next to me, Kai is glaring at the phone like he can tell my mom off with his mind, and Willa looks like she's about to swim across the ocean to beat some sense into her. I can't see Mav from where I'm standing, but I doubt his reaction is any less violent. The immediate support from everyone around me gives me the strength I need to finish this conversation.

"This isn't up for discussion. If you called to discuss my relationships or my career, then I think we're finished here."

"You're making a mistake," she argues.

"I'm not. Even if I were, it's my mistake to make. Good-bye, Mom."

"Wait! That's not why I called. Your aunt Valerie died." Valerie is my mom's sister and our only cousin, Millie's mom.

"What? When?"

"A few weeks ago. Neither of my children's numbers worked, so I couldn't get in touch with you."

"You clearly have Willa's number," I point out.

"Yes, but I just realized that."

"Thank you for letting us know. Please text her address to Willa's phone," I tell her and hang up.

"We need to fly out immediately after the show tonight."

"What? Why?" Cal asks, surprised.

"Aunt Val died. Weeks ago. We need to see Millie."

Cal's face goes from shock to anger. Millie was not only our only cousin, but she was also one of our closest friends when we were kids. Kai and Willa know her too. A phone call won't be enough.

"Fuck. That's Millie's mom? I'm sorry, guys. She was really amazing," Kai says.

My mom and her sister couldn't have been more different. My mom is snobby and opinionated. Aunt Val went with the flow and could make me laugh so hard I'd feel it in my abs for days.

"I booked us on a private jet out of Dublin. We'll be cutting it close, but we should make it to Germany in time for the show," Cal says. I nod in agreement.

I plop myself back down on the couch next to Mav, and he throws his arm around me.

"That was a rollercoaster of emotions in a really small amount of time. I could use a drink or a nap. Maybe both," he says.

I laugh humorlessly in agreement.

seventeen

BRAD

THE FLOOR of my room is littered with tabloid articles I printed about Belle. The idiots reporting on the band seem to have figured out who Belle is. Took them long enough. They just immediately assumed she was Kai's bimbo of the week.

Not that I cared. She's a whore and would deserve the negative attention.

But I need them to know who she really is for my plan to work.

I pick up one of the papers to my left and examine the article. Some tabloids are reporting that the band is breaking up since they're at the end of their contract and haven't resigned. They're calling her this generation's Yoko.

I snort. I would love for that dumb band to be no more, but claiming Belle has that power is laughable. Continuing to shuffle through all the articles provides no new information. She's on tour and sometimes she's seen with Malikai. I can't fathom how this is print worthy.

Then my phone pings. I set an alert with Belle's name attached so I would know of anything new immediately. I frown with confusion at what I see.

"Belle and Cal are back in the States?" I mutter to myself. I read the article and there's a picture attached of them at a private airstrip in Boston. "What the fuck?" The article doesn't know why they're here or where the rest of the band is. Maybe that article about the band breaking up is accurate. Either way, it's made this job a little easier.

That bitch filed a restraining order against me when she left. There's no way authorities wouldn't be alerted if I left the country. But driving from Maine to Massachusetts? I can easily do that without them knowing.

I quickly grab my keys and race to my car. I'm backing out of my parking space when my phone rings over the car's Bluetooth.

"What?" I bark.

"Mr. Foley? This is Martha with Maine Medical. Your mother has made progress in her speech therapy and was able to ask for you just now. Will you come see her?"

Fuck! I sit in my car, halfway out of the parking spot and not sure what to do.

"She's asking for me?" I reiterate. My mother hasn't been able to speak for months. I've been using funds I skimmed from her company to pay for her care since my boss stopped the payments until I get Belle back under control.

"She was quite demanding that I call you and get you here."

Belle is within reach, and I need to go get her. But there's always a chance her brother will be stuck to her side like glue. It might take longer than I'd like before I can see my mother.

"I'm on my way," I hang up before the nurse has a chance to respond.

The drive to the hospital is short, and I stride by the nurse's station without bothering to glance their way. I've been here enough. They know who I am and should know better than to stop me.

"Mother?" I ask quietly, stepping into the private room her company is now unknowingly paying for.

"B-B-Brad," she stutters. I contain my wince at her muddled words. She wouldn't be happy to see that look on my face, even if she doesn't have the strength to slap it off me right now.

"You asked for me?" I take the seat next to her bedside. You'd think with all the money I'm paying for this room; they would provide more comfortable chairs.

"Belle?" she asks simply.

Oh, she can say Belle's name, but not mine? What is with everyone's obsession with this girl? She's as boring as a fucking brick.

"Apparently, she's in Boston. I just got the alert on my phone before I was summoned here."

My mother tries to glare at me, but the left side of her face is still frozen.

"I'll get her back."

"Y-You b-bet-ter."

I contain my eye roll. My mother is the reason I have to deal with Belle in the first place. She made a deal with a man way more powerful than she is and now I'm somehow stuck facing the consequences of that. I don't even know what the fucking deal was. I can guess, though. Her company was going under and then suddenly it was super successful, and I had a girlfriend I didn't want.

"Did you just want a status report?" I ask, trying to keep my tone from betraying my annoyance. I could be halfway to Boston by now and not listening to the stuttering the nurse is calling 'progress.'

"C-Company f-f-f-fails. We f-fail. You f-fail."

"I get it, Mother. If I don't get her back, we're both fucked." I wouldn't normally speak to her this way, but there isn't much she can do about it right now.

She shakes her head like I don't understand. She's basically speaking in a fucking riddle, so I don't know what she expects right now. "M-Money."

Oh. *Shit.* She found out about the money I've been taking. "I'll put it back once I have Belle. He'll pay me back," I say with more confidence than I have. He'll at least restart payments for Mother's care. That's about all he's promised.

She doesn't look convinced. Or maybe she does. I don't fucking know. I don't have time to figure out her new disappointed face right now.

"I best be going," I say, leaning forward to place a kiss on her head. She makes a noise that sounds like a protest, but I ignore her and walk out of her room.

"Martha!" I bark at the pudgy nurse sitting in the chair at the nurse's station. She doesn't jump like most would at my tone. Instead, she plasters on a fake smile and waits for me to tell her what I want. "Don't call me again unless it's an emergency. I will visit Mother when I am able, and not a moment sooner."

I don't wait to hear a response. I need to get to Boston and get Belle. She has somehow become the only way to get my life back on track. I knew the stupid bitch was trouble when I first met her. She'd be better buried.

Hmm. Now that's a thought.

eighteen

KAI

"STOP PACING. IT'S ANNOYING."

"I can't help it," I grumble.

I've been an anxious mess since Cal and Belle left for the airport a few hours ago.

"They won't be back until tomorrow night at the earliest. You need to relax," Willa says, not even trying to hide her annoyance.

"I can't relax. She's going to be too close!" I shout while pulling on my hair.

"I'm going to need you to explain that one," Mav says, rubbing a hand over his tired face. It's late and we should be sleeping. We fly out to Germany in the morning.

"To Brad. She's going to be too close to Brad!"

"Oh. I didn't even think of that," Willa says, frowning.

"Unless someone spots them, they'll be fine. He thinks she's here with us and there's no reason to think she would fly out because her aunt died. If she was going to do that, she would have done it weeks ago. As far as he knows anyway," Mav says before yawning.

"She's also with Cal. Belle claims Brad is a coward and would never interact with Cal so I'm sure she'll be ok even if someone sees them," Willa says before standing and stretching.

"Right. Yeah," I say, feeling only slightly better.

"I'm going to sleep. They're in the air for another few hours, anyway," Willa says and Mav seconds.

"Good idea," I say as I follow them towards the bunks.

I know I won't sleep. I haven't felt this type of panic since Ezra went missing. Belle could be walking into the lion's den and there's nothing I can do to protect her.

nineteen

BELLE

WE LANDED in Germany with enough time to check into our hotel and rush to the venue. We missed sound check, so the best we can do is hope our friends did it for us.

"You made it!" Willa yells as she barrels into me.

"Five minutes!" Nate yells as he passes us.

I look around and see Kai talking on the phone. He seems angry.

"What's going on?" I ask Willa, pointing to Kai with my chin.

She winces. "There are more tabloid stories about you and Kai. He's just talking to our PR team."

"How bad?" I ask. Stories about us have been popping up here and there these past weeks, but nothing has come of it.

"Not bad. They just got pictures of you two talking closely. They left out that the restaurant was so loud, the only way you could speak was if you got right in the other person's ear," Willa says with a shrug. It's annoying the way rumors spread so easily. I guess that's part of this life that I need to get more used to. "They also knew when you landed in Boston somehow. He's been an anxious mess."

I feel bad about worrying Kai, not that it was my fault. He's used to life in the spotlight, and I don't think tabloids bother him. Until now. Until they started writing about me. The one thing that hasn't changed about Kai is how protective of me he is.

"Showtime people!" Nate yells, ushering us on stage.

We play our set to a sea of screaming fans. That part never gets old. The rush I feel while playing and the adrenaline high afterward are addicting.

"This is a new one," Willa says as we enter our dressing room. As usual, there are flowers there waiting for me. Mav follows in behind us, probably having heard Willa. He plucks the note from the front of the vase.

They're a strange but pretty flower. There are five blue pointed petals with a small white flower on the inside. I've never seen them before.

"The note still doesn't have a name," Mav says, handing it over.

I take it and read it out loud.

> You are mine, little liar.
> Do they know? Do they see?
> It's your fault, this fire.
> I'll never set you free.

"Well, that's the first one that feels threatening," Willa says, reading it next to me.

"It's a columbine. It means foolish," Mav supplies. He's used to looking up the meaning of flowers by now.

I sigh before taking the usual pictures and sending them off to the lawyer.

"So, how was your trip?" Willa asks.

"Good, but too short. Millie is married. His name is Logan, and he seems nice. He's definitely obsessed with her."

"And he owns a record label!" Cal yells as he barges into our room.

"I spent eight hours on a plane with you and you didn't mention that once," I say to Cal as I glare at him.

"I wanted to tell everyone!" Cal says defensively.

"Kai isn't in here," Mav points out.

"I'm here now. Why'd you guys ditch me?" he asks, in a more playful tone than I'm used to.

"Three out of the four were in this room, and I couldn't hold it in anymore," Cal says with too much excitement.

"Logan owns a record label?" I ask, making sure I heard him correctly.

"He does! He has no idea how to run it, but he said the woman he has in charge is fantastic. I have her email, and I already sent her clips of our shows. I think we need something new to send if we want to sign, though."

"Can't you get a deal just for being family?" Willa asks.

Cal just shrugs. "Probably, but I'd rather do it because we're wanted."

I can't blame my brother for feeling that way. It would be hard to know if we were successful or just related to someone who is.

"I have some things we could try, but they're not great," I offer.

"They're probably amazing, Belle," Kai says, surprising me.

"I think we need to have a lawyer go through the contract and make sure that anything we perform or produce during the tour is our property and not theirs. I don't want Sparks owning our new stuff," Mav adds.

"Ok. I'll send the emails. Belle, work your magic," Cal says, hugging me.

No pressure.

Two more shows. Two nights with no flowers or vaguely threatening notes after. Tonight is our last show in Germany. We only have one more show total and then we're done.

The show is going like all the others. The crowd is singing along to our second to last song. I'm sweaty and can't wait to shower. Then Cal decides to switch things up without consulting anyone. Honestly, I'm surprised it took him this long.

"Did you guys know that the original version of "Shattered Dreams" had Belle and Kai singing together? What do you think about asking them to do it again?" Cal asks the crowd, who seems not only really into the idea, but is now chanting my name.

I look at Cal, but he's gesturing for someone backstage and mouthing 'mic' at them. I'm going to fucking kill him. I chance a look at Kai to find him already looking at me. His features are hard, but he must read the panic in mine because they soften. He picks up his mic stand and swings his guitar to his back before making his way towards me.

The guy Cal gestured to must be adjusting the volume of my mic. I usually sing background, so it shouldn't be as loud as Kai or Cal's. I see the man give Cal a thumbs up before Kai sets his mic up, so he's facing me. His eyes never leave mine and he nods slightly. He's asking me if I'm ok. So I return the nod and look to Willa. She looks concerned but smiles once I nod at her too. I've only been singing the backup vocals, nothing that would put my voice to the forefront like this will.

This song doesn't start with drums like most of our songs do. It starts with the slow strum of Kai's guitar. I sing first about unattainable love and angst. Kai's voice joins mine soon after, singing about wanting from afar. His voice is raspy and warm. Together, we sing a tale of the love I once held for him, and maybe still do. Part of me always thought he knew this song was about him, but lately I'm not so sure.

Kai's eyes hold mine the entire time, keeping me with him and in the moment. I sing to him, not the audience. I let the longing I felt while writing the song mix with the pain and confusion of the present. I don't know if the emotions are as identifiable in my voice as I think they are, but Kai's are. All I hear from him is suffering.

The moment the last note leaves my fingers, and the song ends, his eyes leave mine. I feel the loss of his attention immediately. I watch as he smiles and waves to his fans before bowing and leaving the stage.

Willa said Kai was hurting, and I believed her. I got glimpses of it in his eyes here and there, but this, that suffering. . . I could feel it as if it was something I could reach out and grab. And I want to. I want to take that from him to see him smile again. Watch him laugh and tease me like he used to.

I follow him offstage and make my way to the dressing rooms, assuming that's where he's going. I don't know what I plan to say or do, but I feel like I need to be with him right now. I stop when something catches my eye. The door to mine and Willa's dressing room is open.

"Why are you standing there?" I hear Willa, but I don't move. "Oh fuck. Not again." Willa moves past me and into the room, picking up the note and reading it. "Fuck!"

"What's going on?"

I snap out of my stupor when I hear my brother's voice and go grab the note from Willa.

"What's going on is we need to clean house of our entire security team." Willa barks. We told them not to let any flowers be delivered to us from anyone.

I ignore them and read the newest note.

> Run, run, little liar
> I dare you to
> If you spread your legs for him
> It'll be the end of you

"Is this where the party is?"

"Motherfucker!" I scream, crumpling the note and throwing it across the room.

"Nope. Definitely no party here."

I turn to see Mav with his hands up, slowly backing out of the room.

"We need that for evidence!" Cal yells, going after the note and smoothing it out to take pictures. "Who did you sleep with?"

"Not that it's anyone's business, but I haven't slept with anyone!" I yell, frustrated at the wrong people, but unable to contain it.

"Google says it's a geranium, and it means stupidity," Willa says, gesturing to the plant with her phone.

"That seems pretty fucking accurate right now," I say as I pace the room and run my hands through my sweaty hair.

"You're not stupid, Belle," Willa says, touching my arm to slow down my pacing.

"Aren't I? I put myself in this situation. Every decision I've made so far has landed me here. *I* chose to go to college. *I* said yes to a date and everything else with Brad. *I* agreed to come on tour with you. *Me*, Willa. I'm more than stupid." I plop down on the couch so hard it slides back a little.

"Did you hear from Frank yet?" Willa asks Cal. Frank is the band's lawyer and has been handling the Brad situation for me. It's proven to be difficult since we're all Americans and no one has been able to prove Brad has left the states. We also can't seem to prove the notes and flowers are from him. Since everyone I'm with is part of a famous rock band, it's being blown off on both sides.

"Yeah. He said to just keep taking pictures of everything and sending it to him. Homeland has assured him Brad's passport hasn't been used to leave the country. He has a call out to Bangor PD to do a wellness check. Just to make sure he's still there."

I snort. Willa and Cal look at me, probably questioning my sanity. "He's still there. His mother never leaves Maine. Which means Brad never leaves Maine. Honestly, if I found out he was still breastfeeding, I wouldn't even be surprised."

"That's a disgusting image I didn't need," Willa says, her nose scrunched up in horror.

"You think he hired someone?" Cal asks.

"He must have. I don't think these flowers are coming from a delivery service. It would be too easy to figure out where they came from."

"You're thinking pretty clearly right now. I would be freaking out," Willa says, looking at me warily. She definitely thinks I'm going to have a mental breakdown at any moment now.

"I'm just so sick of being the victim, Willa. I will not let him bully me into submitting to him. We've been traveling all over the place for six weeks, surrounded by security and loads of other people. I'm not alone anymore," I tell them, trying to convey how much I mean what I say.

"Is now a bad time to ask how your first time singing lead felt?" Cal asks, clearly wanting to change the subject.

"That reminds me. I'm going to kill you!" I say, leaping up from the couch and smacking him on the arm.

"Ow! What was that for?" he whines, rubbing the spot.

"Don't put me on the spot like you did with the last song!"

"Oh. That. I just kind of had the idea and went with it."

"You and Kai killed it though," Willa offers.

"Fuck! I meant to go find Kai," I say before running out of our room and into theirs.

"Hey, Belle. Everything ok over there?" Mav asks with a smile.

"I got another note and a whole damn plant," I grumble while looking around. Mav is the only one in here.

"He went to the hotel bar already."

"He doesn't even like bars," I say, like that's going to change his location.

"I know. He said he's getting a table. Which we know is bullshit. I think he needed a minute to himself."

I nod and thank him.

"I'm going to the bar!" I yell as I pass my dressing room. Willa hurries after me and links her arm with mine. I didn't bother to shower off the sweat and makeup from the show like I usually do, and I know I'm preventing Willa from doing the same. She doesn't seem bothered by it as she walks by my side.

"Never alone, remember?"

I force a smile and continue to the bar with her.

KAI

I'M busy sulking in a dark back corner of the small hotel bar. Everything in here is dark. Dark wood, dark walls, dark tables. It's easy to hide back here, away from anyone that would recognize me. Except Belle. She just walked in and locked eyes with me immediately. Like she has some sort of a homing beacon on my location. The thought would make me smile if I wasn't so pissed.

She slides into the booth next to me and takes my hand. It's wet from the condensation on my glass. I've been gripping the ice water I ordered for a better part of twenty minutes.

"That wasn't fair of Cal to do, but neither was you taking off on me," she says, not a hint of the anger I was expecting.

"I know. I'm sorry. That song just brings me back to nights in my garage with all of us. It's difficult for me to sing it every night," I tell her, not mentioning that singing it with her brought me straight back to watching her and Ezra compose it. That memory is painful for several reasons.

"I get it. I've been writing. Maybe you can help me with it and "Shattered Dreams" can be a song we only sing occasionally?"

Her compassion is something I love the most about her. It's moments like these when I just want to pull her into my lap and kiss all the bad memories away.

"Think about it," she says when I take too long to answer. "I need to shower the show off." I nod, which makes her smile. She leans over and kisses me on the cheek before sliding out of the booth and walking to where Willa was waiting by the elevators.

I watch them as they enter. Belle smiles at me when she catches me watching right before the doors shut. I try not to picture a naked Belle in the shower, but she put that image there and it won't leave. The last thing I need is a hard on in a hotel bar.

The part of me that used to drown my pain in whiskey is itching to order a drink. That part of me is kept at bay more easily than it used to be. Just Belle's smile alone keeps me from self-destructing.

I love her. I love her so fucking much, and I have no idea what I'm supposed to do about it.

"You're joking. This is a joke. Ha ha. Very funny. You got me!"

Belle is panicking, her eyes are wide, and all the color has left her face. Cal just informed her they want her on the morning show with us, and he's pushing it because he thinks she's going to save the band. I can't blame her for her reaction. He's thrown a lot at her at once. We've managed to keep her from the few interviews we've had, but this is the last one and it's also the one with the biggest audience. I'm not sure she would have been able to avoid it, even if Cal didn't suggest it.

"Please, Belle! The producers promised to keep you out of most of the discussions. They know you're a newborn when it comes to this. Still slimy and everything," Cal says.

"That's disgusting," Willa mutters next to me.

"I'll wear a full shirt for tomorrow's show!" Cal says, eyes pleading, hands folded together in front of him.

Belle considers for a moment. "Full shirt and you get me the most expensive room at the hotel."

"Deal!" Cal shouts before grabbing his sister and spinning her around.

Belle came with us to the tv studio this morning under the impression she was just going to watch it. I think she was the only one that believed that.

"Alright. The set has a loveseat with three stools behind it," one producer, I think he said his name was Don or Dave, something with a D, tells us while pointing. "When you're introduced, you'll enter Willa and Bellamy to the couch, then Callahan, Maverick, and Malikai. In that order. We've framed it perfectly, so no rearranging." Then he points at Belle. "You need to hurry to hair and makeup!"

We all tell him we understand and wait for Belle to come back. They must have given her the basics because she comes rushing back a few minutes later, looking just as beautiful as she always does. The only difference I notice is the smoky eye they gave her, and her hair seems to have a product in it to tame it a little. She's in tight red jeans and a black crop top, looking every bit the rockstar she's becoming.

They call the morning show Rockin' 'Round and it's hosted by two former rock stars, Billie and Stevie. Both women. They're badasses and this was the only interview I've been looking forward to. The only part I dislike is the amount of fan interaction they allow. It's filmed live and fans can ask questions. Sometimes they're even allowed to interrupt the interview. Makes for great TV. Especially in Scotland, where heckling is part of the culture.

"They brought down the house in Munich last night, and now they're here in Glasgow to chat with us! Please welcome, Shattered Halo!" Billie growls out our band name, making it sound cooler than it is.

We file onto the stage in the order Don Dave told us. Shaking hands with both hosts and smiling politely. Four of us are at least. Belle looks like she's about to be led to her death. I squeeze her shoulder reassuringly, and I feel her relax under my hand. Interviewers can sense fear and they'll pounce on her. Cal shouldn't have pressured her into this. Stevie is short, with long, straight, black hair, and a tiny waist. Billie is her opposite, a tall and curvy blonde.

The interview gets underway quickly, and like it always does, veers toward my missing twin. You'd think they'd leave it alone after five years.

"So, Kai. What would Ezra say if he were here today?" Stevie asks. That one is a favorite. No fucking idea why.

I put on my tv smile and answer. "Well, I can tell you

right now that he would have loved your introduction, Billie. Ezra was a huge wrestling fan, and you sounded like a ring announcer." Am I trying to deflect? Yes. But it wasn't a lie. Ezra would have had her saying the most random things he could think of.

"I love that! How would Ezra feel about Belle joining the band?" Billie asks.

Dammit.

"Belle was always part of the band. She just stepped away to focus on her education. Ezra was proud of her, no matter what. He'd be thrilled she was back," I answer honestly.

"What would he think about you dating her?" Someone yells from the audience.

Billie's bleached eyebrows shoot up. "You two are dating?"

Before either of us can answer, someone else shouts, "If you don't want her, I'll take her!"

"Yeah! Is she single?"

"Can I get your number, sexy?"

The audience is shouting and heckling Belle. It's the end of the interview and this is how this show works. Stevie and Billie are allowing it and eyeing us for a response. I chance a look at Belle and see a subtle shake in the hand she has resting on the arm of the couch. She's terrified. And why wouldn't she be? She has men shouting at her and trying to claim her like predators.

Fuck. She going to hate me for this.

"Yes. We're dating," I say, stepping off the stool and pulling Belle up off the couch. I put my arm around her waist and pull her into me. "Stay away from my girl," I say to the audience, trying to make it seem like I'm joking. "Thank you for your time." I shake Bille and Stevie's hands, then wave at the audience before leading Belle off the sound stage.

"What the fuck was that?" she hisses the minute the producers remove our mics.

"I was just trying to stop them from heckling you," I say, lifting my hands in surrender.

"You just announced on live tv that you're dating me the day after I got a note threatening my life if I was with someone else!" she whisper-shouts at me.

"What note?" I ask. I haven't heard anything about another note.

"You kind of took off after the show last night and missed the whole thing," Cal says, handing me his phone. I look down to see a picture of the note in question.

"Fuck. Belle, I didn't know. I swear," I plead with her. She scoffs before turning on her heel and walking away.

"You shouldn't have done that anyway, dude," Cal says, putting his hand on my shoulder.

"She was shaking, Cal! I didn't know how else to stop them," I say as I knock his hand off.

"We should go. I think she's heading back to the cars," Willa says as she passes us.

We find Belle pacing in front of our rented SUVs. I've never seen her this angry before.

"Why, Kai?" she screams the moment she sees me. "Why are you doing this to me? Acting like you can't stand to be around me one moment and then telling the world you're dating me the next! I can't keep doing this with you! It's been weeks, and I feel like I'm losing my mind!"

"I was trying to protect you! Ezra would want me to protect his girl. That's what I'm trying to do!"

Belle pauses her pacing and stares at me like I just insulted her grandmother. "What does that mean? What are you talking about? I'm not Ezra's girl!"

Now I'm frustrated. It's been five years, and she needs to stop pretending.

"I saw you that night! In the woods, in each other's arms. You were happy. Stop pretending you weren't together!" I yell at her.

Belle is suddenly eerily calm. Her features even out, and her posture straightens. I don't think I've ever been more scared in my life.

"You're telling me that for five fucking years, you've been an absolute dick to me because of something you *think* you saw?" she asks in an even voice.

"I know what I saw, Belle." I'm trying to hold my ground, but it feels like the earth I'm standing on is about to swallow me.

"What you saw, Malikai, was me hugging my friend. And do you know why I was hugging my friend? Because he told me he was in a relationship and in love. That he was happy. That's what you fucking saw." Her features are still blank, but her eyes are blazing.

"Who the hell would he have been in a relationship with if it wasn't you?" I ask, trying to find the lie in her words. Because if she's telling the truth, then the foundation of the wall I've built around myself is about to crumble.

Belle keeps her mouth shut and doesn't answer. I've

caught her. "I knew it. Stop lying Belle! It doesn't matter anymore."

"I'm not lying!" she yells, the mask she was holding on to cracking.

"Stop!" I turn around to see Maverick. He's crying, but I can't tell if it's from anger or sadness. "It was me. Ezra was with me."

Belle walks past me to Mav's side, hugging him.

"What are you talking about? Ezra wasn't gay. Are you gay? I've never seen you with a man." I wanted to call him a liar. My brother would have told me if he loved someone. He would have told me if he was gay. But at the moment, I realize that's not true. I've spent years assuming he loved Belle without telling me. Why would this be any different?

"Ezra is the love of my life, Kai. Being with another man feels like a betrayal," Maverick tells me. The love of his life? My brother was that in love and never said a word.

Belle looks up at Maverick and nods. He swallows before speaking. "The night he went missing, we were going to tell everyone about us. Then I got a text..." he pauses and shakes his head, tears flying from his face. "I had to leave. I had to leave, and I never got to be with him in the open. Love him out loud. We were robbed of that."

"Why did you leave that night?" Belle whispers to him. I'm close enough that I hear the question too. I look at Mav and he somehow looks even more miserable.

"My mom texted me. My dad was drunk, and he was —" he pauses and looks at Belle. "He was beating her. She texted me to save her from him."

"Maverick," Belle says before hugging him tightly.

Willa comes up from Mav's other side and hugs him too.

I didn't even register she was here. I look around and notice Cal is standing next to me, his jaw hanging open.

"It's not your fault. You did the right thing," Willa assures him.

"No, I didn't. I always ran to save her. I've even offered to buy her a house away from him. But she won't leave. She stays with that piece of shit." A heart wrenching sob breaks free from his throat. "If I just stayed with Ezra, he would still be here. It's my fault he's gone."

I un-stick my shoes from where they seemed to be glued to the pavement and make my way over to Mav.

"It's not your fault. It's not anyone's fault. You were in an impossible position." I grab him, pulling him out of the girls' embrace and into mine.

"I don't know why Ezra felt he had to keep who he was and who he loved a secret from me, but I don't blame you for anything. Thank you for loving my brother."

I hold him until the sobs cease. Then I watch as he enters one of the SUVs, shoulders slumped, head down.

"You knew this whole time?" Cal asks Belle. There's hurt lacing his words. Cal and Belle have always told each other everything.

"Ezra asked me not to tell. Then when he went missing. He wanted to be the one to tell everyone, and I've been hoping that he still would."

Cal nods. "Come on, Willa." They walk away, leaving Belle and me in the parking lot alone.

"Belle, I'm so fucking sorry."

"I don't want to hear it, Kai."

"Please, just listen," I beg, getting as close to her as I

dare. I wouldn't blame her if she kicked me in the nuts right now.

"Listen to what? You hated me because you thought Ezra was in love with me. Now you know he's not, so you're going to be nice? It doesn't make any fucking sense, and I'm too emotional to deal with your bullshit." She tries to walk away, but I grab her.

"You don't understand!" I yell, causing her to pause, eyes wide. "From the moment your eyes found mine when we were kids, I have loved you. I love you, Bellamy. I tried to stop. Tried to forget you. Tried to accept that you were Ezra's. But I couldn't. I can't. I love you."

Belle's eyes go impossibly wide, and her jaw hangs open in shock. "I was never Ezra's," she whispers.

"I know that now."

I watch her eyes fly back and forth as she looks off into the distance. She's trying to process everything I just said and I'm letting her, but all I want to do is kiss her. If she even lets me kiss her.

"I can't do this, Kai," she says, tears in her eyes as she pulls away from me.

"Belle, please. Just think about it. I can wait. Take as long as you need," I beg. I'm begging for something I didn't know I could have until seconds ago, and it's already slipping through my fingers.

"You hurt me worse than anyone else ever has. Brad hurt me physically, but you... Kai, you destroyed me." Her words are like a shot directly to my heart. "I just. . . can't."

I drop to my knees in front of her. "Please, mo chridhe. I know I fucked up. I'll do anything to fix it. Don't give up on me. Please, Belle." She continues to back away from me as I beg for her to stay.

She runs up to the first SUV. The back door opens, and she climbs in. They take off immediately after. I watch her go from my knees. The pain I felt when I thought I lost her five years ago is nothing compared to what I'm feeling right now.

I think I just lost her for good.

"I KNOW," Willa says patiently. She's been listening to me complain about Kai for hours at this point. He never came back, but Cal went after him. He texted that they're fine and will be back later.

"I don't know what to do, Willa."

She sighs. "What are your feelings for him? Separate from everything that just happened. I know you're pissed and hurt right now. But deep down, what do you feel about Kai?"

I think about that. I'm not really sure how to answer. Do I love him? Yes, I always have. That doesn't mean he deserves my forgiveness, or to. . . date me? Is that what he was begging for?

"Can we stop tiptoeing around the shit?" Maverick exclaims. His hair is sticking up at all angles, and his eyes are red and puffy.

"Mav..." Willa warns.

"No! Look where keeping shit bottled in got us. She deserves to know so she can understand. You and Kai are both asking her to make an uninformed decision, and honestly? Fuck that."

"What are you talking about?" I ask him. I'm not really ready for any more bombs to be dropped today, but he's right. We need to drop the bullshit.

"Kai has major abandonment issues. Ezra left him. Then you left the band, and him by proxy. His dad walked out on their family and his mom can't even look at him because he has Ezra's face," Mav explains.

"I think he's unfairly putting a lot of that on you because of the timing of when you left. And he seems to have always loved you and thought he lost you to his brother. So I don't think that helped either," Willa adds.

"He's been dealing with all of that, and no one said anything?" I ask as my brain slowly processes how deeply Kai is hurting.

"I think it's becoming pretty obvious we suck at communicating," Mav mutters.

"Even if I forgive him, and I'm not saying I do, he's just going to assume I'll leave the band again." Kai has a way of making me feel like no matter how many times I include myself with them or say I want to stay, he just won't even believe me.

"Are you? Going to leave the band?" Mav asks. He asks kindly, but the question is still loaded.

"I have no idea! I don't want to, but there's still a chance there won't be a band soon, anyway," I say, standing to pace while I rant. "And why does my status with the band matter? Is that a requirement to be with Kai? Is loving him not enough?"

"You love him?" Willa asks with a knowing smirk.

"Of course I love him! I've always loved his stupid ass! I'm just furious with him right now. Furious and confused."

"I think that's fair, considering everything," Mav says.

"I don't know what to do. I've wanted to be with Kai my whole life. I loved him even when I thought he hated me. But he's not..." I search for the words I want and come up empty.

"He's not okay. You don't need to find a complicated term. Kai isn't okay. He has a lot of things that weigh heavily on his shoulders. You can help him carry that weight, maybe even offload some of it, but it has to be something you're willing to do. Something you know you're signing up for and won't back down from. He loves you, Belle, but he won't survive losing you after he's had you."

"Jeez. No pressure, Mav," I try to joke.

"He's right though. Think about it. Don't decide anything now. I love you both, and I know someone is going to get hurt no matter what, but at least make the choice that's best for you," Willa says, giving me a quick hug.

I wander like a zombie to my bed and lay down. Napping seems like a better idea than thinking right now.

"Belle, wake up!"

I shoot up immediately and look around. My heart is racing out of my chest.

"What? What is it? Was I dreaming again?" I ask Willa, feeling embarrassed for constantly waking them with my screaming.

"I got a text from Cal. Kai is at a pub with a glass of

whiskey in front of him. He won't leave, and Cal thinks you're the only one who can get him out," she explains in a rush, seeming panicked.

I try to shake the fog of sleep from my brain to process what she said. Kai is in a pub. Cal can't get him to leave. Does he need to leave?

"Why do I need to get him?"

"Whiskey, Belle. Kai went to rehab for alcohol abuse. He's been sober for three years, and he's about to blow it," Willa says, pulling me out of bed.

"What? No one told me that! Fuck!" I sprint to the door, looking around for my shoes. I find them near the couch and quickly put them on.

"Coat!" Mav yells, throwing it at me. I scramble to pull it on as I push the door open and run outside. Cal booked a house for the last show, so luckily, I'm not running through a hotel looking like a crazy person. Which I'm not telling him. He was supposed to book me a fancy hotel room for going on that stupid show this morning. He knew the whole time he had a house planned.

"I don't know where to go!" I yell.

"I know. Let's go!" Willa says, grabbing my arm and pulling me into a cab. She must have called one already.

My leg bounces anxiously, and I'm tempted to ask the driver to move faster. I had no idea Kai ever had any trouble with alcohol. But as I sit here thinking about it, we've been in pubs and bars almost every night, and he's never had a drink in his hand.

"This is all my fault," I cry into my hands.

"It is not."

"He thinks I've abandoned him for good, Willa. Left him to his pain just like everyone else he loves."

"Save it for your song writing. That will probably be a hit."

"This isn't funny!"

"And I'm not laughing! Kai is hurting, yes. I told you this before we even left home. The fact that his communication skills are on infant levels is not your fault." She pulls my hands away from my face and forces me to look at her. "No matter what we walk in on, you didn't put him in that pub, you didn't order him that drink, and you sure as fuck didn't force him to drink it. Do you understand?"

I nod, pulling myself together just in time for the cab to drop us off.

I start to walk and notice Willa isn't following. "Aren't you coming?"

She shakes her head. "He needs you or no one. Me going in there won't help. Trust me."

I pull the door open and immediately spot my bother hovering around a very depressed looking Kai. The moment Cal sees me, his shoulders relax slightly, and he walks over.

"He hasn't had anything to drink. All he does is stare at it. He won't even talk to me," Cal explains, running a frustrated hand through his hair.

"Willa's outside. I'll stay with Kai."

"I'm sorry to do this to you, Belle."

"Don't. Kai is my friend too, even when I hate him."

"You hate him?" Cal asks.

"Not even a little."

SOMEONE TAKES the seat next to me, and I'm about to ask them to kindly fuck off, but then I smell her. She's always smelled sweet, like sugar and jasmine.

"Kai," she says softly.

"Why are you here, Belle?" I ask, my voice breaking.

"Why are you staring into a glass of whiskey like it's going to tell you the meaning of life?" she asks with more snark than anyone would dare around a recovering alcoholic that's about to end that recovery.

I chuckle. "It doesn't tell me anything. But it will make me forget for a while."

"Are you sure about that? Did you forget me when you were drinking before?"

I look up at her, expecting to see the same hurt and anger that was there earlier. Instead, she's smiling softly.

"Nothing could ever make me forget you, mo chridhe," I whisper.

"You keep calling me that. What does it mean?" she asks me, her eyes searching mine. They've never once looked at the glass in my hand. Cal couldn't stop looking at it, like he was waiting for a moment to snatch it from me. Belle's only focus is me, and I'm about to melt under her attention.

"It means 'my heart' in Gaelic." I look down as I answer, too scared to see her reaction.

"Maverick told me about your parents and how you felt about me going to college instead of signing with the label."

I nod. I figured someone would.

"Why didn't you tell me?" Her voice is gentle and soothing.

"I couldn't. I didn't know how," I say, a tear racing down my cheek. I don't bother to wipe it away. I'm sure more will follow. "I was young and so fucking angry at the world. It wasn't fair of me to put that on you. I know that now. I've known that for years." I look up, meeting her curious gaze.

Belle keeps her eyes on mine and doesn't interrupt me, but I can see in her eyes she wants to ask questions.

"But then I never saw you. You never came home after school. Or if you did, we were touring. I felt like you left us all, left me, to go live a different life. And with everything else going on. . . Ezra and my parents. . . I just couldn't handle any more pain. So that pain turned to anger."

"Kai..." she starts.

"I know it was wrong, Belle. And I had no idea how having you in my life again would affect me. I tried to push you away to save myself from breaking, and that wasn't fair to you. I'm so incredibly sorry for that and for hurting you."

"Can I ask you something?"

"You just did."

She rolls her eyes and laughs. "Would you consider therapy? I'm working with a therapist online. I need help to process everything with Brad, and I think maybe it would help you too."

Belle asked so sweetly that I can't deny her. Usually people scream it at me in anger, like therapy is a punishment. I knew about her therapy sessions. She never kept them a secret from us.

"I'm not sure it's my thing, but I'm willing to try it," I tell her honestly.

"Can I ask you something?" I ask her, using her words.

"You just did," she says in a deep voice that I think was supposed to sound like me but sounds more like Cookie Monster.

"Is there a chance? For us, I mean. I know I have no right asking you, but I need to know. I can't handle one more moment thinking I've lost you forever while also wondering if I can win you back."

Belle considers me with her beautiful ocean blue eyes. I would drown in them if she let me.

"Why do you love me?" she asks. Hope and disappointment swirl around in my gut.

I let go of the glass and take both of her hands in mine. "I love you because when you laugh, your nose scrunches up and makes you look adorable. I love you because you're smart and funny and creative. I love the way you look at me. I love how strong you are. You're so fucking strong, mo chridhe. I love the way you smile to yourself while you're playing music on your keyboard. I love how you get a line between your brows while you write songs. I love the way you love the people in your life. I just love you, Belle. I always have."

Tears are streaming down her face, but she's smiling. That's... good? I think.

"I love you, Kai."

The words are barely out of her mouth, and I'm claiming her lips. They're soft and warm and taste like magic.

She pulls away too soon, her hand on my chest and for a moment, I'm worried I misread the situation.

"We need to go slow. We both need to process a lot, but I think we should do it together," she tells me while staring at my lips.

"Whatever you want, mo chridhe. I'll do anything you want me to." My lips are back on hers and the hand that was on my chest has turned into a fist that's gripping my shirt and pulling me into her.

"You need to take me on a first date. And then lots of dates after that," she says against my lips.

"I've never been on a date before. I'd be happy for you to be my first," I mumble before capturing her lips again.

"Wait," she says, pulling away again. "You've never been on a date before?"

"No one was going to compare to you. So I didn't see the point." I shrug.

She pulls me by my shirt so she can kiss me again. "You should've told me sooner."

"I know."

"We need to get back to the house before Nate has a stroke. We were supposed to have that video call with the label at some point, and I'm sure we're past that time."

I lift a brow in question.

"I was taking a nap and Willa woke me up. She told me

you needed me, so I ran out the door. I don't even have my phone. I know we were supposed to be on the call by four."

"It's after four," I tell her with a smile. I toss a few bills on the bar to cover the whiskey I ordered but never touched.

"Let's get back," I say, holding my hand out to her. She takes it happily. I wrap my arm around her waist and lead her out the door. For the first time in years, I feel happy. I don't care how slowly she wants to take this. I'll take anything she'll give me.

"YOU GUYS ARE HAVING the lamest makeup sex I've ever heard!"

I look up from the song I've been working on. Kai is next to me on my bed, strumming mindlessly on his guitar. We made it back in time for the second half of the meeting. Sparks is willing to resign us with a worse contract and a ridiculous six album clause. Cal said no immediately and shut the computer down.

"If we were having sex, you and the entirety of this city would know!" Kai shouts back, causing my face to heat. I can hear Willa's snort from the other side of the door.

Cal bursts through the door, a look of excitement on his face that morphs to disgust and goes right back to excitement.

"I never want to hear you talk about having sex with my sister ever again. As far as I'm concerned, you're a Ken doll down there," Cal says.

"We need to lock that door," Kai grumbles.

"Frank called!" Cal yells, waving his phone in front of

our faces, changing the subject to something he can stomach.

"Ok? Why?" I ask, not following why a call from his lawyer is exciting.

"He went through the contract. We can perform a new song tomorrow, and Sparks won't own it! It's exactly what we need!"

"We don't have a new song," Willa points out, having followed Cal into my room.

Cal just gestures wildly between me and Kai. "Belle writes, Kai composes. Simple."

"Says the man who has never written a song," Willa says.

"We need this! If we can pull off a new hit song on the last show of the tour and send it to *Nep-Tunes*, it could be our new beginning!" Cal says enthusiastically as he paces the room.

"The label that Logan owns is named *Nep-Tunes*?" I ask, wondering if the terrible name is a bad omen.

"Yeah. That was already the name when his company purchased it. He kept it because he said the old man that owned it named it that. I guess he let his son name it when he was a kid or something. Sentimental shit. Doesn't matter. This needs to happen."

"You want us to have a song ready from start to finish that not only will be a huge hit, but guarantees our future? And that has to be done in the next..." Kai looks at the time on his phone. "Eighteen hours, so we can practice it during sound check?"

"Exactly! I'm going to go tell Mav!" Cal practically sprints out of the room.

"I'm going to try to reel him in." Willa leaves the room after him, pushing the lock in on the knob before shutting the door.

I laugh but quickly stop when I see Kai's face. "What?"

"He just came in here and put an insane amount of pressure on us, and then skipped out of the room like he's solved world hunger." Kai says, his eyes wide.

"Cal is an idiot on a good day, but I actually think this is doable," I tell him, taking his hand in mine.

"It's impossible! I'm not as good as Ezra at composing. That's even if you can get a song done in enough time for me to even try it."

"I have a song," I say with a smile. I wrote it the moment we got off the call, and Kai and I went to my room. It took me less than an hour. I've just been smoothing it out while I enjoyed being next to him.

"You do?" he asks, eyebrows shooting up to his hairline.

"I do. We have eighteen hours to compose it. Which I can help with too."

Kai smiles and kisses me quickly. "I'm going to grab the computer! There's composing software on there that can help us."

He hops off the bed and runs out the door. I don't remember the last time I saw him this happy. I feel like I got *my* Kai back, and I'll do everything I can to hold on to him.

"What do you think?"

Mav, Cal, and Willa are staring at Kai and me with identical expressions of shock.

"Guys? You're making me nervous," I say, shifting closer to Kai on the couch in the living room of the house. We just played the song we've been working on all night for them. It's like "Shattered Dreams," in that the only instruments we use are Kai's guitar and my keyboard. I think a piano would sound better and probably look better stage wise, but we don't exactly have time for that right now. I can experiment with that after the tour.

Kai is beaming next to me. Apparently, their inability to speak isn't bothering him at all right now. I know he's proud of what we've accomplished. I am too, but I need someone to say something before I explode. I look over at Willa to see a tear slip down her face.

"Are you crying? Why are you crying?" I ask her in a panic. Willa doesn't cry.

"You did it. You fucking did it!" She says before launching herself at me.

Kai is laughing on my other side, and I look over to see my brother hugging him. Mav throws himself on top of all of us.

"Do you think he's proud of us? Wherever he is?" Mav asks quietly, still spread out on top of all of us.

I chance a look at Kai. Usually the topic of Ezra has his shoulders stiffening and some remark about his brother being dead leaving his lips before he storms off. I'm happily surprised to see him looking contemplative.

"Yeah, Mav. I think he is," Kai says before he turns his head to look at me. I can see it in his eyes. He's allowing himself to hope.

"Always and forever?" I ask.

"Always and forever, mo chridhe."

twenty-four

KAI

I'M ALWAYS calm before a show. It's the only time I feel completely at peace. Cal gets so excited, I'm afraid he's going to have a stroke one of these days. Belle and Mav are always nervous. Willa is the only other one that gets calm like I do. It's like this is where we belong, and our bodies can sense it.

Tonight though. Well, tonight is feeling very different. I've been nervous about our entire set. The song we wrote is going to be played last. I've helped compose all our songs since we started playing professionally, but none of them have mattered like this one.

"You've been amazing, Glasgow!" Cal yells into his mic. "So amazing, in fact, we decided to debut a new song for you tonight!" The crowd goes wild, screaming at us in excitement. I pick up my mic stand and make my way over to Belle. We're skipping "Shattered Dreams" tonight. We didn't want the new song to be overshadowed by the well-loved classic.

"Ready?" I whisper to her. She rewards me with a big smile before she nods.

"Hold on to your butts and get out your phones! We want your reactions streamed live!" Cal says. "Make sure you tag us in your posts! We want to see it all!"

Live streaming from the fans was part of the plan. We're hoping any media hype we get around the song helps with getting signed at the new label.

Belle locks her eyes on me, and her fingers start expertly gliding along the keys. I add in my guitar and start singing. The first verse is just me, and then Belle comes in on the next. Once her soft and clear voice mixes with my deep and raspy tone, I know we have the crowd hooked. They've gone silent, and I know they're hanging on every word.

That's the thing about rock fans. They'll let you know immediately if they're not feeling what you're giving them. Silence is just as telling.

Belle and I wrote a love song. Most of the words are hers with little input from me, but it tells our story. At least the beginning of it. A story of two people that have loved each other silently throughout the years and finally get together.

The song ends on one last note from my guitar. I don't even think. Emotions overcrowd my brain. Grabbing Belle by the back of her neck, I bring her lips to mine and kiss her like no one is watching. She lets out a small gasp before returning my kiss.

The crowd is going wild, chanting for more.

"That was 'Always and Forever!' Tag us in your posts!" Cal tells the fans. "You've been amazing Glasgow! Goodnight!"

I put my guitar down, take Belle's hand, and leave the stage. Hopefully not for the last time.

"Holy shit! We need to send that to Logan right now!" Cal yells the moment he sees us, ushering us both into a sweaty hug.

"It's like five in the morning for him," I point out.

"Don't care. I have to send it, or I might die," Cal says, and I honestly believe him. The man is vibrating.

"I sent the video to your email. I booked your flights. You leave tomorrow at four pm," Nate says as he passes us and starts directing the staff packing our equipment.

"I need my phone!" Cal yells as he darts away towards the dressing rooms. I hear him yelling sorry as he probably knocks people over on his way.

"I'm going to stop him before he calls Logan too," Mav says, following Cal.

"You guys coming out with us tonight?" Willa asks.

I look down at Belle, who is still smiling, but I know she has to be as tired as I am.

"Nah. I think we're going to get some sleep before we pass out standing up."

"You've earned it," Willa says before leaving us too.

Belle snuggles into my side, her hand still firmly clasped in mine. "I'm exhausted and wide awake at the same time."

I chuckle. "That would be the combination of the adrenaline high and lack of sleep."

"Can we get snacks and then go to sleep?" Belle asks me with a yawn.

"Nate! I need a car!" I yell before scooping Belle up into my arms. She yelps in surprise but throws her arms around my neck and kisses my cheek.

"You got it, Kai!" Nate yells back.

"Can I take you on a date tomorrow?" I ask her. I'm a little nervous. I don't think she'll say no, but this is still brand new, and I'm half afraid I'm dreaming.

"A first date in Scotland with the hottest guy I've ever seen? How could I say no?" Belle teases.

"Hottest guy you've ever seen, huh?"

"I take it back," she says and rolls her eyes.

I tickle her side, causing her to squirm.

"Okay, okay! I would love to go on a date with you."

I lean down and capture her lips with mine. I groan from the contact, taking the kiss deeper. Every touch from her ignites a fire in my body.

"Car's here, Kai," Nate says.

I reluctantly part from Belle to thank him.

"Let's get back and get some sleep. I've got a hot date tomorrow," Belle says before laughing at her own joke.

I chuckle as I carry my woman out of the venue. I can't think of a time I've ever been this happy. And fuck, it's terrifying.

twenty-five

BELLE

"SLOW DOWN! I HAVE LITTLE LEGS!" *Willa calls from behind me.*

We're getting ready to ride our bikes to the ice cream stand in town. Everyone is meeting in our driveway since it's at the end of the street.

I turn and notice Willa running towards us without her bike.

"I can't go with you guys. My dad wants me to stay home," she says when she comes to a stop in front of me.

"He never lets you go anywhere anymore," I complain and immediately regret it when I watch her face fall. Ever since her mom died a few years ago, her dad has tried to keep her home more and more.

"I know. He just gets scared if he can't see where I am."

"Can we come over after?" I ask.

"I'd love that! I have to get back though," she says and turns around to run to her house before I have the chance to say anything else.

"Her house is so boring," Cal whines.

"You're boring!" I retort.

"You're annoying!" he shoots back.

"Are you guys going to start this again or can we go get ice cream?" Ezra asks. He and Kai are straddling their bikes at the end of our driveway, waiting for us. Kai's arms are crossed, and he has an amused look on his face, while Ezra is glaring at Cal. He hates when we fight.

"Why do I have to take Belle? She's twelve. She can go hangout with Willa without me," he complains.

"She's our friend too, and we want her to come with us," Ezra says, making Cal pout more than he already was. Our mom has always made Cal take me everywhere. I feel a little bad about that, especially during the times I didn't want to go with him. But Kai and Ezra are my best friends too. No matter how much that annoys him.

"Fine. Let's go," Cal grumbles.

We sit on a sticky, red picnic table with our ice cream in hand. Chocolate for me, peanut butter Oreo for Cal, mint chocolate chip for Kai, and a monstrous abomination for Ezra. He gets one scoop of pistachio and one scoop of bubble gum. Then he mixes and mashes it together into some sort of melted ice cream vomit. He swears it's good, but none of us will try it.

I know the current silence is because we're eating ice cream, but I'm still feeling a little awkward. Am I intruding on my brother hanging out with his friends? Are they just being nice to Cal's little sister and not really my friends?

"What are you thinking so hard about over there?" Ezra asks me.

"I'm sorry that I always have to come with you guys, and you can't play with Cal alone," I blurt out.

"Aren't we your friends?" Kai asks, surprised by my confession.

"Well, yeah. You were kind of forced by my mom, though."

"No one forced us, Belle. You're our friend and we're yours."
Kai elbows Cal, who is sitting next to him, in the ribs.

"Ow! What was that for?" Cal asks while rubbing his side
dramatically.

"For making your sister feel like she's bothering us, you dick,"
Ezra says, not bothering to look up from his ice cream. They have
that weird twin thing going on. He didn't need to see Kai elbow
Cal to know it happened.

Cal sighs. "I'm sorry, Belle. I didn't mean it like that."

He did. I don't blame him. Mom doesn't let me hang out with
Willa without him tagging along either. It's why the five of us are
always together.

I just give him a small smile.

"We're always going to be friends. Our group will go to a
nursing home together and terrorize the staff. We'll be there for
each other no matter what. You know that, right?" Kai asks me.
The stern look on his face matches the seriousness in his tone.

"Always and forever?" I ask him, my tone defiant, but my
eyes pleading.

Kai gives me one of his lazy smirks. "Always and forever."

Cal snorts. He hates conversations involving emotions. He's
too tough for that or something.

"Hey, Ez. To infinity..." he says.

"And beyond!" Ezra finishes for him. We all fall into a fit of
giggles.

***

"What were you dreaming about?" Kai whispers, his face
buried in my neck. We went straight back to the house after

our last show. Both of us passed out together after having been awake for so long. You'd think taking things slow would include not sleeping in the same bed together, but since Kai was already sleeping next to me to keep my nightmares away, it just felt natural.

"That day we went to get ice cream. When always and forever first started with us," I tell him, pulling his arms tighter around me. I love the feel of him this close. The warmth of his chest pressed to my back and his breath on my neck. The heat pooling between my thighs is not helping to keep my brain on track. My vagina doesn't agree that we should take things slow.

"That explains why you were smiling."

"Maybe I was smiling because I love you." Just saying it out loud makes me smile again. Kai groans and pulls me closer until I'm flush with his body.

"I love hearing you say that," he says in my ear before nipping at my lobe.

"I can feel that." I grind my ass against his rock-hard erection so he doesn't miss my meaning.

Kai lets out a deep moan before holding me still. "That's mean, baby. We're taking things slow. I want to do this the right way. I love you too much to fuck this up."

"I love you too much to let you. So stop worrying and get to wining and dining."

Kai chuckles, his face still buried in my neck.

"What should I wear?" I ask him as I try to squirm out of his grasp.

"Something light. It's going to be warm." Kai gets up, and I watch as he runs his fingers through his sleep messy hair. My eyes travel down his muscular arms, but snag when I see a small tattoo on his ribs.

"Kai..." I gasp.

His brows pinch together when he sees my face. He follows my gaze to see what I'm staring at.

"It's always been you, mo chridhe," he says softly.

I already believe him, but the proof is right there, forever marked on his skin. *'Always & Forever, Belle'* in my handwriting. He must have used one of the many birthday cards I signed like that for him over the years.

"When? Has Cal seen it?" I ask while trying to hold back tears.

"When we got home after our first tour. It was right after Christmas and your mom said you had gone back to school the day before," Kai says, his eyes look far away like he's lost in the memory. "I just really fucking missed you, and I was so gone for you. I didn't know how to express that to you, so instead, I grabbed the birthday card you sent me that year and went straight to the tattoo shop."

I walk into his arms and run my fingers over the tattoo.

"Cal saw it later that night and was less than happy about it. I was drinking a lot by that point, and he flat out told me I wasn't good enough for you."

"Cal has known how you've felt about me this entire time?" I'm more shocked than anything. Cal can't keep a secret to save his life.

"He has, and he was right. I was a mess back then. I'm still a mess now, but I'm working on it. And one day, I hope I'll be worthy of you. Until then, I'll keep working on my bullshit." Kai wraps his arms around me and squeezes me tightly to him.

I want to tell him he's worthy. I want to tell him *I'm* the one who doesn't feel worthy of him. But I know Kai. I know better than anyone that he won't believe me if I tell him. He needs to make himself believe it. So instead, I kiss him quickly and get ready for the day.

"Kai. . . this is. . . wow." My words fail as I look around me. We're surrounded by flowers of all different sizes and colors. The air is heavy with the different floral and fruity scents.

Kai took me to a botanic garden he rented out. He didn't want to chance being interrupted by fans.

"I wanted you to have good memories of flowers too. Not just ones tarnished by weird and threatening notes."

"I love this," I tell him honestly.

Kai takes my hand and leads me down a path surrounded by leafy plants and large red and yellow flowers. There's a small alcove where a tea table has been set up. Intricate iron chairs sit on either side of the matching table.

"I thought we could have lunch here, but I didn't think about how overwhelming the smell would be," Kai says, scrunching up his nose.

"It's not bothering me, but we can go somewhere else if you want."

"There's something else I want to eat, but not today," he growls in my ear. I can feel my entire face heating. I turn to him, grab his shirt, and pull him down to me. I kiss him with desperation. With a longing I've held in for too many years.

"Belle," Kai groans, returning my kiss with just as much

fervor. His hand is in my hair and the other is on my hip, pulling me into him.

A throat clearing has us jumping a part. I guess we weren't as alone as I thought we were.

"Your tea is ready, Mr. Irons."

I turn to see an older man smiling at us as he gestures towards the table. I didn't even hear anyone setting it up. It now holds a white and blue teapot with matching cups and saucers. In the middle is a three-tier tray of small sandwiches and small cakes.

"Thank you, Felix," Kai says. He puts his hand on the small of my back and leads me over to the table.

"This looks like something out of a movie!" I exclaim. Kai just laughs and takes his seat.

I pour tea for both of us before picking out a sandwich and taking a bite.

"So, tell me what I've missed with you." Kai's tone is casual, but I know the question is hard for him. He's beating himself up for pushing me away. But he also knows those missed years include an abusive boyfriend. He wants to hear about it, but he knows it's going to hurt.

"I originally majored in education. Swapped to forensic science. Ended up with a business degree."

Kai listens to my not so exciting retelling of my college years. I spent most of it missing my friends and not really trying to make new ones. So there wasn't a lot to tell.

"How did you meet Brad?" he asks, his voice and body tense. I don't really want to talk about this on a first date, but I know it needs to be said.

"We met senior year. He was in one of my classes. Brad was nice, handsome, said all the right things. I moved in with him after graduation. He got me a job at his mom's finance company. I worked there for six months, during which he slowly talked me into staying home." I take a deep breath, keeping my eyes on my plate so I don't have to see the anger I know is simmering in Kai's.

"Once I quit, it was like I locked myself in a cage. The fighting started. Yelling at first. Then he hit me. Apologized, and I believed it. Then he kept hitting me, and I was too scared and too alone to stop him."

"Why didn't you tell Cal?" Kai asks, his voice barely containing his rage.

"I was embarrassed. I know now that I shouldn't have been, and that Cal would've helped get me out of the situation immediately. But when I was in it. . . there was nothing and no one else. I felt alone." I've been working through all this with a therapist, so it's a lot easier for me to talk about now than it had been a few weeks ago.

"I'm so fucking sorry," he says, getting up from his seat and kneeling next to me. "I should've been there for you. You never should've been with him in the first place."

"Stop. We can't live like that or move forward in our relationship thinking that way. We're together now, and we have our own memories to make. Hopefully, good ones." I run my fingers along the stubble on his jaw.

"Sorry. That was a terrible first date topic," Kai says.

"But you needed to know, so you could stop guessing?" I supply for him.

He smiles sadly. "Yeah."

Kai makes his way back to his seat. We eat the delicious food and chat about much lighter topics.

As we're getting ready to leave, Kai's phone rings.

"Yeah? Okay. We're on our way."

I arch an eyebrow at him in question.

"It was Cal. Isla and Logan want to have a video confer-ence about signing us," Kai says, a huge smile spreading across his handsome face.

"Isla?" I ask, trying to remember if I've heard that name before.

"Cal said she's the one that really runs *Nep-Tunes*. He seems to think her opinion matters more than Logan's."

"Let's get back and make sure Cal doesn't do anything to ruin this."

Kai nods and we rush out of the garden. I'm excited and nervous and happy. I look at Kai as we rush through the rain and into the waiting cab and see similar emotions running across his face. We put all our eggs in one basket. All our hopes in one company. It's reckless and a little stupid. But I have a good feeling.

"CLOSE YOUR MOUTH, YOU'RE DROOLING," I whisper to Cal while nudging him with my elbow. He's been staring at Isla without blinking since she appeared on the screen five minutes ago. It's unnerving.

"Our lawyers went over your previous contract, and you were right. They don't own any of the rights to your newest song. They do, however, own all previous songs recorded with them." Isla is a blonde-haired, blue-eyed, no-nonsense type of woman. The complete opposite of Cal, which is making it hard to keep my attention on what she's saying and not snicker at my best friend.

"What does that mean for us if we go forward with a contract with you?" Mav asks, always the practical one.

Isla sighs and leans back in her chair, eyes darting between all of us. "I'm going to be straight with you. We only want "Always and Forever." Ideally, we would love to have "Shattered Dreams" too, but that isn't a deal breaker. All your other songs are subpar in comparison."

"Ouch," Willa says quietly next to me.

"We can give you "Always and Forever." I doubt the other label will part with "Shattered Dreams," though," Mav says, scratching at his stubble covered jaw.

Isla nods and turns her attention to Belle. "You wrote both songs, correct?"

"I did," Belle answers, pride clear in her voice.

"Then this decision is about to fall heavily on your shoulders," Isla says while Belle looks at her with confusion written across her face. "I'm willing to sign you to a deal. It would be for one album and one US tour. 75/25 split. We would be responsible for distribution, but that would leave you in charge of marketing and recording costs. You would also own all the rights to your music, not us."

"Okay..." Belle says slowly. We're all staring at her, trying to figure out why Isla is only talking to her. Judging from how scrunched up her brow is right now, Belle seems to be wondering the same thing.

"We're only willing to sign if you agree to be the song-writer on the album. Once we see how the album and subsequent tour go, we can talk about signing you to a more traditional deal."

I hold my breath, waiting for Belle's response. Trying to tell myself that if she leaves, it's not me she's leaving. That she can't be responsible for saving the band.

But she is. Isla just told her it's her or nothing.

Belle looks at me with shock on her face. I lean in and kiss her forehead.

"What do you want to do?" I whisper to her. "Don't worry about us."

When I pull back, I see her look of shock has been

replaced by one of determination. I smile to myself. *That's my girl.*

"I'll do it," Belle says without an ounce of hesitation.

"Belle, you don't —" Willa starts.

"I know I don't. I want to," Belle says, cutting her off and effectively ending anyone else's arguments.

Isla looks at Belle for a moment, seeming to come to some sort of conclusion that makes her smile. "Logan West is your cousin."

It's not a question, but Belle answers anyway. "By marriage."

"You could've gone to him. Been handed a contract with very little stipulations."

Again, not a question, but the implication is there.

"My dad always taught me that everything tastes sweeter when it's earned. We don't want to be handed an opportunity based on who is in our family. We want to earn it based on our talent. I think we've done that and will continue to do so."

My girl. My Belle. She's so strong and so damn smart. Sometimes I wonder if she really knows how amazing she is.

Isla smiles again. "Perfect. If there are no further questions, I'll have our team send the contract to your lawyer."

"You're beautiful!" Cal blurts. Isla stares at him like she just noticed he was in the room with us.

"Thank you for your time, Isla. We look forward to working with you," I say while shoving Cal out of the frame. She nods and ends the call.

"Smooth, buddy. Real smooth," Mav says, chuckling at Cal.

"Did no one else see her?" he asks with complete sincer-ity. "I think I'm in love."

"Well, I think you're an idiot," Belle says while laughing. "She looks like she's probably old enough to be our mom."

"She looks nothing like Mom," Cal says with a dopey smile on his face.

"Ew. That's disgusting." Belle pretends to gag.

"Name one thing that happened in that meeting," Willa challenges.

We all stare at Cal and wait for his answer.

"Uh…"

"Exactly." Willa rolls her eyes at Cal. "They're sending the contract to Frank. We can go over it with him."

"We need to finish packing and head to the airport soon," Mav points out.

I look over in time to see all the color leave Belle's face. I pull her into my lap quickly. "What is it? What's wrong?" I ask her, trying to keep my voice calm. Her sudden change in mood has me panicked. I hold her tight and rub my fingers up and down her back.

"I've been so distracted with the shows and the traveling and —" Belle pulls back to look at me, her tears threatening to fall from her beautiful eyes. "And finally being with you that I haven't thought about Brad."

"He won't touch you, Belle. I won't let him."

She looks at me and my heart breaks. She's terrified. I want to kill him. Hurt him for hurting the woman I love. Stop him from hurting her or anyone else ever again.

"I've felt safe with an ocean separating me from him. Now we're about to be in the same state again."

If I could keep her at my side every minute of every day

for the rest of time, I would. But she's come so far from that battered girl in her brother's kitchen. Her spark is back, and I don't want him or anyone else to take that away from her. Me included.

"What can I do to make you feel safe?" I ask instead.

Belle snuggles into me, resting her head on my shoulder. "You're the only place I feel safe."

Fuck. She has a way of knocking me off my feet while simultaneously lifting me to heights I've never imagined. I hug her tightly to me and kiss the top of her head.

Having her in my arms, seeking me as a comfort, just solidifies what I already know to be true. I will do anything and everything I can to keep her safe.

twenty-seven

BELLE

"HELLO?" *I shout into the darkness.*

I look around, trying to make out anything that would tell me where I am. It's so dark that I can't even see my hand in front of my face.

"Is anyone there?" I yell, unsure if I want an answer.

I put my hands out in front of me and take small steps. The only sounds I hear are the shuffling of my feet and the blood pounding in my ears.

"Where the fuck am I?" I mutter to myself as I shuffle along slowly.

Eventually, my hand comes in contact with rough fabric. I curl my fist around it and pull. Moonlight streams in from a hidden window, and I have to blink rapidly to get my eyes to adjust to the sudden light.

I look around and find I'm in my old bedroom at my parent's house. Everything is the same as it was the day I moved out.

"Mom?" I yell, not expecting a sudden answer, but trying anyway.

Opening my bedroom door, I peek out into the hallway and listen. The house is silent, and the hallway is empty.

The stairs creak and groan as I make my way down to check for any signs of my family. My hand runs over the old banister. I freeze.

"What the fuck is that?" I gasp, lifting my hand that just touched something slick. My face pales when I see what it is. Blood. There's blood on the banister.

My breathing increases rapidly, and I try not to move.

"What am I doing? I haven't been quiet, and no one has murdered me yet."

I take a deep breath and run down the remaining few stairs and toward the front door. Something catches on my foot, causing me to trip and land on my side.

"Shit. That hurt," I groan and roll onto my back. I sit up to see what tripped me. A scream leaves my throat before I fully process what I'm looking at. Milky white eyes and gray molted skin are the first things I pick up on.

"Ezra," I say on a sob. My hands shake over him, but I can't bring myself to make contact.

I look up, trying to find someone to help him, even though he's clearly been dead for a while. The living room is dark, but I see the outline of someone laying on the couch. I get my wobbly legs underneath me and carefully step over my best friend's body.

"Dad? Cal?" I ask between sniffs. Whoever is on the couch doesn't answer.

I quickly find the light switch on the wall and flip it on. What strength was left in my body gives out when I see who is in front of me. I drop to my knees.

"No no no no..."

A sound leaves my body that's as primal as it is broken.

"Kai no," I cry, scrambling on my hands and knees to get to the man I love.

His skin is pale, and his body is covered in blood.

"Please, Kai. Open your eyes," I beg, shaking his shoulders. He's cold. His skin is waxy and feels like ice. As I'm shaking him, I notice the large gash across his throat.

"No!" I scream to him, to the universe, to whoever will listen and bring him back to me.

Then I hear it over my pleas, the low chuckle. The one that still haunts me. I turn my head quickly to see him sitting in my dad's chair.

"This is your fault, Bellamy."

"Brad. You did this? You took him from me?" I scream at him as I tremble. He's holding a bloody kitchen knife and smiling.

"You're mine. No one else can touch you," he laughs again.

And all I can do is scream.

I wake with a gasp.

"Belle! Are you ok?"

I look up to see Kai staring at me, concern etched into his perfect face. His perfectly alive face. Before he has a chance to say anything else, I fling myself into his arms, breathing in his scent and listening to the beat of his heart.

"It felt so real," I whisper. Kai's warm arms are wrapped around me, calming my racing heart and slowing my breathing.

"Mo chridhe, it's ok. It was a nightmare," Kai murmurs into my hair. We're in my bedroom at Cal's house. Kai refused to let me out of his sight once we landed, and Cal didn't want me out of his either.

"Midnight Macaroni?" Cal yells from the other side of my door.

"Yes, please!" I yell back.

Kai snickers as he tries to pull away. I'm clinging to him too hard to let him.

"I've got you, baby. He can't get to you here."

"I don't usually have nightmares when you're next to me," I whisper into his chest. I feel him flinch and pull away so I can look at him.

"I was downstairs with Cal. He texted me that the contract was in his email, and we were reading it over." Kai looks guilty, like he was cheating on a test and not just downstairs. I hate I make him feel that way. That he feels like he needs to be with me at all times or I'll break.

And isn't that the truth? He was a floor away, and I woke up screaming and crying like an infant.

"Come on, let's go downstairs before Cal comes back up here to get us," I say, climbing out of bed and putting my hand out for Kai. He smiles and grabs it, probably thinking I'm letting the nightmare roll off me like I had been doing.

But I can't. Not this time. I need time to figure out what I want to do, but dream or not, it was too real. Kai is in danger from just being near me. And why was Ezra there? Was I the cause of his disappearance somehow?

"Stop overthinking. You said Brad is a coward and won't come near you when there are other men. Has that changed?" Kai asks, reading my thoughts.

"I doubt it." I don't even try to deny what I was thinking about. He would know I was lying. "But I can't live my life worrying I'm in danger or that you are for being with me."

"We've been home for less than a day, Belle. We're going to figure this out. I promise." Kai sits on the couch and pulls me down onto his lap. "There's nothing I won't do to make sure you're safe."

That's what I'm worried about.

———

"It smells so good in here!"

Kai comes around the corner to meet me at the front door of his house. He told me to just let myself in, and I did. Cal dropped me off, and I wasn't risking him coming in and interrupting our date night.

His house is the opposite color scheme of Mav's. Apparently, they thought it would be funny. Which I guess it may have been at first, but they both need to add some color. I won't lie, though. I kind of love the black floors.

"Thanks, baby," Kai says with a lazy smile before he pulls me into him for a sweet kiss. Taking my hand in his, he leads me into his spacious kitchen. Like the rest of his house, it's black and white. Black floors and cabinets with white walls and countertops. Even the appliances are black.

"What did you make?" I ask him, taking in the colorful assortment of veggies on the counter.

"Buffalo chicken mac and cheese is in the oven. I was just about to make a salad to go with it."

"My favorite!" I exclaim, bouncing on my toes.

Kai just chuckles and pulls me into his side, kissing the top of my head.

"I know," he whispers, putting his finger on my chin and titling my face towards him. He captures my lips with his. The kiss is slow at first, soft. It soon turns hungry, both of us wanting to devour the other.

"Kai..." I pant breathlessly into his mouth.

"I know, mo chridhe," he says quietly before sealing his lips over mine again.

"I don't want to wait," I manage to mumble between kisses.

He pulls back to look into my eyes. I don't know what he sees in mine, but all I see in his is love and lust. He quickly spins around to turn the oven off and then lifts me off the ground. I squeal as he throws me over his shoulder and quickly walks towards the stairs.

"But the mac and cheese!" I yell with a giggle.

"I'll fill this whole house with mac and cheese for you for the rest of our lives. But right now, you're mine." The growl in his voice shoots right between my legs and suddenly I'm no longer laughing.

The next thing I know, my feet are back on the ground and we're ripping each other's clothes off.

"Want you so bad," Kai groans into my neck, trailing his words with hot kisses.

"Take me. I'm yours," I moan as he backs me up to the bed. When the back of my knees hit the mattress, he picks me up and tosses me to the middle before crawling between my legs.

I'm so worked up just from the anticipation and kissing him that I shatter the moment his tongue touches my clit. I can feel the hot breath from his laughter as I come down.

"That was a little too easy, baby," he chuckles as he makes his way up my body. I can taste myself on his lips as he kisses me greedily. "I love you so fucking much."

"I love you too," I moan as the head of his cock pushes against my entrance.

Kai stills and drops his head. "Fuck!"

"What is it?" I ask, confused about why he's stopping and angry. I'm suddenly self-conscious and if I could move easier, I would try to cover myself.

"I don't have condoms. I never bring women here so there was no need. Fuck."

"I have an implant. The hospital tested me for everything when Cal brought me. So I'm ok if you are," I tell him, smiling shyly and pointing to the two tiny white dots on the inside of my bicep that are the only indications of the implant. I know he's been with a lot of women. He's a rockstar and it kind of comes with the territory.

"I've been celibate for almost two years now, mo chridhe. They weren't you, so I didn't see the point."

I look into his eyes and see the honesty shining through them. He's always loved me just as much as I've always loved him. My heart breaks for all the time we lost together, but the love in Kai's eyes quickly repairs it.

"Make me yours, Malikai."

twenty-eight

KAI

WITH ONE QUICK THRUST, I'm buried inside her. Nothing else will ever compare to this moment. Our bodies are joined in the way that our souls have always been. I feel complete in a way I never thought I would again. A way I never thought I would deserve.

I'm trying to give her a minute to adjust to my size. "I need to move, baby," I groan into her neck.

She responds by pulling my hair to give her better access to my mouth and grinding her hips against mine. I take that as my invitation to move and start rutting into her ruthlessly. Years of pent-up lust and feelings are being worked out between our bodies.

I can't get enough of her. I capture every little gasp and moan with my lips, like I can breathe in how much she loves me. I cover her body with nips and kisses, putting everything I feel for her into every touch.

I meant our first time to be slower, more romantic. But the moment she asked me to make her mine, I lost control.

Every inch of my skin feels alive and needy. I need to be touching her everywhere, and I need her touch in return.

Her hands are everywhere, my hair, my ass. Her nails are digging into my back one minute and my scalp the next. Every touch sends electricity straight to my balls. I'm not going to last at this pace, but I can't slow down either.

"Kai, I need..." she gasps.

"I know, baby," I tell her before moving my hand between us and circling her clit. She comes screaming my name. Her walls squeeze me so hard that I shoot myself into her. Her pussy milks me for everything I have.

"Belle," I whisper, kissing her softly. She snuggles into me, and I let her for a moment before getting up to get her a wet cloth.

"Where are you going?" she asks while giving me the most adorable pout I've ever seen.

"I'll be right back," I say and laugh. The sight of her laying naked in my bed is enough to get me hard again, but I shake my head and try to focus on the task at hand.

"Kai! Not to rush you or anything, but I really want that mac and cheese," Belle calls from the bed, causing me to chuckle.

God, I fucking love this woman.

"If you make that noise one more time, I'm going to bend you over the arm of this couch."

Belle looks at me with one eyebrow raised, like she's considering it. We're sitting snuggled up together on the couch, eating our dinner. She's been moaning with every bite.

"We can come back to that later. I'm too full right now."

I just laugh and shake my head. Moments like these make me so happy that in the back of my mind, I think I must be dreaming. She can't be here on my couch, eating my food, and looking at me like she loves me more than anything.

But she is.

And she's smiling, but a tear is streaking down her cheek.

"What's wrong?" I ask, alarmed at the conflicting emotions on her face.

"You're back. *My* Kai. Not the grumpy jackass that's invaded your body for the past five years." Her eyes are shining as she speaks, and the smile is still on her face, but her words make me feel like the world's biggest asshole.

I pull her into my arms and kiss her with a ferocity that I hope conveys how much I regret every moment I treated her poorly.

"I'm so fucking sorry, Belle. You have to know I hate how I treated you all those years," I practically plead.

"Kai. I know. Stop apologizing. You acted like an ass, and I ran. Neither of us handled losing Ezra, and it cost us each other," she says quietly, the smile slipping from her face. "But we're together now."

For-fucking-ever is what I want to say. I know it's true in the deepest, darkest parts of my soul. This woman is it for me. She is my other half and my only love. I'll marry her one day.

I keep all that to myself because it's still new, and this

conversation is too heavy already.

"What do you think about me hiring a private investigator to look into Ezra?" she blurts.

So much for lightening up the conversation.

My mood instantly plummets, and I can feel the muscles in my body locking down.

"I don't want to have this conversation right now," I say as evenly as I can manage.

"But Kai, he's still out there somewhere and —"

"I said no!" I scream, getting up from the couch and pacing in front of her. I run my hands through my hair and tug, trying to calm the anger that's surging inside of me.

I take one look at Belle and seeing the tears in her eyes and the shock on her face feels like a knife to the gut.

"Belle. . . I just. I can't," I try to explain but the pain that surfaces when my brother is mentioned, the pain I can usually force down, is forcing its way to the surface.

"He's out there somewhere, Kai! What do you mean you can't? We're not giving up on him!" her tears are replaced with a look of determination and fury. How do I explain to her he's not out there? And if he is, he doesn't want to be found. The look on her face tells me she won't listen to anything I say right now.

"How about we watch a movie and talk about the new album?" It's taking every ounce of self-control I posses to keep my anger in check right now.

"How about we talk about the fact that you're abandoning Ezra?" She counters in a loud voice that penetrates my already thin control.

"Fuck you for saying that to me! He's my brother! My twin! Don't you think I looked for him? Don't you think I want him back?" I watch her reel back at my harsh words and even harsher tone. I do my best to calm my voice before speaking again. "I can't go down that road again. It almost killed me."

Belle's wide eyes don't soften in the way I'm used to. They harden as she spins on her heels and takes off running to my bedroom.

"Where are you going?" I call out after her, but she just ignores me. I follow her and find her putting her clothes on. "Belle —"

"Don't," she says with a hardness and finality that throws me off. "Cal is going to pick me up."

"Please. Stay. We can talk about something else. Get back to our date," I plead with her.

"I don't want to talk about something else! I want to find my best friend!" she yells, throwing her hands up in exasperation.

I open my mouth to argue, but I'm interrupted by the blare of a car horn.

"That's Cal," Belle says with sudden sadness.

"Mo chridhe, please..." I beg. I'm not sure what I'm begging for at this point. For her to stay? Drop the Ezra topic? Keep fighting for him because I'm clearly too weak to do it myself? All of the above? None of the above?

"I'll talk to you later," she says softly and then rushes past me to the bedroom door.

I let her go. Stunned and stuck in place by how quickly the night went from being the best night of my life to one of the worst. The sound of the front door slamming and then a car door gets my feet moving. I walk over to the window and watch my best friend drive away with my heart.

twenty-nine

BRAD

SHE'S NEVER ALONE. Never fucking alone. What twenty-four-year-old has their brother drive them to and from their booty call?

"Fuck!" I shout for the millionth time into the universe.

I've been watching her since the moment her plane landed, waiting to get her alone. If I can just get her back, I can break her again. Make her push everyone else away.

Make her mine.

Mine.

Make her pay.

Pay for what she's done.

Pay for what it's cost me.

Pay.

Do I keep sending her flowers? Mess with her some other way? I could. It would be easy.

But it would also make it easy for her stupid brother to figure out it was me. He has his fucking lawyer up my ass as it is.

So, here I am, sitting in the fucking shadows.
Waiting.
Watching.
Until the opportunity arises.
Until I take back what is mine.

BELLE

"ARE you just going to sit there grumbling to yourself, or are you going to tell me why you're mad?"

I shoot my brother the most annoyed look I can muster, and he just laughs at me. Full on, head thrown back, laughing.

"Nothing is funny right now, Callahan," I snark.

"It's not my fault you look like a grumpy puppy when you're mad," he says with a shrug, not caring that he's just making me angrier. I'm about to tell him off when the doorbell rings.

"If that's Kai, tell him I'm not here."

Cal looks over his shoulder as he walks towards the door, giving me the look that says he thinks I'm an idiot.

"Where is that asshole? I'll kill him. Guitarists are easy to replace!"

I smile when I hear Willa's voice coming from the front door. Cal must have called in reinforcements. She storms into the room where I'm sitting on the couch and looks around. Satisfied that she doesn't have to commit any murders at the moment, her gaze narrows on me.

"What did he do?" she asks as she takes a seat next to me.

I sigh before leaning back to stare at the ceiling, collecting my thoughts.

"It's more what he won't do."

"Anal? Breath play?" she asks with complete seriousness. "Oh! Wax play? You've always liked candles."

"I don't need to hear any of this," I hear Cal mutter as he hightails it out of the room.

"It's not related to sex, Willa," I tell her, completely ignoring my brother.

I can see her overthinking, so I hold up my hand to stop her before she goes on another tangent.

"I brought up looking for Ezra. It... didn't go well," I admit, suddenly feeling guilty. Not for wanting to look for him, I will never apologize for that, but for the way I reacted when Kai pushed back.

Willa sighs and looks at me with disappointment for the first time since we argued over who the best Chris was (Hemsworth, obviously) and she thought it was Pine.

"I told you how hard that was on him, Belle. Why did you think that conversation would go well?"

"Honestly? I just kind of blurted it out. It's been on my mind for years, and I just... I just want to find him, Willa. I hate that he's out there somewhere. Alone." I look up and expect to see sympathy or empathy in my best friend's eyes, but I see anger instead.

"Belle, you know I love you, I do, but you're being self-centered," she states plainly. I open my mouth to argue, but she continues. "You were isolated. You left us and went to school, and honestly, I don't hold that against you." I give her a look that says I don't believe her, but she smiles slightly and says, "I don't."

"Then why are you acting pissed with me right now?"

"You weren't here, Belle. That was your choice, and I respect that, but you weren't *here*. You didn't see what trying to find Ezra did to Kai. You didn't hear him crying every time he was called with a lead that went nowhere." Her words hit me like a truck and it's suddenly difficult to breathe. "You weren't the one pulling him out of bars as he tried to numb the pain or try to find the right words to reassure him that his life wasn't over. That was us."

Hot tears fall down my cheeks, and I do nothing to stop them or wipe them away. She's right. I wasn't thinking about how any of this would affect Kai. I was only thinking of the guilt I was feeling from being away for so long.

"We all love and miss Ezra. But we decided years ago that we won't sacrifice Kai, hoping Ezra might be alive. Otherwise, we risk losing them both."

I sit with that for a moment, and Willa lets me, keeping quiet by my side. I love Ezra as much as I love Cal, but Kai... Kai holds a part of my soul. Even now, not being in the same room as him, feeling his warm gaze on me or the heat of his touch, makes me feel empty.

"So I just let Ezra go?" I ask, my voice barely a whisper.

"No. You hold him in your heart, and maybe one day he'll come back. Or maybe Kai will find the strength to look again, but you can't force it. Promise me you won't force him." Willa's voice has lost its anger, but the sternness is still there.

"I promise. I never meant to hurt him."

"I know. I'm sure he knows that too," she says before squeezing my hand.

"I need to go back. I can't leave him like I did," I say, shooting up from my seat.

"I'll drive you!" I hear Cal shout from where he was clearly eavesdropping.

I roll my eyes. I have my car here still. The one time I tried to drive myself to pick up a coffee, Cal followed me there and back. I went through a drive through. I didn't even get out of the car. It's not worth the argument anymore. I haven't heard a peep from Brad since we've been back. I can't decide if that's good or bad. The hovering my brother is doing is grating on me, though.

I hug Willa quickly and follow Cal out the door to his car.

"He's definitely not here," Cal states like I couldn't tell from the dark house and missing car.

"Where would he go?" I ask as another wave of guilt hits me. I know I shouldn't feel guilty for picking college over the band, but the distance I'm feeling from everyone paired with what Brad did makes that hard.

"Mav's? Maybe," Cal says, pulling his phone out and texting someone. I'm assuming Kai or Mav.

"Can we go over and see?" I ask while gnawing on my bottom lip.

Cal's phone pings with a new text. His brows furrow as he reads it. "I know where he is," is all he says before pulling out of Kai's driveway and back onto the street.

We drive for fifteen minutes before Cal pulls over onto the side of a back road. I know exactly where we are and my entire body tenses. I can see Kai's car a little further ahead of us.

"He's in the woods?" I ask, my voice higher than normal.

"He sits by the river sometimes. Mostly when he wants to talk to Ez. Says he feels closer to him there." Cal is staring out at the dark sky over the tall trees. "I have a flashlight in the trunk. I'll walk you over to him so you can talk."

Cal is out of the car before I can respond. His temper is even, which is strange for Cal. I can't tell if he's upset or angry or just worried. Once I see the beam of his flashlight, I get out of the car and silently follow him into the woods.

The leaves on the ground are wet from the rain we had recently. The trees are blocking the wind, but it's still pretty chilly. It smells like wood and decaying leaves and fresh air. I used to love that smell. Now it's part of my nightmares.

"He's right up there," Cal says, using the flashlight to point. I follow the beam to see the hunched shoulders of a defeated man.

"Kai!" I yell, running to him. I watch as he turns. His eyes are red and puffy in the bright light of Cal's flashlight. I can see the shock register on his face before he stands and quickly makes his way to me.

"I'm sorry," he mumbles into my hair after he scoops me into his arms.

"You have nothing to be sorry for. I wasn't thinking

about how much this would hurt you. I'm the one who's sorry."

"If you two are good here, I'm going to head home."

I look over my shoulder at my brother and then back at Kai.

"I've got her," Kai says. Cal nods like he knows.

Kai's gaze returns to me, and I can see the torment there. The torment *I* put there and tears instantly well in my eyes.

"I'm so sorry," I hiccup.

"There's nothing to be sorry for, mo chridhe," he says softly. "I love how much you love my brother. I love how much you're willing to fight for him."

My feet are still dangling off the ground, so I lift my legs and wrap them around his waist, locking my ankles behind his back. "But I love you so much more."

Kai smiles sadly and presses a quick kiss to my lips. "I love you too, baby."

I look around. Kai brought a camping lantern that he has sitting on a rock near the river. I can see the small area it illuminates.

"Cal said you come here to talk to Ezra."

He nods. "It's the place I feel closest to him. Probably because it's the last place I saw him."

Kai has made no attempt to put me down, both of us trying to stay as close to the other as possible. I tighten my grip on his neck and snuggle in closer.

"I don't believe he's dead. There were times when I thought it would be easier to think of him that way, less painful. But I don't think I ever truly believed he was. I still can't." Kai pulls back so that he can see my face. "I'd know if he was dead, wouldn't I? He's my identical twin. I'd feel it."

"I think we would all feel it."

Kai nods and pulls me into him once more.

"I don't want to do anything to cause you more pain. We can miss Ezra without kicking over stones and hurting people, without looking for him," I offer. I can't tell what Kai is thinking right now. After my talk with Willa, I wish I could go back and stop myself from even suggesting it. But it's out there and Kai has clearly been thinking it over. I don't want to do anything to hurt him further.

"I know, but I think I want to try to find him. Maybe hire a better PI that will weed out the false reports before calling me about them." I nod into his neck, letting him speak. "I need to know what happened to him, Belle. Even if what the police reported was correct and he is dead —"

I kiss his neck, feeling his racing pulse under my lips. I just want to let him know that I'm still here with him while he sorts through his thoughts.

"I need to know, and I think that with you by my side, I'll finally have the strength to find out."

I lean back so I can look at his handsome face. His eyes are shining with unshed tears and the small smile on his face is sad.

"Are you sure?" I ask him. Even with the tiny spark of hope I feel that he's agreeing to look, I still don't want him to if it'll hurt him. He's the most important person in my life.

"I'm sure. I need answers and hiding from them won't change what they are," he says before kissing me softly.

"If it gets to be too painful, tell me. Promise to tell me and we'll stop." I grip his face in my cold hands, making sure he knows how serious I am.

"I promise."

With that, he carries me all the way back to his car and into his bed.

thirty-one

KAI

THE SUN slowly shines in through the large picture window in my living room. I've been sitting here since early this morning with a picture of my brother and me in my hands. Belle is asleep on my lap. I took her straight to my bed for make-up sex. Then we had hot chocolate on the couch. We stayed up for hours talking. At one point, Belle even called Willa and had her on speakerphone. She was making sure that I was absolutely certain about searching for Ezra before she agreed to help me.

Willa, understandably, was skeptical. But she eventually agreed when Belle told her I promised to back down if it became too much. Unlike last time, when I tried not to give up until I had nothing left to give.

Belle groans next to me, slowly peeling her eyes open. Once she spots me, she smiles, warming every cold crevice of my heart.

"Good morning," she says, her voice thick with sleep. Her brown hair is a mess around her face, but she's never looked more beautiful. I lean down and kiss her. Loving that it's something I get to do. Kiss her whenever I want.

She gets up, stretching her arms above her head. The shirt of mine she's wearing rides up so I can see the tops of her toned thighs. I reach for her, grabbing the backs of her legs to pull her towards me. She giggles and presses a kiss to my forehead.

"I'm going to make some breakfast. Do you want coffee?" she asks, pulling away from me, causing me to pout. Belle just laughs. Her fucking laugh kills me. I'll never get tired of it. "We can play after we eat," she calls as she walks away.

I grumble to myself, knowing her well enough to know that if she's hungry, we have approximately thirty-eight minutes until she turns into a monster. I'm not stupid enough, or horny enough, to fight her on it. Instead, I pull my phone out to text the group.

ME

Belle and I have decided to get a new PI to look into Ezra.

WILLA

Couple things! You guys are so cute!

ME

That doesn't even make sense.

MAV

What are you hoping to get out of this?
More bullshit like last time?

I sigh. I knew Maverick wasn't going to be thrilled. He had just as much trouble as I did the first time around. But the difference is, his trouble never stopped. It makes me mad that I didn't see how much he truly loved Ezra before. It's so obvious now.

ME

Answers.

CAL

I'm on my way!

BELLE

On your way where?

CAL

To Kai's for the meeting?

ME

We're not having a meeting.

WILLA

I'll head over too.

ME

We're not having a meeting!

MAV

I don't feel like going to Kai's today.

BELLE

I'm going to make pancakes if you guys are hungry. I already have the coffee on.

MAV

I actually decided I need to get out of the house. Be there in five.

ME

I hate all of you.

Except Belle.

WILLA

Aww! Barf!

"Where are you going?" I ask as I watch Belle run by.

"To put my clothes back on. I love my brother and my friends, but they don't need to see me mostly naked."

I groan and stare at the ceiling. I wanted a quiet morning with my girl. Now I'm about to have a loud one with the idiots I've chosen as my family. I'm annoyed at that thought making me smile.

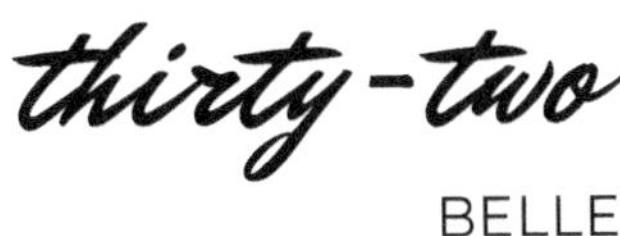

thirty-two

BELLE

"OKAY. We're all here. What did you want to talk to us about?" Cal asks from his spot on the couch between Mav and Willa. All three are looking at Kai and me expectantly.

"I didn't invite you here, and I already told you everything," Kai says, sounding annoyed. I know he secretly loves when we're all together, though. You can see it in his relaxed body language and the smirk he's trying so hard to keep off his face.

"Right. Well, after you called me last night, I started researching private investigators —" Willa starts, but Cal scoffs, interrupting her.

"Willa knew? How come she got to know, and I didn't?" he whines.

Willa hits him in the face with a black throw pillow and continues speaking like he isn't even here. "I made a list of those that seem most reliable. The one at the top of the list was interesting."

"Who was it?" I ask, not at all surprised that Willa has already done some research.

"Harrison Ray," she says. The name sounds familiar, but I'm not sure why. I look over at Kai to see his eyebrows have shot up, and he looks completely shocked.

"Sheriff Ray?" he asks.

"Yeah. I called his office and his daughter answered. I guess he resigned after Ezra's case. He felt it wasn't handled well, and they took the power to keep the case open from him. She said she thinks he would be willing to work with us, but he's currently away on a different case, and she doesn't know when he'll be back."

"I remember him coming to our house to tell us that Ezra had been declared dead. He made it clear he didn't agree, but at the time, I blamed him for not doing something about it," Kai says, almost to himself. "He took a phone call while he was there. Whoever was on the other end was the one with the power."

"How do you know that?" Mav asks, leaning forward and planting his elbows on his knees. Suddenly more interested in the conversation than when he arrived.

"I listened in. I was angry and thought I might overhear something that could be used as blackmail or something. I don't know. I wasn't in the right frame of mind. All I heard was him talking to someone he called 'sir' and arguing that the case was being closed too soon."

"He seems like a good choice if we want to wait for him," I say, looking between Kai and Mav and trying to figure out their moods. They both seem lost in their own thoughts.

"I'd like to start now," Kai says eventually.

"I have a few other options," Willa says, handing Kai her phone. I get closer to them to see the list she's made with a ranking system next to each name.

"Willa," Kai sighs, handing her phone back to her. "Please, just tell me what the next best option is, and I'll give that person a call."

"Fine," Willa mumbles under her breath. "I just sent you her contact info. Her name is Kelly Boswell."

"Thank you," he says. "I'll call her now."

I watch as he walks away, looking for any sign of doubt in his movements. I see nothing but his normal confidence. His normal confidence and how great his ass looks in the gray sweats he's wearing. It's unfair how hot he looks in sweatpants and a plain white t-shirt. If I wore that same outfit, I would look like a sick rat.

I take the moment of silence to really examine Maverick. His brown hair is messy and sticking up everywhere. His honey eyes are dull and dark bags hang underneath them. Everyone has assured me that this is how he gets when they're home, but I don't know how much longer I can let it slide before I try to do something about it.

"Stop looking at me like that," Mav huffs when he notices my stare.

"Like what?" I ask, not so innocently. He needs help, and I'm not about to pretend he doesn't.

"Like I'm a project you can fix with some inspirational quotes and a hug," he grumps before crossing his arms and leaning back on the couch.

"I'm just trying to figure out how you're feeling about all this," I tell him. "And honestly? I'm a little afraid to ask you. You look one minute away from a nervous breakdown."

I hear Willa gasp quietly, and I can feel Cal's stare on the side of my face. But Maverick just looks at me, silently. His face not giving a single emotion away. Hopefully thinking about what I said and not about to lose his mind and leave. I hate that they all walk on eggshells around him, but I also understand why they do. It's just how they've coped all these years.

And yes, I've been removed from that, so maybe I don't get it. Willa has reminded me of that in Kai's case more than once. But I'm here now and maybe a fresh perspective is what they all need.

"Since you're being honest with me, I'll be honest with you," Mav says with a quirk of his lips. Like maybe he wants to smile but can't. "I'm fucking terrified."

"Mav —" Cal starts softly, like he's trying to calm a rabid dog. But Mav's mood is even, and he holds up his hand to stop my brother from interfering.

"I will not go off the deep end from answering her question, Cal," Mav says, effectively shutting Cal up, even though I can see in his eyes he still wants to argue.

I move from where I've been standing next to the fireplace and sit on the coffee table in front of Maverick so that we're eye to eye. This feels like a conversation where I want him to know he has my undivided attention.

"I'm terrified we're going to find out he's dead. I'm terrified we're going to find out he's alive and chose to leave us all. I'm terrified that he's out there somewhere with no memories of us. I'm terrified he misses us and can't come back," Mav looks me in my eyes as he explains, tears forming and slowly falling. "No matter what happens, it's going to fucking hurt, and I'm so damn sick of hurting, Belle."

Hot tears prickle at the back of my eyes as I lean in to pull Maverick into a hug. "Does it hurt less not knowing?"

"I don't know," he whispers, voice cracking.

Arms wrap around us tightly from both sides. I don't have to look to know it's Cal and Willa. They're silently letting Mav know they're here for him, no matter what. That quiet support seems to be exactly what he needed. His stiff shoulders fall, and he leans his head on Cal's.

"Thank you," he whispers to all of us.

"Kelly said she can get started right away," Kai says, the sound of his footsteps coming to an abrupt halt. "What did I miss?"

"Just hug us," Cal yells, getting a laugh from everyone. Kai comes up behind me and does just that.

thirty-three

BRAD

I NEED to isolate her somehow. Make her mad enough to go on a walk alone. Or drive somewhere alone. Or fuck, I don't know. Be fucking alone.

BOSS

You have a week.

ME

I don't understand why we need to get her away from them. She's weak. I doubt they let her cut her own food herself.

I pace in the shitty hotel room I've been renting. It smells like mildew and poor people. When he asked me to seduce her a couple of years ago, I had no idea it would turn into this bullshit.

BOSS

I don't pay you to understand. You have a week.

ME

What do you want me to do?

BOSS

Figure it out or I will.

I know what the threat is. Figure it out or he'll destroy me. My career and life as I know it will be over. Because I agreed to make Belle my girlfriend. FUCK.

ME

Yes, sir.

I continue my pacing, pulling at my hair and trying to think of what to do.

My eye catches on what my mother likes to call 'trash-zines' or celebrity tabloids. I used them once to mess with Belle while she was in Europe. It was stupidly easy to get the Irons woman to give a shitty interview about her son. Only took some cash and a bottle of Xanax.

Pathetic.

I quickly find the contact for the woman at one of the most popular tabloids and hit call.

The moment she answers, I tell her my plan.

"I have a perfect story for you about the newest member of Shattered Halo."

I don't contain the smile on my face as she jumps on the story.

If I can't get to you, I'll make you come to me, Bellamy.

thirty-four

BELLE

"ARE you sure you want to do this?" Cal asks me for the eighth time in the last few minutes.

"Of course I don't want to do this. If I don't, she's going to show up at your house," I point out. . . again.

I'm meeting my mom for lunch and Cal is driving me. Because of course he is. We haven't heard a peep from Brad in the weeks we've been home. I think it's because he can't leave his mom. She had a stroke right before I fled. I can't say I feel sorry for her. The woman makes the evil Disney stepmoms look like nice ladies. I don't think Brad is willing to sacrifice his visits with her by hurting someone who is now in the public eye and ending up in prison. No one else agrees with me, so here I am, being dropped off by my brother like I'm in high school again.

Cal's offered to stay, but I know if he does, it'll turn into a fight. Cal can do nothing wrong in my mom's eyes, and all I can do is screw up.

My big brother hates that she sees us the way she does and constantly defends me. My mom hates that he's always

218

defending me. So they fight. It's a cycle that I'm not really in the mood to witness today. So I'm sacrificing myself on the altar of sibling-dom and having lunch with her. That should buy us another few months of peace.

"Fine, but I'm sitting in the parking lot the whole time," he says, and I just laugh. There's no point in arguing. I know him too well. Even if he agrees not to stay in the parking lot, he'll just be circling the restaurant until I'm done.

"Feel free to leave when people notice there's a famous rockstar sitting in his car like a creep," I joke. He shoots me a dirty look, making me laugh again.

He pulls his car up directly in front of the small steakhouse my mother chose. I'm sure it costs a fortune, and she expects me to pay. We got an advance from the label so I can afford it.

Cal shrinks in his seat, pulling his baseball cap down lower on his face, like hiding his hair and forehead suddenly makes him look less like Callahan Griffin. His antics make me chuckle again.

My good mood is ruined the moment I walk into the restaurant and see my mom waiting for me with a scowl on her face. Looking at my watch, I see I'm early, not late, like the scowl would imply.

The restaurant is nice. Dark wood floors and light blue walls. The tables are all square with white cloths and black metal chairs. The light fixtures hanging from the ceiling are long and black metal that match the chairs, with those old school looking light bulbs. I like the atmosphere of the place. I'd like it more without my mom here.

"Hi, Mom." I take my seat across from her at the small square table, offering a smile that I hope seems genuine.

"Bellamy," she replies, looking put out even though she's the one who asked me to meet her here. Typical.

"So, how have you been?" I'm trying my hardest to be nice. I never understood my mother's contempt towards me, and as I've gotten older, I've cared about it less and less.

"Have you heard from your father recently?" she asks, completely ignoring my question.

"Oh, uh, yeah. We text occasionally." My dad hasn't been around much since my parents divorced. I haven't actually seen him in years, but we've always texted to stay in touch.

"Hmm," is her only response.

Thankfully, the server picks that moment to come and take our orders. As expected, my mother orders the most expensive steak on the menu. I opt for a steak salad, which apparently was the wrong choice from the scoff coming from my mother.

"What's wrong with salad?" I ask her once the server is out of earshot.

"Trying to be skinny for your current fling while being chunky when you were with the man you cheated on is absurd."

I'm not chunky. Never have been. Even if I was, fuck changing how I look for a man.

Wait...

"Cheated? I never cheated on anyone." Now it's my turn to scowl. First, she's telling me to go back to the man who abused me, now she's saying I cheated on him? What the fuck?

She just scoffs again before placing the cloth napkin on her lap.

"Did you ask me here to see if Dad talks to me and accuse me of cheating on my abuser? Because if that's the case, I'm going to be leaving." I push my chair back and go to stand. Before my butt is even off the seat, she's throwing a magazine at me.

Right on the cover is a picture of Brad and me in college. His arm is around my shoulder, and I'm smiling up at him. My hair is down and straightened because that's how he liked it. His eyes are directly on the camera. I don't know how I didn't notice the coldness in his baby blues back then, but it's obvious now. Brad has those all-American good looks with his blond hair and blue eyes. He's attractive, and this picture was picked perfectly to highlight that.

"Shattered Halo's Cheating Angel," I read the title out loud. It's not even a good title. Not that I expect much from these garbage people calling themselves reporters. I know what they're doing. They picked a picture of Brad, front and center, where you can barely even see me, to garner sympathy for the handsome man who was wronged. It's such a typical story and it always works. It might work on me if I wasn't so over all this and ready for Brad to be out of my life for good.

"You stepped out on Bradley and he's generous enough to forgive you. Yet you're gallivanting around with that Irons boy and playing rockstar with your brother," my mother says, looking at me through her cold, calculating eyes. Eyes that are the same dark blue as mine, but so much more piercing.

I pushed back on the self-doubt that I've been working so hard on. My mother has a way of bringing it rushing to the surface. Like maybe she wants me to break.

"I left him because he put his hands on me. Because he manipulated me into giving up family and friendships," I say as calmly as I can, trying not to cause a scene in the middle of a restaurant. "And not that it's any of your business, but Kai and I didn't start dating until two months after I left Brad."

"That's not what the article says," she sneers.

"I don't care what the article says! Your daughter is telling you it's not true. That the man you're so keen on defending is a monster, yet you sit here and attack me." My voice rises as I stand from the table, completely done with this conversation.

"You had a man that was well off with a stable income and instead you settle for the back-up twin," she says, her voice even like she isn't breaking my heart.

She was never warm or really even kind as a mother, but I guess some part of me hoped she loved me. Now I'm not even sure of that.

"Back-up twin?" I say with utter disbelief.

"Adira and I still talk. I read her interview. I know you had a thing with Ezra before he died. Now you're with his identical twin brother. That's a little trashy, don't you think?"

I blink slowly. Almost convinced I'm dreaming and not actually having this conversation in public. Unable to believe that my own mother just called me trash without asking me a single real question about my feelings or my relationship.

I want to scream. I want to scream until my lungs give out and my throat bleeds. It's no wonder Ezra hid his sexuality from these people. I'm in a loving, committed relationship with a man, and I'm being attacked. I couldn't even imagine the reactions if Kai was a woman.

"I'm going to give you the courtesy you don't deserve," I say, still standing in front of the table. I can feel the eyes of everyone else in the place on us. I'm sure there are a few phones out taking videos right now. So I say the next part clear enough for everyone to hear, phones included. "I have never been with, nor have I had any interest in being with Ezra. Kai is the love of my life. I've loved him since I was a child, and he feels the same way. I don't know why his mother or mine are trying to pin us against each other, but it won't work."

Mom rolls her eyes, and I can see she wants to speak, but I don't give her the opportunity.

"As for Brad, he abused me. There are medical and police records. I will be handing this article over to my lawyer and filing a defamation suit against the publishers." I grab the magazine that was sitting on the table and turn to leave. Before I do, I look over my shoulder at the woman who raised me. "Don't contact me again unless it's with an apology. Even then, I probably won't answer."

I walk as casually as I can out of the restaurant, holding my head high and trying not to break down. As predicted, I see my brother's car in the spot right up front. I make a beeline for it and practically throw myself into the passenger seat.

"What the — Belle?" Cal asks, eyes wide. I definitely startled him. "What happened?"

I burst into tears and can barely hear Cal's panicked questions over my sobs. I hand him the magazine that I have clutched in my fist. It's the best I can do at the moment.

The tears slow and my vision clears enough to see the anger on my brother's face as he reads the article. I didn't even bother. The title was enough to tell me it was full of lies.

"I'm calling Frank," Cal says, pulling up the contact on his phone. They quickly discuss the article and Frank says he'll get right on it. It's a quick conversation and I'm starting to really like how quickly and efficiently Frank works.

I find some fast-food napkins in the glove compartment and clean up my face.

"What can I do?" Cal asks quietly.

"It wasn't the article. It was Mom," I tell him, looking at my hands instead of his face. He didn't want me to go in there alone, and I insisted I would be fine. I don't want to look at the *I-told-you-so* expression on his face. So I recap my very quick lunch with our mom while picking at my cuticles and sniffling.

"Speak of the devil," he practically growls. I look up at him. That reaction was unexpected. I knew he wouldn't be happy, but he usually makes excuses for Mom. His face is red, and he looks angrier than I've ever seen him.

Our mother is striding up to his car, looking like someone peed in her martini.

"What?" Cal barks as he puts down his window.

I watch my mom's steps falter. Cal never speaks to her with anything more than minor annoyance.

"Callahan. Your sister left without paying her bill," she whines. My jaw drops at the utter audacity of this woman.

"And what did my sister order?" Cal asks while gripping the steering wheel with white knuckles. The car isn't even running. Which might be a blessing, considering Cal's current state.

"A garden salad with steak tips, but I don't see why that matters," my mom says while looking at the door to the restaurant. I can see the server there, his arms crossed. Clearly, she told him she was going out to get the money to pay the bill, and he's babysitting her. A small spark of petty joy hits me when I realize how embarrassing this must be for her.

Cal reaches into his back pocket, grabs his wallet, and throws a couple of bills out of the window.

"This won't be enough to cover the entire bill," she says as she scrambles to get the bills he dropped.

"It's more than enough to cover Belle's salad. Goodbye, Paula." Cal puts his window back up and starts the engine.

Once we're away from the nightmare that birthed us, I feel like I can breathe.

"How can I help?" Cal asks, like him standing up for me didn't do everything I needed from him.

"Do you think Dad would come visit?" I ask in a small voice. I miss my dad. He moved out of state when he divorced my mom. Texting just isn't the same as seeing him in person.

"If you want Dad, I'll get you Dad," Cal says with absolute certainty.

"You can't send me a text like that, you asshole!" Kai yells at Cal the moment we walk through the door.

Kai has me in his arms before I can ask questions. His warmth and strength immediately calm me.

"What happened, mo chridhe? Are you ok?" he asks into my neck, gently placing kisses after each question.

I mutter a summarized version, keeping myself in his hold. Cal fills in any missing information. I can feel Kai stiffen the moment I mention the article and then relax when Cal tells him he already called Frank. It would be funny if it was happening to someone else, and it wasn't my life filled with the drama.

"What did he text you?" I ask Kai after we'd told him everything, and he's moved us to the couch with me sitting across his lap and Cal in the recliner across from us.

"The asshole said I need to get here immediately because you needed me. Then didn't answer when I called him. I tried calling you, but you didn't answer either." I can hear the slight panic in his voice, and I feel guilty, even though I wasn't the one who texted him in the first place.

I glare at my brother, who just shrugs. He really can be an asshole sometimes.

"I'm sorry. My phone is in my purse, and I didn't hear it." I don't mention I was probably too busy sobbing to hear it. He's already ready to go to war with anyone hurting me. I don't need to add ammo.

"You don't need to apologize," he says with a pointed look at Cal, who just ignores him. "But I was going to take you on a date. We can do it on a different day if you just want to stay home. We could even watch a movie with that idiot," he offers, gesturing at Cal with his chin.

"Hey! I said you needed to be here, and you are. You're welcome," Cal says, standing and stomping off dramatically.

I laugh for the first time since lunch, feeling a little lighter just from being near Kai. "I want to go on the date."

"That's my girl," he says, kissing my temple and scooping me up into his arms. "Don't wait up!" he yells to Cal. I can hear my brother's disgusted groan coming from the kitchen, and that just makes me laugh some more.

"They look closed," I point out as Kai pulls us into the empty parking lot of our favorite childhood hangout.

"They are."

I look at him, knowing full well he can see how confused I am, but he just smiles and gets out. I watch as he walks around the car to open my door for me. His ass looks amazing in the tight jeans he's wearing. The navy Henley that stretches deliciously across his muscles is making it difficult to want to go anywhere other than a bed.

"I'm not really sure that breaking and entering is a good date idea," I tell him, accepting his offered hand to help me out of the car. That just makes him laugh. His laugh makes me weak in the knees, and I'm helpless to follow him into whatever illegal activities he has planned.

He leads me into the building. The smudged glass doors are unlocked. The familiar smell of burned cheese and hot plastic permeate the air of the arcade. The purple and gold carpet hasn't changed since we were kids. It's like a memory hitting you in the face. We spent hours here, all five of us, trying to beat each other's high scores on the machines and track times on the go-karts.

"How is no one here in the middle of the day on a Saturday?" I ask, looking around and realizing I don't even see any staff.

"I rented the place out for the day," he says, flipping the lock on the door behind us. "It's hard to go out and have fun like this when you have a recognizable face. I appreciate our fans, but sometimes it's nice to be left alone."

"This is perfect. Thank you for doing this." I lean up on my toes to kiss his jaw and the rough stubble tickles my lips. He turns his head to capture my lips in a quick and sweet kiss.

"What do you want to do first? I can kick your ass in mini golf. Or I can kick your ass on the go-karts. Maybe you want to get your ass kicked playing ski-ball?"

I elbow him in the ribs playfully. "I think there's something wrong with your memory if you think you beat me in any of those." If we were really being honest, Willa beat all of us. But out of just Kai and me, I was definitely the winner.

"Willing to put your money where your mouth is?" he asks, a sly grin taking over his face.

And because I'm feeling bold, I say, "I'd rather put your dick where my mouth is." I watch his jaw drop and the fire alight in his eyes before I take off running. I'm out the back door and halfway down the path to the go-karts before I hear him chasing me.

Kai crashes into my back and sweeps me off my feet right before I reach the gate to the track. I'm giggling like I haven't in years.

"You're mean, baby," Kai murmurs in my ear. He puts me on my feet, but immediately grabs me by the back of my neck and pulls me into a searing kiss. Just a simple peck from this man makes my heart race, but he's kissing me now like he wants to devour my very being. By the time he pulls back, I'm breathless and ready to ride him like a rodeo champ.

"We're going to have some good, clean fun first. Then I'm going to take you home and show you what you can do with that dirty mouth of yours."

"Promise?" I ask, my voice sounding husky in my ears.

Kai grips me to him harder, his erection pressing firmly into my stomach. I know exactly what I'm doing to him, and I love that I have that power. That this incredibly sexy, famous, amazing man wants me and only me. It blows my mind every time I think about it.

"Promise," he growls, kissing me hard, then spinning me around to land a swift slap on my ass. "Now let's get started before I decide to take you in the middle of the mini-golf course."

I raise an eyebrow as I look back at him over my shoulder.

"Baby," he growls again. I know he's only holding on by a thread, but I'm having fun playing with him. So I blow him a kiss and skip off to pick my go-kart.

thirty-five

KAI

I CAN'T GET her clothes off fast enough. Belle has been teasing me through our entire date. Shaking her sweet little heart-shaped ass every time she took a swing on the mini-golf course. Bending over just enough so that I could see right down her shirt every time she picked up her ball. She knows exactly what she's doing to me. My cock is so hard behind my zipper, it hurts.

"What's the rush?" Belle giggles, trying to wiggle out of my reach. All she manages to do it grind her ass against my dick, making me groan.

I freeze when I think I hear a twig snap. We're outside my house, surrounded by trees and the sun just set. So far, we've been lucky with the paparazzi. They don't bother us here, at least they haven't. Not one for taking chances with my girl, I scoop her up and rush into my house. Belle is stiff in my arms.

"Is someone out there?" she whispers, even though we're safe inside and the door is locked.

"I don't know, and I wasn't risking it."

I turn to Belle, expecting the moment to have passed. But I see her smiling at me with a sparkle in those beautiful blue eyes of hers.

Her lips meet mine in a slow and sensual kiss. Squeezing her tightly to me, I kiss her back, pouring every ounce of feeling I have for her into it.

"No one has ever made me feel as safe as you do," she murmurs against my lips.

"You'll always be safe with me," I tell her as I back her into the wall. She moans into my mouth when she feels how hard I am.

My plan was to take it slow. Worship her with my mouth and show her how much she means to me. But then she teased me all afternoon and now I'm not sure I'll be able to restrain myself.

Her jeans are already unbuttoned from when we started outside. My shirt and her sweater are somewhere in a bush, I think. In the back of my mind, I know doing anything outside, even on my sleepy street, is reckless. But with Belle's lips on my skin, my mind goes blank and all I can see is her.

"I need you." Belle's words are breathy and thick. I can feel her hot breath against my neck, sending shivers down my spine.

"Tell me what you need, baby." I lick and suck the spot where her neck meets her shoulder, loving the way her body shudders beneath me.

"I need you inside me. I want you to fuck me so hard that I still feel you in the morning. I want you to own every part of me," she says, looking into my eyes with a fire so hot I could turn to ash on the spot.

"If you think you can handle that," she adds with a knowing smirk.

Watching my girl come back to me, back to herself, has been as much of a relief as it has been a turn on. I fucking love every version of her, but this bossy little brat is my favorite.

I let her go long enough to rip down her jeans and remove her sneakers. She peels her shirt and bra off herself. She's standing in front of me in nothing but a black thong. I give myself a few seconds to appreciate her body before I'm ripping the thong from her body. She gasps, her plump, pink lips falling open slightly. I picture my dick between those perfect lips and groan.

Later. Right now, I need her as much as she needs me.

I capture her lips hungrily. Her hands are on my belt. She quickly gets my jeans and boxers off until we're both naked and panting. I lift her in my arms and walk to the couch, sitting so that she's on my lap.

"Ride me, baby. Show me how much you need me."

Belle doesn't need to be told twice, and soon she's lowering herself onto my length.

"Fuck fuck fuck. You're so fucking perfect," I tell her, keeping her steady with my hands on her hips. I can already feel my balls clenching and that tell-tale tingling at the base of my spine. Belle can undo any control I have in a way no one else ever could.

"Oh my god, Kai. Right there," she moans as I take control and pound into her. I know I'm hitting the right spot from the noises she's making and the way she's tightening around my cock.

"Fuck, baby. You need to come for me." I reach between

us to play with her clit. I'm not going to last much longer, but I refuse to come without her.

"Kai," she says my name like a prayer right before she tumbles over the edge, taking me with her. I piston into her wet heat, helping her ride out her orgasm as long as I can before I'm emptying myself into her.

Looking down at where we're connected, I smile. "You were made for me, mo chridhe. Look how well you took me."

Belle smiles. Her eyes are still a little glazed over from her orgasm, but there's no mistaking the happiness on her face. My chest swells knowing that I'm part of the reason for it.

She's mine.

She's everything.

thirty-six

BELLE

"YOU'RE STAYING HERE TONIGHT?" I ask Kai, slightly embarrassed that I can't sleep without him anymore. Like I'm a little kid who can't sleep without her favorite teddy bear.

Kai just smiles and pulls me in for one more kiss. "I'm just going to check on Maverick and then I'm yours."

I snuggle into his chest the best I can manage with the console of the car between us.

"I sleep better than I ever have when I'm next to you, Belle. You never need to ask if I'll be staying with you. Next to you is the only place I plan to sleep for the rest of my life." Sometimes I think Kai knows my mind better than I do. One look at me and he knew what I was thinking.

"I could come with you to Mav's," I offer, not really wanting to be parted from Kai. It feels like part of me is missing when he isn't with me.

Kai just chuckles. "Go hang out with Cal so he doesn't start whining in the group chat. I'll be back in a couple of hours." He leans closer to kiss me quickly.

I want to argue, but I can't. Cal texted me this morning complaining that we don't get any sibling time, and I needed to come over and hang out with him. If I ditch him to go to Mav's with Kai, no one will ever hear the end of it.

"Fine," I grumble as I get out of the car, stomping dramatically.

Kai just laughs again. "I love you," he shouts out of his window before pulling out of the driveway.

I turn to see Cal waiting for me at the front door. His face is a mixture of excitement and that weird face he makes when he tries to hide it. Like he's about to sneeze or something.

"Who says your big brother doesn't come through with his promises?" He yells, raising his arms like he's preaching to a crowd.

"What are you talking about? What promise?" Cal says dumb things when he's excited. That's not new. Usually I can figure out what he's talking about, though. "I don't think anyone says that." Cal is a lot of things, unreliable isn't one.

He ignores me, grabs my hand, and pulls me into the house. He's practically running, and I have to jog just to keep up.

"Ta-da!" he yells, bowing like he just performed a magic trick.

"Your living room has been vacuumed?" I ask, looking around the room to try to figure out what he's so proud of.

"What?" he asks, jerking upright and looking around. "Dammit! Stay here," he orders before running off toward the kitchen.

"Did you buy me a puppy?" I call out after him, knowing

full well he doesn't want something that could pee on a carpet in his house.

"Better than a puppy," he calls back, really upping my curiosity. "He's potty trained!"

He? What?

"Dad!" I scream, rushing into my father's arms as he comes around the corner.

"Told you I'd get you Dad if that's what you wanted," Cal says smugly, but I can see the emotion in his eyes. My big brother is the biggest softy I know.

"Why didn't you tell me you needed me, my beauty?" Dad asks, hugging me tightly and kissing the top of my head. He's called me his beauty ever since we watched *Beauty and the Beast* together when I was little.

I pull back and take a good look at my dad. He's wearing old, worn jeans and a red flannel. His eyes crinkle around the edges when he smiles. My dad and Cal are almost identical. Same brown hair and dark brown eyes. Same build. Cal is just the younger and more excitable version.

"I didn't want to worry you," I tell him honestly. I love my dad, but he worries more than Cal does. The two of them are like mother hens when they're together.

Dad frowns but doesn't say anything. Instead, he takes my hand and leads me to the couch to sit with him.

"Tell me everything. Callahan will fill in the blanks if you try to leave something out," he says sternly. I glance at my brother to see him shrug. There's really no arguing with Dad.

So I spend the next hour with my dad's hand in mine, telling him my story. From the moment I left Brad, right up until I hugged him, he now knows everything. I watch his facial expressions vary from anger to surprise back to anger but kept going. I knew if I stopped, Cal would have to finish for me. My life has been dramatic enough without him adding his flair to it.

"I thought you were becoming more and more distant from us. I thought it was the actual miles between us, not..." I watch my dad swallow hard, knowing what I told him is hurting him.

"Dad —"

"I should have been here for you, Bellamy. I should have seen what was happening and pulled you out of that situation. I'm so sorry," my dad says. His grip on my hand tightens, and his eyes are pleading with me to either forgive him or scream at him. I'm not sure which.

"Cal said something similar, but neither of you would've been able to do anything. You know how stubborn I am," I remind him.

"I almost shit my pants when she asked for my help," Cal adds, causing me to snort and my dad to laugh. Cal is always good at lightening the mood. Except I think this time he was serious. I've always valued my independence and asking for help felt weak. It's taken a lot of work with my current therapist to realize that line of thinking will get me nowhere.

"Where's your lawyer on this?" Dad asks Cal.

My brother rubs the back of his neck, and his face turns red.

Shit.

"What aren't you telling me?" I ask calmly, even though I want to throw things at Cal right about now.

"Brad is. . . missing," he admits sheepishly.

"I'm sorry. What?" I ask, dumbfounded. I look at my dad, who looks just as confused as I do. Though, to be fair to him, he's getting a lot of information in a short amount of time and seems to be handling it pretty well.

"Frank had some people monitoring him while we were overseas. They lost him after we landed," Cal says, staring at his feet instead of me.

"And you didn't think this was important information to share with me?" I ask angrily. I can't even tell if I'm more angry or hurt right now. I stand up and start pacing.

"I hired a whole team to track him down. I thought they would've found him by now and you wouldn't have to worry."

"What? Are we employing every private investigator on the East Coast now?" I'm still pacing. I can feel both my dad's and Cal's eyes on me, but I don't look at either of them. I can understand Cal's reasoning. I was a mess when I showed up on his doorstep months ago because of Brad. His brotherly instinct is to protect me.

But I'm far from that girl. I don't think I realized it until this moment, but I'm not scared anymore. Just angry.

"Actually, they're technically bounty hunters," Cal says. I look up to see my dad looking between us, his face showing every ounce of confusion he's feeling.

"And they haven't come up with a lead?" Dad asks, clinging to the one bit of information he understands.

"They think he's in the area. He's been smart and hasn't used his credit cards or anything they can easily track him with. Even his phone is off."

"Does Kai know about this?" I ask, suddenly wondering how many people in my life have been keeping this from me.

Cal shakes his head. "Only me."

I stare at my brother, looking for any sign of a lie in his face, but I don't see one. I sigh, glad I don't have to confront Kai later. I'm not sure I can handle him lying to me.

I thought everyone was overreacting and just being overprotective this whole time. Which isn't out of the ordinary, especially where Cal is concerned. I should've known it was more than that.

"Don't," my dad says, grabbing my hand and pulling me down next to him again.

"Don't what?" I ask, my voice suddenly sounding defeated.

"You have an uncanny ability to blame yourself for things that are out of your control."

"But —" I try to argue.

"No buts. We will figure this out. Together."

I nod and look up at Cal. He's hunched over, looking like a sad puppy.

"Please stop hiding things for me. Especially things like this where my safety is at risk." It's the closest thing to an olive branch Cal is going to get from me. The smile that spreads across his face tells me he knows that.

"I promise!" he says quickly and way too loudly. My dad and I both flinch at the volume.

"So, you're with Malikai now?" My dad asks, not so smoothly changing the subject.

"I am." I can feel the blush creeping up my neck. Talking to your dad about your relationships never gets easier. Luckily, he's a lot easier to talk to than my mom.

"I always knew you two would find your way," he says.

My jaw drops for a moment before I smile. He knew. Of

course, he knew. My dad was always the most preceptive person I know.

"Am I the only one that didn't know?" I ask, more to myself, but Cal's snort is answer enough.

"I'm going to go order lunch," Cal says, hopping up to grab his phone from the coffee table.

"How long are you staying?" I ask my dad.

"I'm staying as long as you need me, my beauty. My bags are already in one of the guest rooms upstairs. I'm sure as hell not leaving when my daughter is being stalked."

I throw my arms around his shoulders and squeeze. I missed him so much. Cal always made fun of me for being a daddy's girl, but in this moment, I couldn't care less.

thirty-seven

KAI

"FUCK," I mutter under my breath as I let myself into Maverick's house. It's the usual mess, but something stinks.

"Mav?" I shout. I have to dodge dirty clothes and empty pizza boxes before I find him on the couch.

He's staring out into space, clutching a picture frame. I can see dried tracks on his face from where tears have fallen. His white shirt has food stains on it, and he's not wearing any pants, just black boxer briefs.

"Mav?" I try again, gently. I'm pretty sure the smell that's assaulting my nostrils is coming from him. His blood-shot eyes find mine, and there's nothing but misery in them.

"You should go," he says, his voice like gravel. He probably hasn't used it since the last time I saw him.

"You know that won't work," I tell him, moving the empty beer bottles from next to him and taking a seat. "What's that?" I ask, gesturing to the frame he's clutching with my chin. He looks down, seeming to register that he's even holding something, then hands it to me.

My heart drops into my stomach when I see the picture.

It's of Mav and Ezra when they were in college. My brother's face is smiling happily at me while Maverick is kissing his cheek.

"I've never seen this picture before," I say, my voice hoarse from trying to contain my emotions.

"It was at the top of my closet. I hid it." There are no emotions in his words, and that concerns me more than anything.

"Is Ezra why you get like this? When we're not on tour, I mean." I've been dancing around Mav's depression for years because I know he snaps out of it the moment we leave. But I don't know how long we'll be home this time, and I just can't risk it anymore. I need the truth from him, but I'm afraid he'll shut down. It's like trying to play the game *Operation* while wearing oven mitts and a blindfold.

Maverick sighs and leans his head back to rest on the couch cushion. "Partially," he admits. I have to lock my muscles up to prevent myself from jerking upright at his honesty. Usually he just tells me he's fine and then won't talk.

"What's the other part?" I ask softly.

Mav turns his head to look at me, like he's taking my measure and deciding if I'm worthy of the truth.

"My parents. They never liked my career choice," he snorts. "When I'm back in town, my mom is constantly trying to get me to meet her, and my dad pretends I don't exist."

"You don't want to meet up with your mom?" I ask, trying to remember a time that Mav has ever mentioned his parents. I immediately feel like an asshole when I realize that I never even asked about them. The only information he's told me voluntarily is that his dad abuses his mom and was upset that Mav didn't follow in his footsteps and go to law school.

"All that happens when I do is her trying to set me up with one of my dad's political friend's daughters. Then we get into a fight about the bruises she's trying to hide and the help from me she immediately turns down. It's exhausting."

I nod, understanding the parent problem better than most. I've avoided checking in on my mom since we've been home. I need to confront her about the interview she gave, but I'm not sure it would be worth it.

"This isn't sustainable," I tell him, gesturing to the mess around us.

He nods but doesn't move.

"How about you shower, and I'll pick up?" I offer.

"I'm fine," he says. I can feel him shutting down again. He's not as different from his mom as he thinks he is.

"You can either get in the shower or I'm calling Willa."

His eyes snap to mine at the threat. Willa might be tiny, but the girl is fierce. She'll get him in the shower and probably make him mop every floor in this house while she watches.

"You wouldn't."

I lift my brow and shrug. "Dude, you smell. You need to shower, and I'm willing to call in the calvary if I have to."

He grumbles something under his breath that sounds a lot like *asshole,* but he gets up and heads towards his room anyway.

I spend the next thirty minutes filling trash bags and taking them to the bin in the garage. Eventually, Mav comes and helps me. His hair is wet, and he's wearing clean clothes. He even put pants on this time.

We work silently next to each other to get his space back to something that won't be hindering his mental health. He needs help in that department, but just getting him in the shower and cleaning is a pretty big accomplishment for one day. I'll work on more tomorrow.

I got back to Cal's to find Belle and her dad in a heated game of Rummy.

"Full house is poker! You can't put that down!" Belle is yelling while her dad looks happy just to be here. He probably did that on purpose just to get a reaction out of her.

"Can I talk to you?" I ask Cal. He frowns but nods and follows me out to his back deck.

"You better not be keeping secrets from Belle. I got in trouble for it earlier today," he says, looking slightly scared when mentioning his sister. I found out about the Brad situation while I was at Mav's. Cal wanted to warn me, at least according to him. I think he just wanted me to come defend him. I'm pretty pissed at him for that too, but right now I have something else on my mind.

"What do you think about moving?"

His brows furrow. "Moving where? I thought you wanted to stay in this area?"

He's not wrong. Part of the reason we all live in our hometown is that I wanted to stay close to where Ezra was last seen. No one argued with me about it, since I think they all felt similarly.

"I did, but Mav is a mess when we're here. The new label isn't going to work us to the bone the way the other one did. We'll have a lot more time at home, and I just…" I trail off, sighing.

"Yeah, I get it. I checked on him a couple of days ago, and he's worse than ever." Cal rubs his chin as he thinks. "Where are you thinking?"

"Well, the label said they rent studio space in Boston for the artists on this coast. What if we moved closer to there? As it is right now, we're like three to four hours away and that could get annoying." Cal looks at me and I know he's thinking the same thing. We want to get Belle away from here too, but if we make that decision for and about her, she'll refuse.

"Do you think Willa will agree?" he asks. Willa still lives in her parent's old house. Her dad died a couple of years ago, and she hasn't wanted to part with it.

"She doesn't need to sell that house. She can always keep it and get a condo or something. It's not like she can't afford it."

"My dad lives close to Boston now. That could be a good sell for Belle too," Cal adds. "And Mav?"

"He hates it here. If we tell him we want to move to be closer to the studio —" I pause for a moment to think about it. "Well, I think he'll be suspicious, but I'm sure he'll go with it, anyway."

"So, Willa and Belle."

I nod, knowing that the girls were going to be the harder sell.

Cal and I decide to wait until the band meeting next week to bring it up. We have a virtual meeting with Isla to go over the songs Belle and I have been working on. It'll be easier since Mav already knows about it, and we won't have to drag him out of his house or ambush him to talk.

I just hope my plan works, and I can keep both the love of my life and the love of my brother's life safe.

<h1 style="text-align:center">thirty-eight</h1>

BELLE

THE LATE SPRING weather is surprisingly warm, so I decide to sit in one of the white Adirondack chairs Cal has overlooking the cliff. I'm trying to finish writing a song before our meeting with the label later today. I was going for something more upbeat, but I can't seem to get in the right mood for it.

My dad left to go home yesterday. He needed to show up to a few in-person meetings for work, but he promised he would be back in a few days. I miss having him around. He kept Cal from hovering.

A chill races down my spine. The creepy, itchy feeling you get when someone's watching you pricks at the back of my neck. I turn my head towards the house, fully expecting to see Cal watching me out of the window, but he's not there.

I look around, but I don't see anyone. Cal's yard is fenced in, the only opening being the cliff. Unless someone is looking over the fence, I should be alone. Since I'm pretty sure the fence is way too tall for that, I try to get back to writing.

I can't shake that uneasy feeling, so I pack my stuff up and head back into the house.

"What are you doing?" I ask my brother as I watch him dart around the kitchen.

"Nothing. Snacks. Meeting." He doesn't stop to explain any of that. I'm assuming he means he's making snacks for the meeting, but who knows with Cal.

"Did you let Jon know what time the meeting starts?" I ask. We hired a new agent this week after firing Linsey, our old agent. Jon is in his mid-thirties and a lover of all things music and horror. Cal clicked with him instantly. It's unusual to sign a record deal and then hire an agent, but this band hasn't exactly been known to do things the normal way.

"He thinks I need an assistant," Cal says, continuing to dart around the kitchen like a ping-pong ball.

"I agree, but that doesn't answer my question."

"3:30 our time," Cal says, taking a veggie tray from the freezer. I'd really like to know what it was doing in there, but considering I still don't have an answer to my first question, I leave it for now.

"Yes. That's when the meeting is. Did you tell Jon?"

"Of course I told him," Cal says, looking at me like I'm the flustered one and not him.

"Why are you acting so weird?"

"It's an important meeting!" he shouts. "It would be easier from Boston, don't you think?"

Considering the label is based out of LA, I can't see why being in Boston would be easier. Cal is currently rummaging around the pantry, though, so I leave him to it and head up to my room.

Kai went to get Mav about an hour ago. My guess is that he's cleaning since they're not here yet.

"What the hell is wrong with your brother?" Willa asks, stepping into my room and sitting on my bed.

"I have no idea. He seems nervous."

"Why? It's basically just a status report meeting. You're the one who has to pitch songs. He doesn't have to do much of anything."

"I know that. You know that. He apparently thinks his life depends on this," I say with a laugh.

Willa just rolls her eyes, fully aware of how worked up Cal can get. "Where's your man?"

"Getting Mav."

She nods and bites her lip. "I'm worried about him."

"Me too. Kai said he's worse than he's ever been."

Willa just nods, lost in thought. I have no idea what to do to help Maverick, but something needs to be done. He's barely surviving at this point.

"Ten minutes!" Cal screams up the stairs.

"Did that sound weirdly high pitched to you?" Willa asks.

I laugh. "That's how you know he's nervous. That and the veggie tray in the freezer."

"Again?" Willa sighs, following me out of my room and down the stairs. "I almost broke a tooth on a baby carrot the last time he did that."

We both laugh as we make our way into the kitchen. I can always count on my best friend to lighten the mood.

The meeting is almost over. Kai and Mav never showed. The three of us have been playing it off like they caught a cold and are just resting. I pitched my songs as best I could while half my focus was on the missing members.

"I think that about covers it. Studio time is scheduled for next month. I'll send over the demos when they're done," Jon says to Isla. Cal, Willa, and I just nod along. This meeting needs to end so we can find the guys. Cal is pissed, but Willa and I keep exchanging worried glances. This isn't like Kai. Mav? Sure. When he's home, he's likely to sleep through something important. But Kai never misses anything.

"You know how to reach me with any questions," Isla says.

"Sure do. Thanks for your time," Cal says and hits the end call button.

"Hanging up on her probably wasn't smart," Willa chastises, but Cal ignores her and answers his phone.

"When? How? Why are you just calling me now?" Cal is screaming into his phone, which is very unlike him. The tone and volume of his voice are enough to immediately put on edge. "And they're both there? They're both alive?"

I glance at Willa to see her face is as pale as I'm sure mine is. He has to be talking about Mav and Kai. I want to interrupt and ask him what's going on, but my tongue feels heavy, and I'm not sure I remember how to breathe.

"I'm on my way." Cal hangs up the phone and immediately starts heading for the door. Willa and I follow him straight to his car. The moment our doors shut, Cal is putting the car in drive and peeling out of the driveway.

"Someone hit their car when they were on the way over. I don't know anything else. Kai is in surgery. Maverick is unconscious, but relatively unharmed." Cal's eyes haven't left the road, and his knuckles are white from how hard he's gripping the steering wheel.

My first instinct is to ask a million questions, but I know Cal doesn't know the answers to any of them. He just said as much. Instead, I sit next to him and try to focus on my breathing.

"Cal is the emergency contact for all of us. Kai is his," Willa says, answering one of my unvoiced questions. If I wasn't so panicked about Kai, I would probably be offended at not being my own brother's emergency contact, but I don't have room in my brain to think that over right now.

The rest of the short drive to the hospital is silent. Cal screeches to a halt in front of the hospital, which, thankfully, has a valet. Otherwise, he would definitely get towed. There's no way he was wasting time finding a parking spot. He tosses the keys to a teenager, and we follow him through the emergency room doors.

The hospital had to clear out a waiting room for us. It's nice to have fans, but a hospital waiting room isn't the place to ask for pictures or autographs. We were swarmed the moment we sat down.

Willa is pacing, Cal is standing up and then sitting back

down in thirty-second intervals, and I'm curled up in an uncomfortable chair while rocking back and forth.

There was a police officer here to greet us. He explained that a driver hit Kai's side of the car and then took off from the scene of the accident. They're running through traffic cameras to see if they can get a plate number or car model. He gave us his card to call him when Mav and Kai can speak to him.

Maverick is getting an MRI to check for swelling in his brain, and Kai is still in surgery. He's been in surgery for over four hours now. The nurse couldn't give us much information and said we would have to wait for the surgeon. I thought Willa was going to climb over the desk and try to check the computer herself. The only thing that stopped her was the promise that we could go in and see Mav once the doctors were done with all the testing. Willa wasn't going to chance getting kicked out of the hospital. Not today anyway.

"Mr. Griffin?" We all turn to see a nurse in the doorway of the waiting room.

"That's me," Cal says, practically rushing at her.

"Mr. Wolfe is awake and can have visitors. If you're ready, I can show you to his room."

Cal nods but doesn't move. "What about Kai? Malikai Irons."

"Mr. Irons should be out of surgery soon. I can tell the surgeon to meet with you in Mr. Wolfe's room."

"Okay, yeah. That works. Just make sure he does," Cal says as more of a demand than anything. "Please," he adds as an afterthought. The nurse just smiles. She's probably used to panicky family members.

"He's going to be okay," Willa says, taking my hand as

we follow the nurse to see Maverick. I just nod. I haven't spoken a word since Cal got the phone call. I'm afraid I'll lose any control I have and break down if I do.

Mav has a bandage on his forehead and a nasty black eye, but otherwise seems to be doing alright.

"Where's Kai?" he asks the moment we walk into his room.

"Surgery," Cal answers before pulling a chair over to the side of Mav's bed. "The surgeon should meet us here soon to let us know how it went." I watch as Mav visibly relaxes. I wish I could. Knowing Kai's alive isn't enough. I need him to stay alive.

I take Mav's hand in mine and squeeze. He turns to me and smiles weakly.

"So, what's the damage?" Willa asks, plopping herself on the end of his hospital bed.

"Six stitches in my forehead, mild concussion, and bruised ribs. They were worried about swelling in my brain, but it's gone down. I need to stay overnight for monitoring, just in case," Maverick answers.

"What happened?" I whisper.

Maverick's warm brown eyes meet mine and start to fill with tears. "I don't know. Kai and I were talking about therapy. I got so mad at him for trying to talk me into something I don't want to do. Then I remember hearing a crash and glass shattering." Mav swallows and wipes at his eyes. "Then I woke up here."

I nod, and Willa squeezes his leg.

"What if —" Mav chokes on a sob. "I said some shitty things. What if he —"

Hot tears drip down my face, matching the ones on Maverick's.

"Don't," Cal says firmly. "He's going to be okay, and then you can argue some more."

"Mr. Griffin?"

We all turn to see a woman in green scrubs and a hair net standing at the foot of Maverick's bed.

"Yes?" Cal asks with a tremor in his voice. The confidence he was pretending to have a moment ago has vanished.

"Mr. Irons is out of surgery. We repaired a punctured lung, severed artery, and some smaller internal bleeding. He has a torn bicep that will need to be surgically repaired once he's more stable and we're confident he could withstand the procedure. He also had several deep lacerations that we stitched on both his arms and his face. We've given him two blood transfusions, and he's currently in recovery."

"When can we see him?" Cal asks immediately.

"He should be moved to the ICU within an hour. I doubt he'll wake up soon. He lost a lot of blood, and his body needs the rest to heal. I would estimate him being responsive in twelve to thirty-six hours."

"He's going to be okay?" I ask, my voice thick with barely contained emotions.

"The next twenty-four hours are imperative to his recovery. As long as everything goes well, he should make a full recovery."

That was a non-answer, but I'm willing to take it anyway.

"I'll send the nurse in to retrieve you once he has a room.

ICU only allows one visitor." She doesn't wait for a response before she's back out the door.

The next hour creeps by slowly. I keep my grip on Maverick's hand, which he doesn't seem to mind. Willa and Cal fill him in on how the meeting went. My eyes are glued to the door, waiting for someone to take me to Kai. We didn't discuss who the one person to go to his room would be, but they're nuts if they think it won't be me. It feels like my whole heart is outside of my body and somewhere else in this hospital.

The moment the nurse appears to take one of us to Kai's room, I'm jumping out of my seat to follow her. Cal and Willa tell me to give him their love and to text them with updates. I promise I will as I'm halfway out the door.

"The ICU has a small room attached to all the patient rooms where you can sleep," the nurse tells me as we walk into the unit. I thank her, knowing full well there's no way I'm going to be more than a few inches away from Kai.

The tears that I thought had dried up return the moment I lay eyes on Kai. He's pale against the white sheets, his dark hair a stark contrast to the pillow. He has cuts and bandages along both his arms and the left side of his face. He's covered in bruises where I can see his skin, and I'm sure it's just as bad where I can't. Cords and tubes connect him to multiple machines.

"He looks worse than he is. Most of those cords are just recording his vitals. His color should return by morning," the nurse assures me before leaving me alone in with him.

I take a seat in the chair that's already next to his bed and carefully take his hand in mine. The slow beep of the machine above his head lets me know his heart is beating steadily.

"You scared the shit out of me, Kai," I say with more anger than I was expecting. "You can't leave me. Not now and not like this. We're supposed to get old and yell at the kids on our lawn. Or retire to some tropical island." I sniff, wiping my nose on the sleeve of my shirt. "You promised to sleep next to me every night for the rest of our lives. This isn't it. Not yet."

I lay my head next to his leg and keep my hand in his. I close my eyes and pray to whoever will listen that he wakes up.

I woke up a few times to nurses checking Kai's vitals or lab techs, drawing blood, but so far, I'm the only one who's woken up.

Once the twelve-hour mark hits, I get more nervous.

WILLA

They said twelve to thirty-six hours. He's still well within the given time, Belle.

CAL

He'll come back to you.

MAV

He's too stubborn not to.

ME

I know, but it's hard to wait.

CAL

Do you want me to swap with you so you
can get something to eat?

ME

I don't think I can eat. My stomach is in
knots.

WILLA

Mav is going home soon; we can bring you
something if you want. Like a book or a
toothbrush?

ME

The nurse actually gave me a toothbrush
and some magazines. I appreciate it
though.

CAL

I let the nurses know that no one is allowed
in to see him other than us. His mother
included. So you should be safe from any
unwanted visitors.

Fuck. I wasn't even thinking about reporters or fans trying to get in here. This lifestyle is something I'm seriously not used to. I'm glad Cal thought of it.

MAV

His mother would have to care to show up.

WILLA

She cares about money and it's a story she
could sell...

ME

She's seriously become that bad?

Kai has mentioned it, but I didn't realize the extent she's

fallen. She was always a little cold, but never cruel. Losing Ezra really changed her for the worse.

CAL

She took money to give a bullshit interview saying Kai was stealing you from Ezra…

ME

Yeah, I get it. I was trying to forget about that.

WILLA

Keep us updated on your man.

ME

Will do.

"Mo chridhe?"

My head jolts up from my phone at the gravelly sound of Kai's voice. His bright blue eyes connect with mine and it takes everything I have not to throw myself at him in relief.

"You're awake," I sob, grabbing his hand and gently kissing his knuckles like I have been all night.

"What happened?" he asks. "My throat feels like I drank sand."

I jump up from the chair and rush to get him some water. He quickly sucks down the first cup, and I refill it for him before talking.

"You were in an accident. Do you remember anything?"

Kai frowns as he concentrates. His brows jump into his hairline suddenly. "Mav! Is he ok? He was in the car with me."

"He's fine. Just a concussion and some bruised ribs. He's

actually about to head home with Cal and Willa," I reassure him. Kai lets out a breath and relaxes into the bed.

"Someone crashed into me from a side street. I didn't even see the car until it was too late."

"There was an officer here when we arrived yesterday. He said the other driver took off. They're trying to find witnesses or camera footage to track down who it was." I can't keep my eyes or my hands off him. I know he's too hurt, but all I want to do is crawl in bed next to him and hear the beat of his heart with my own ears.

Kai nods and his eyes slowly start to close again. I leave him long enough to let the nurses know he had been awake and talking for a few minutes before I'm right back in my spot by his side.

ME

He woke up. He remembers the accident but didn't see the car or the driver. He's asleep again for now. The nurse said a doctor will be by to check on him soon.

WILLA

Told you he would wake up!

MAV

That's the best news I've had since they told me I could leave!

CAL

Does he remember you? Do you have to remind him who you are and why he loves you? Oh! I can make a slideshow of pictures of the two of you to help jog his memory.

"Jesus Christ, Callahan," I mutter to myself.

WILLA

She just said he remembers the accident.
Why would he remember that but not her?

CAL

How should I know? I'm not a brain doctor.

MAV

That's pretty obvious.

I snort, feeling lighter than I have since Cal got that phone call.

"What's so funny?" Kai asks, apparently not as asleep as I thought he was.

"I think Cal is disappointed you don't have amnesia, and he can't come up with crazy schemes to get you to remember me."

Kai starts to laugh and then groans in pain.

"Shoot. Sorry. Don't laugh. You broke some ribs." My hands are hovering over him, not quite touching, but acting like I can magically take the pain away or something.

"What else is wrong with me?" he asks, looking down at the arm that's wrapped securely against his body. I explain the punctured lung and the surgery he had, plus the one he has to have for his torn bicep.

"Aren't we due in the studio next week? How can I sing if this lung is going to take six to eight weeks to heal? And how the hell long will my arm take? I can't play guitar with one arm," Kai asks, clearly frustrated.

"I don't know or care. You could've died, Kai!. Delaying the album is the last thing I care about right now."

Kai squeezes my hand and smiles sadly. "I know. I'm

sorry, mo chridhe. You're right. That doesn't matter right now."

The doctor comes in a few hours later and explains the next surgery. It should be fairly quick, and they scheduled it for first thing in the morning. If everything goes well, Kai can go home by the end of the week. He'll still have physical therapy and appointments to check how his lung is healing, but they seem confident he'll make a full recovery.

thirty-nine

KAI

I'VE BEEN in this hospital for over a week. By the time I'm discharged, I won't be able to leave here fast enough. Belle is happy I'm not dead, but I think she's about to leave me in the morgue if my attitude doesn't change.

"I'm sorry," I say to the nurse I just snapped at for the third time in as many minutes. Belle is glaring at me with her arms crossed.

"I get you're antsy to get home, Mr. Irons," the nurse says before snatching the discharge papers I just signed. She leaves the room without another word. Not that I blame her.

I sigh and drop my face into my hands. I haven't slept well the entire time I've been here. My mom has been trying to get in to see me, and the police have no leads on who hit me. I just need to get home to my own bed with my girl next to me and get some actual sleep.

I feel the bed sink next to me and Belle's hand curling into mine. I look up to see a mix of annoyance and under-standing on her face. She's been with me this entire week, only leaving to shower. She slept on the small bed in the room next to mine once I assured her I wasn't going to suddenly drop dead.

"I know you're in a mood because you need sleep and real food, but that isn't the fault of anyone here."

"I know. I'm sorry," I say, kissing her temple.

"I have an idea that might cheer you up," she says as a devious grin takes over her face. She leans in, whispering her brilliant idea to me, making me laugh.

My girl. She can bring a smile to my face in the worst of times. I fucking love her.

Belle pulls her car into Cal's driveway. Willa had dropped it off for her earlier in the week for when she needed to take me home.

"You'd make a terrible actor," Belle says, laughing at the smile that's already on my face. "You have to act serious if this is going to work."

"Right," I nod, smoothing the features in my face out.

I gingerly exit the car and follow Belle into the house. I'm still sore as fuck, but movement gets easier by the day.

"Welcome home!" everyone screams as we enter the house. The usual suspects, Willa, Cal, and Mav are front and center. I also see our new agent and manager, Jon, standing off to the side wearing a shirt with Michael Myers holding a coffee on it. Cal and Belle's dad, Jason, is standing next to Jon.

Cal immediately rushes up to me. "It's good to see you alive and kicking, man," he says, patting me on the back.

"Thanks. Have we met?" I ask him, trying to contain my smile when his face falls and his eyes widen in shock.

"I thought you didn't have amnesia! Belle said you know who she is!" Cal is balancing on the line of shock and outrage. I look over his shoulder to see a confused Maverick and an excited Willa.

"Of course I know who Belle is. She's the love of my life. Why wouldn't I know who she was?" I ask him, feigning confusion.

"How can you know who Belle is and not me? I met you first!" Cal exclaims, pulling on his hair in frustration.

"By like eight seconds," Belle mutters behind me. Willa is outright cackling and Maverick is smirking. Everyone seems to have caught on except Cal.

"Are you sure? I think I would remember if that was true. Are you like some weird fanboy or something?" I'm managing to keep a straight face, which tells me that I would actually be an amazing actor.

"Fanboy? Fanboy!" Cal's scream is getting higher as the minutes pass, and I think he may have actually pulled some hair out of his head. "This isn't funny! Why are you laughing? He probably forgot you too!" he yells at Willa.

I look around Cal and wave. "Hey Willa. How's your head Mav?"

Willa laughs so hard she's bent over, and Maverick starts to snicker. Jason and Jon are smiling at the entire scene.

"How can you remember them and not your best friend?" Cal is pacing and his face is so red he might pass out if I don't relent soon.

"What do you mean? My best friend is right there," I say, while pointing at Maverick.

Cal is so outraged he starts to storm away, probably just to scream.

"Cal, come back! I was kidding. I could never forget you!" I call after him. He spins around and narrows his eyes at me, like he isn't sure if he believes me or not.

"Tell me something only you and I would know," he says, still suspicious.

"Remember that time we played a show in Vegas, and you took these two redheads back to your room and —"

"Shh! My dad and sister are here, dude. Jesus. I believe you," Cal says, putting his hand on my mouth to stop me from finishing my story.

Belle and I spend the next hour catching up with everyone and ignoring Cal's glares. That's about as much time as I had in me before my girl was ushering me out to the car and getting me home to my bed.

Belle helps me shower before we both settle in. It's only early afternoon, but I don't think either of us can keep our eyes open any longer. Belle tried to sleep in the guest room, scared that she was going to hurt my injured ribs in her sleep.

"I need you next to me. I won't sleep without you, and you know it."

She narrows her eyes but gets into bed with me anyway.

"I'll hold your hand, but that's as close as I'm willing to get to you until you're healed more."

I groan out a complaint but do as she says. Holding her hand is better than nothing. Soon I hear her breathing even out, and I know she's asleep.

I take a second to check my emails from the PI looking into Ezra. So far, all she's been able to dig up is people claiming they saw him in a small town in New Hampshire three years ago. She's currently following that lead. I sigh and plug my phone in before following Belle into sleep.

"Fuck." I peel my eyes open and look down. Belle has her mouth wrapped around my cock and is sucking with a desperation I feel in my balls. "Baby," I moan.

"I needed to feel you. I needed to taste you. You can't move like you want to for sex, but I can still do this," she says before descending on me again.

"Holy fuck, baby," I moan, unable to control the way my hips thrust up into her mouth. "I'm not going to last. Your mouth feels too fucking good." It doesn't feel as good as her pussy, but it's pretty close.

"Stay still or I won't let you come," she says, holding my dick in her hand, but not moving. I nod quickly so she'll continue. Belle usually doesn't take control in the bedroom, so this is a hot as fuck surprise.

I stay still like she ordered as she takes me to the back of her throat and swallows. "Fuck!" I shout. She seems to like how vocal I've been and moans. The vibrations are my undoing, and I shoot myself down the back of her throat. She swallows me before pulling away with a satisfied grin.

"Sorry for waking you up," she teases.

"No. If that's how you're going to wake me up, always wake me up. Please. I don't care if I just fell asleep. Wake me the fuck up."

Belle giggles before settling into my side gently.

"It's my turn to taste you."

"Nope! We have a meeting," she says, rolling off the bed. I watch her strut to my closet, where she keeps some of her clothes.

"No fair," I grumble. Getting up much slower than her. "The meeting is just with the band. They can wait."

"You just had the stitches in your chin and cheek removed. You're not doing anything with your mouth until I'm sure you won't rip anything open."

"Don't come at me with your logic! I want your taste on my tongue. Just ride my face," I argue. Belle just laughs and continues to get ready.

"The meeting was your idea, so you better get dressed."

"Fine, but I'm keeping a tally and paying you back when my face is better."

"You say that like it's a threat," she calls from the bathroom.

I grumble and complain to myself as I get dressed. Whoever hit me is really going to pay. Not only have they caused me a lot of pain, but now I can't even eat out my girlfriend. Fucking asshole.

***

Cal and I just pitched the idea of moving to everyone. Belle was immediately in, and Willa followed shortly after. Maverick is the one teetering on the edge, just as I predicted.

"Is this because I said no to therapy? Moving seems like a really dramatic response to that."

Cal rolls his eyes at Mav, who, luckily, can't see him.

"Cal and I talked about this before the accident," I tell him. "And honestly, I'm not so sure I want to be in a car that long all the time anymore." Was that a cheap shot? Yes, but I'm willing to take all the cheap shots if it gets Maverick out of this town and out of his head.

"He's telling the truth. We don't have to live directly in Boston, but I think it would benefit us to be a lot closer," Cal adds.

Maverick sighs and looks around. He knows he's outvoted, but he also knows we won't force him. "Alright. Let's move."

"This is so exciting!" Willa exclaims before pulling up real estate listings and looking them over with Belle.

My phone vibrates in my pocket, and I pull it out to see a text from Kelly Boswell, the PI looking into Ezra.

KELLY

I'm resigning from this case.

ME

What? Why? I can pay you more.

KELLY

Not worth the money.

ME

Did something happen?

KELLY

There are bigger players involved than you realize.

ME

Who? Did someone threaten you? Please give me something.

KELLY

Please don't contact me again.

But I can give you this. Whatever
happened, it wasn't an accident.

"What the fuck?" I mutter.

"What's wrong?" Cal asks, trying to read my messages over my shoulder.

"The PI just quit. She wants nothing to do with this case and wouldn't give me an explanation."

I don't even have time to process that before I notice the look on Willa's face as she reads something on her phone.

"What now?" I ask her.

"Uh..."

"Willa," I urge, not in the mood for more games.

Instead of answering, she just hands me her phone. I quickly scan the headline and barely resist the urge to throw the phone against the wall.

"Playboy Rockstar Plays with Heartstrings," Belle reads off the title next to me. "Who comes up with these titles?"

I continue reading as she mutters about morons wanting their fifteen minutes.

"The article is claiming that I cheated on Lindsey Sparks with Belle and then cheated on Belle with Lindsey and several other women in Lindsey's circle," I scoff. "I knew Lindsey was jealous, but this is insane."

"I told you sleeping with that she-demon was a bad idea," Willa says.

"You're not helping," I tell her with a glare. "I need to get Frank on this. This is false. I'm sure there's a lawsuit that can be threatened somewhere."

"Have you noticed that the tabloids are only coming after the two of us?" Belle asks, her brows drawn together as she concentrates on reading the bullshit article. "Cal sticks his dick into anything with boobs and not once has an article been printed about it."

"Hey! I have standards!" Cal argues.

"Sorry. Anything with boobs and a nice ass," Belle corrects, not bothering to stop reading.

"Thank you," Cal says, missing the entire point as usual.

"Do you think someone is doing this as an attack against you guys? Like a jealous groupie?" Mav asks.

"There are quotes in here from Lindsey," Belle says, looking up at me with concern.

"I never cheated on you. I would never do that, I swear," I say, grabbing her face and forcing her to look at me.

"I know that. I don't believe this at all. I just find it strange that someone is able to go around and get people in our circle to give interviews with their names attached. Whoever it is must be offering enough money to make it worth burning bridges for."

"Brad?" Willa asks.

"Maybe. His mom has a lot of money. He doesn't personally, but that doesn't mean she isn't funding this for him."

"What's the end goal, though? Annoy you into going back to him?" I joke.

"He's probably trying to put a wedge between you," Mav says. "Every article is an attack against your relationship. He probably thinks it's new enough that it'll be easy to break."

"Did you tell him that you've been in love with Kai since you were kids?" Willa asks Belle. Even though this situation is serious, I smile, knowing she's loved me as long as I've loved her.

"No. Brad was always insecure. Mentioning Kai would've just led to a fight."

"It makes sense that he thinks he can break them up this way. We should have Frank's team look into it," Mav says.

"I'm going to call Harrison Ray's office again and see when he can start helping us. Whoever is intimidating Kelly won't be able to do the same with him," Willa says, taking her phone from me and walking off to make her call.

"Call Frank and then we're heading home to sleep for the rest of the day," Belle says with a small smile.

"I feel like we can't catch a goddamn break lately. I'm taking one hit after another, sometimes literally."

"And we'll come out swinging," Belle says, kissing me quickly and following Willa.

I fucking love that girl. She's the strongest person I know, and I have a bad feeling I'm going to need to borrow some of that strength soon.

forty

BELLE

"RIGHT THERE. JUST LIKE THAT," I moan. The physical therapist gave Kai the all-clear for normal activity yesterday. It's been six long weeks of him complaining about always being on the bottom. Needless to say, he's been on top and behind me pretty much nonstop for the last twenty-four hours.

My knees are by my ears and Kai is pounding into me like he might die if he stops.

"Jesus, baby. You feel so fucking good," he grunts before pressing his thumb to my clit. "Fuck. Come with me, Belle. Squeeze my cock, baby."

His dirty mouth is all it takes to have me screaming his name. Stars dance behind my vision, and I wouldn't be shocked to learn I'd blacked out for a moment. Kai is growling my name with his release and pulling me into his arms.

"I'll never get sick of that," he says, kissing my damp temple. I giggle into his chest. Kai has a way of making me feel light even when things are heavy.

"What are your plans for today?" he asks as he pulls me closer.

"Well, a shower first," I say, gesturing to our sweat slicked bodies. "Then Willa and I are supposed to go shopping."

It's officially summer and I need cooler clothes. Cal restocked my winter wardrobe when I first showed up, but I still need things to get me through the summer. Willa offered to take me to the mall with her. Kai and Cal are still worried about Brad even though no one could prove he was behind the articles. He's still missing though, so I let them hover.

"Are you sure that's a good idea?" Kai asks warily. He's not as bad as Cal is with the overprotectiveness, but he definitely prefers if I take one of the men with me.

"I'll be fine. We're just going to the boutique in town. Willa wanted to attempt the mall, but I didn't want to deal with the fan recognition when I'm trying on clothes." I've been getting recognized when we go out in public. It's still strange to me. It's both flattering and overwhelming.

"I can go with you."

I kiss him and climb out of bed to head into the shower. "I already agreed to security details when we move. I don't need it here, and I promised to stick with you guys until Brad is handled. Please don't smother me."

"I'm sorry. It's just. . . If anything happened to you—" he stops, swallowing hard.

"I understand. You almost died on me. I promise I'll be safe. Shopping, lunch, then home."

Kai sighs, knowing there's no point in arguing. Especially since I've never fought him on someone always being with me.

We both shower and go our separate ways. Kai is heading to the gym with Maverick, and I'm off on adventures with Willa.

"Have you heard from Cal today?" I ask her while she drives us into town.

"Not yet. Why? He's not stalking us while we shop, is he?"

I snort before shaking my head. Cal would just be shopping along with us. The man loves to spend his money. "No. But I need to talk to him, and it might help if you were with me."

She glances over at me with a question on her face and then looks down at my stomach. It takes me a second to realize what she's asking.

"I'm not pregnant!" I shout, shocked but not surprised that's where her brain went.

"Well, why the hell else would you need me as a buffer?" she asks defensively.

"Because he's looking for houses and keeps asking if I like the layout of the houses because he wants me to like living there," I say, biting my lip nervously. "Kai and I have talked about it, and when we move, I'm going to be buying a house with him. Not living with my brother."

"Ah. Your brother who is not going to take it well because he pretends he loves being single, but actually hates being alone?"

"Yeah. That."

Willa laughs and shakes her head. "I'll be there to kick

him in the shins when he tries to kidnap you so you won't leave him."

"You mean when he cries and whines for hours on end until I just give in?" I say with a laugh.

"Tomato, potato."

Willa and I spend the next few hours stocking up on the summer essentials and chatting over lunch. By the time we're heading home, I realize I still haven't heard from my brother. Kai has checked in a few times and usually Cal is either with him or texting me constantly. Willa's not wrong when she said he hates being alone.

ME

Cal? I haven't heard from you all day.

I wait for a response. Soon Willa is pulling into Kai's driveway and my phone has stayed silent.

ME

Don't make me come over there, Callahan.

"Text me when you want me to go to Cal's with you. I'm going to head home and put all this away. Maybe take a nap."

"Thanks, Willa," I tell her distractedly as I get out of her car and grab my bags from the trunk. She waits as I make my way into the house and then honks her horn as she leaves.

I toss all my bags at the foot of the stairs and call Cal.

His voicemail picks up after a few rings. "Cal. Call me back."

The text to Kai goes unanswered as well. So I head into the kitchen to get my car keys. Something is wrong. I can feel it in my gut, and I'm not going to sit here and wait to find out what it is.

My phone falls from my hand as my body seizes up when I see what's waiting for me on the kitchen island. I don't even hear it hit the floor with the way the blood is rushing to my ears. There, in the middle of the island, is a large crystal vase with black dahlias and black roses. Right in front of it sits a note with familiar handwriting.

I thought this was done. The flowers and the notes had stopped, but I got too comfortable. I run to the counter and grab a knife from the block. I don't think Brad is still in the house, but I can't be sure. I pick my phone up to call the police, but the screen is cracked and unresponsive.

"Fuck!"

I don't have a way to look up the flower meanings, but I don't need to. Whatever the message is, I'm sure it's laced with hatred.

"Kai!" I scream, worried that he was here, and he's hurt. I slowly make my way around the house, checking closets and behind shower curtains.

Kai isn't here. His car isn't in the garage, which must mean he's still with Mav somewhere. At least I hope he is. I can't think about the alternative right now or I might collapse. I take a moment to calm my breathing and make my way back to the kitchen on shaky legs.

I reach for the note, the tremor in my hands making it

difficult. I close my eyes and take a deep breath before reading.

17 Snowflake Lane
Show up or he dies

I can feel myself hyperventilating, but I'm having some sort of out-of-body experience at the same time. My arms feel heavy and disconnected. My legs won't move even though I'm telling them to.

It takes strength I didn't know I possessed to snap myself out of it. I grab my keys and run to my car. Brad has him. My first thought was Kai, but Cal is the one who I haven't heard from since yesterday. If Brad thinks his stupid tabloid scheme put distance between me and Kai, it's Cal he would go for.

I keep my brain thinking as I drive. Summer Bay is divided into two sections. The first one has streets named after types of trees and the other is seasons. Snowflake Lane is located next to Falling Leaves Terrace. I don't know what's at 17 though.

Part of me thinks I should just drive straight to the police station, but the other part isn't willing to risk my brother's life. That's the part driving right now.

forty-one

BRAD

"I'LL HAVE her by tonight, sir."

"This is your last chance. They're looking into things they shouldn't, and I know it's her kicking up the dust. You need to get Bellamy back under your control. If I need to take things into my own hands, both you and your pathetic mother will be sorry."

"I understand, sir."

He hangs up as usual, and I'm left with more threats. If I had known accepting this job two years ago was going to end up with me here, I would've thought more about it.

The money is really fucking good, though. I should've locked Bellamy down. Literally.

I don't understand why he thinks it's her doing all this. She's as weak as a sick mouse on a good day. She cowers whenever I disagree with her. There's no way this is her.

But that's fine. The boss gets what the boss wants. And if he wants me fucking Bellamy again, well, let's just say she has a nice and tight pussy.

I know she's going to show up. I left the letter vague

enough for her to worry about anyone in her life with a penis. Plus, I know the flowers will shake her up.

Black dahlias for betrayal.

Black roses for revenge.

Hopefully, our kids get my intelligence and not hers.

The sound of gravel crunching under tires gets my attention. A slow smile creeps its way up my face.

"Showtime."

"BELLE?" I call into the house. "I'm sorry I missed your text. Someone slashed my tires and Mav was helping me arrange for someone to come change them. I ended up having to have my car towed when the guy realized the break line was cut too. Mav just dropped me off."

I continue walking around and realize I'm talking to an empty house. "Belle?" I call out one more time, just in case.

I quickly call her phone, but it goes straight to voicemail. My concern skyrockets, and I immediately dial Willa.

"I don't care if you don't like the bikinis we picked out. Belle looks hot and you're just going to have to get used to guys looking at her."

"Where the fuck is she, Willa? She's not here and her phone is going to voicemail."

"What? I dropped her off over an hour ago. Are you sure? Have you checked every room?" The panic in Willa's voice isn't helping. I miss the snark from when she answered. It's easier to deal with.

"Yes, I've checked —" My jaw drops when I walk into my kitchen.

"Kai? Are you still there?" Willa asks.

"Yeah, I..." My voice trails off as I grab the note in front of the vase of black flowers I didn't buy. "Willa call the police." I rattle off the address on the note.

"What are you going to do? You can't just march in there alone!" she yells.

"Call the police, Willa!" I hang up on her and grab the keys to my bike. I haven't taken the Harley out in a while, and I can only hope it still runs.

forty-three

BELLE

"OF COURSE it's a fucking haunted house. Why wouldn't it be?" I mutter to myself as I look at the rotting mess in front of me. I'm still in my car, working up the nerve to go inside. I'm sure Brad has seen me by now, but whatever game he's playing seems to require me going in on my own.

The house has peeling orange paint and is surrounded by overgrown bushes. I can see the wooden front steps and one is broken. I'm sure he picked this place just to mess with my head. If I wasn't so angry and worried about my brother, it might work.

I straighten my spine and exit the car. I expect my legs to be wobbly, but they're solid. This ends now. Whatever end that may be.

"Brad!" I yell at the house.

I know what he's expecting. He wants that broken and beaten down girl he created. But she's gone. I found myself these past few months. I found love and strength. No one will take that from me.

The summer sun is starting to set, casting shadows across the already creepy looking house. I make my way to the steps and carefully walk to the front door.

"Come on out, Bradley! I'm here! You wanted me, now you've got me!"

Brad appears in the doorway after ripping open the swollen wood from its frame. His eyes are wide, and his blond hair is sticking up at all angles. He's wearing stained jeans and a black t-shirt covered in dust and holes.

"You look like shit," I tell him, keeping the anger at the forefront and not letting the fear that something has already happened to Cal take over.

"What the fuck do you think you're doing?" Brad asks, looking frantically behind me at the other houses on the street. This one happens to be on a dead end and the other houses really aren't that close.

"Your favorite thing, obviously. Causing a scene," I say, tilting my head and giving him my best *you fucked with the wrong bitch* face.

He grabs my arms, pulling me into the house and slamming the door. The feel of his sweaty palms against my skin is revolting. I'd gag if I didn't think it would cause him to start swinging. I need to figure out where Cal is before I provoke Brad anymore.

"Cal!" I yell into the darkness. "Where is my brother?" I demand as I turn to face Brad.

His hand flies out and slaps me so hard I'm knocked off my feet. I should have seen that coming. Brad is easy to send spiraling, but he's also quick to react with violence. I got too caught up trying to rile him up.

"You stupid, bitch. I don't have him," Brad snarls, spit

flying from his mouth and landing in front of me on the floor.

"Kai?" I squeak. I already thought I was going to lose him once and the possibility of that happening again has my strength quickly leaving my body.

Brad throws his head back and laughs. His laughter is so unhinged that I'm more afraid of him than I've ever been before.

"Nope. I didn't take anyone. You're so easy to fool. So easy to manipulate. So easy to control." His words are like poison, weakening my resolve and my will to fight. But it's the first thing he said that I cling to. He doesn't have anyone I care about. That's the only thought running through my mind as I stand back up.

"You've been trying to get to me for months. It obviously wasn't that easy," I say with a sarcastic laugh. I dust off my jean shorts and get into Brad's space.

"If your loser boyfriend just died like he was supposed to, it would've been a lot simpler." Brad smirks when he sees his words hit like he intended them to. The thought of Kai not being in my life is a hard pill to swallow, and it was one I tried to force down for years. But Kai no longer existing? That's something I can't ever be faced with again. I don't think I'd survive his loss. Even the mention of it, especially from Brad's lips, has my heart hammering and my eyes stinging.

"That was you? You tried to kill Kai?" I ask, even though he's just admitted as much.

"It's surprisingly easy to hire someone to crash into another car. Poor people will really do anything for money." Brad's smirk somehow turns even more sinister, but I don't back down. It's a battle of wills with someone like him. He's not currently using his fists because he wants to brag about how smart he is. The moment that's over, he'll start swinging.

"How did you get the flowers into my dressing room?" I want to keep him talking, hoping someone noticed I wasn't home or that my phone wasn't working. Or that the neighbors heard me yelling at him in the front yard and called the police.

"The same way. I paid your tour manager off."

Fucking Nate. I think to myself. I liked him too. "And the tabloids?"

"Ah! I was wondering if you would figure out that was me. The mom was easy. I paid her off with a bottle of Xanax and a handle of cheap tequila." Brad is so busy bragging that he doesn't notice the way I cringe. The way Kai's mom treats him is bad enough without hearing how quickly she sold him out. "I guess the interview I gave probably made it pretty obvious, huh?"

I notice he's staring at me, expecting an answer. "Kind of."

"Then that chick Malikai was fucking couldn't wait to tell her story. Or the story she believes to be true, anyway. It was pretty simple to find someone jealous of where he was putting his dick." Brad is practically gleeful right now. "And then I find out," he gasps dramatically, "that it's the daughter of the owner of the record label he had a contract with. How scandalous!"

"I don't get it. You don't even like me. Why go through all this trouble?" I ask, genuinely confused.

"You're right. I don't. I never did. You're just part of the job," he sneers, clearly unhappy about it.

"What job?"

"My job! Aren't you listening? The only way to keep my job is to keep you. So we'll be getting married and having kids. As much as it disgusts me to have you as the mother of my children, I need to keep up appearances and pass down the family name."

All I can manage is blinking as I digest that bit of information.

"Your job at your mother's company?" I ask once my brain starts working again.

"I don't work there," he laughs. "Man, you really are stupid."

"Sorry for believing you worked where you told me you did," I mutter, more to myself than him.

"My boss doesn't like you snooping around where you shouldn't. He always knew you would be trouble, Belle. You brought this all on yourself."

His boss.

Always.

As the words sink in, I realize something. "Our entire relationship was just you doing your job and keeping me away from my family and friends."

It wasn't a question, but Brad answers anyway. "That's what I just fucking said!"

"Who is your boss and what does he have to do with Ezra?" Because that's what all this is about. That's the only thing we've been digging into. With the PI quitting and her reasons behind it, it just makes sense.

Brad throws his head back and laughs. "Like I'm going to tell you any of that. It would get me killed."

I'm about to offer to go with him willingly if he tells me the truth, but then I hear the engine of a motorcycle and then distant sirens a few seconds later. I snap my mouth shut and look at Brad. His eyes are wide with panic that quickly morph to anger as he looks at me.

"Who did you tell? How are you this fucking stupid?" He screams. He tries to grab my arm, but I back up quickly and manage to get away from his reach.

I know it's Kai. The note and the flowers were still in the kitchen. He's only been on his Harley once since the snow melted, but it's sitting in the garage. That's his bike, and my guess is that the sirens are the backup he called.

"He was never going to let you take me, Brad." I say softly, trying to keep my voice calm.

"Let me? Let me! No one *lets* me do anything. I'm the one in charge here! I'm the puppet master!" I watch as he becomes increasingly unhinged. I can see it in his eyes.

"Really? Because it seems like you didn't even get a choice of who you marry or have kids with. Maybe it's time to choose yourself and out whoever is doing this to you." I figured trying to reason with him was worth a shot. I can see him think it over for a brief moment before he's snarling like a caged animal.

"No. No! You're trying to trick me. It won't work!" Spit is flying from his mouth again and there's foam forming on the corners of his lips.

"I leave the tricks to you!" I yell, realizing the motorcycle is now pulling onto the gravel. Brad must realize it too because he lunges for me again. I'm not fast enough to dodge him this time, and he grips my arm.

I scream, knowing it'll alert Kai to exactly where I am, but also cause Brad to go into a rage. But if he's raging, he isn't dragging me somewhere else, and that buys me some time.

"Shut the fuck up!" Brad screams and, as predicted, takes a swing at my face. The pain flares across my cheek immediately. Blood gushes from my nose, staining the new lacy yellow tank I just bought.

Old Belle would cower. Old Belle would beg for forgiveness.

Not new Belle. New Belle is fucking pissed and tired of the abuse.

I swing my face back so that my eyes meet Brad's. I know the moment he sees the change because the smugness in his eyes falters. For the first time, he truly seems surprised.

I shove him as forcefully as I can. Between the shock and the broken floorboards behind him, he stumbles and falls.

Laughter explodes from me, like the weight and trauma are leaving my body.

"You will never put your slimy hands on me again!" I shout.

Kai bursts through the front door. The panic on his face breaks my heart.

"Belle!" he yells as he runs to me. "You're bleeding. Are you ok?"

Kai's hands graze my entire body as he looks for more injuries. "It's just my nose."

He nods and then turns his attention to the pathetic

excuse for a human currently trying to sneak away. Kai grabs the back of Brad's shirt and lifts him off the ground.

"You put your hands on my woman," Kai seethes.

"She was mine first!" Brad spits back. "I took her virginity! I was inside her first!"

I'm not sure what reaction Brad was expecting, but it didn't seem to be Kai's fist in his face. He really looks shocked for someone who was just egging another person on.

The sirens are loud, and I can see the lights flashing right outside of the house. Brad makes one more attempt at scrambling away, but Kai stops him with a swift kick to the nuts. Brad groans and collapses in a heap on the ground just in time for the police to come charging in.

Kai wraps me in his arms. I put my ear to his chest and listen to his heartbeat. It's racing, but the sound of it causes me to finally break. I sob into his shirt, soaking it through with my blood and tears.

"It's over, mo chridhe. He can't hurt you anymore," Kai says softly, one hand smoothing my hair and the other rubbing circles on the small of my back.

I lean into him, borrowing his strength. In the safety of his arms, I tell him everything.

forty-four

KAI

I HAVEN'T SLEPT. My eyes haven't left Belle's face. She didn't want to go to the hospital, but I insisted. Her nose isn't broken, thankfully. She has bruises under her eyes that make her look like a raccoon. There's one in the shape of a hand around her arm and the entire right side of her face is swollen.

The officer that followed us to the hospital to get her statement said that the station received several phone calls from neighbors about a break-in and dispute in front of the abandoned house. They came in minutes before Willa's call.

My girl is so fucking brave and so smart. She said she was causing a scene to try to get attention but had no idea if it had worked or not. She knew what she was risking. She knew it would cause Brad to harm her, but at the time, she thought Cal was hurt and in the house.

Speaking of Cal...

I grab my phone to try to text him again. Brad may not have had him, but he's not here either.

ME

Dude. Where are you? We need to talk.

CAL

I'm fine.

ME

That's it? You're not going to explain where you are or why you're ignoring your sister?

I want to tell the asshole she threw herself into danger for him, but she insisted she wanted to tell him herself.

CAL

No. I'm fine. That's all you need to know.

What the fuck? It's so unlike him that I'm actually getting concerned. If Belle wasn't sound asleep in my arms right now, I would be at his house waiting for him.

"Belle?" I hear Willa call from downstairs. I groan. It's not the first time I regret giving my friends keys to my house. "Kai! You are not keeping my best friend from me!"

"We'll be right down!" Belle yells, her voice heavy from sleep.

"I'm sorry. I texted her when we got home to let her know you were fine. Apparently, that wasn't enough."

Belle snorts, not at all surprised. "Have you heard from Cal yet?" she asks as she climbs out of bed.

"Yeah. He says he's fine." I hand her my phone so she can read the messages.

Her brow scrunches as she reads. "This doesn't sound like Cal."

"I agree. I think we should head over there. Maybe take Willa with us."

Belle nods as she leaves the room, her face still scrunched in concentration. I know she's trying to figure out what's going on with Cal, but I doubt she'll have any luck.

I shuffle out after her, mentally exhausted from the day, but not willing to let her out of my sight for more than a few seconds.

Willa has Belle in a tight embrace the moment she spots her. Mav is standing behind them waiting for his turn.

"I didn't realize you were here," I tell him.

He smiles and shrugs. "I told Willa barging in here and screaming was rude."

Once Mav gives Belle a hug, I motion for him to follow me into the kitchen while the girls settle on the couch.

"So it's over?" he asks the moment we're out of earshot.

I shake my head. "Belle said Brad kept talking about a boss. The police are trying to figure out who he means since everyone, including the IRS, thinks his paychecks are coming from his mom's financial firm."

"And it's not his mom?"

"Doesn't seem like it. She had a stroke recently and can barely speak or move. Brad put her in a nursing home and left the business to kind of just run itself with the staff his mother had in place."

"Who would do this, then? And why? Belle isn't exactly an obvious target for any reason. She wasn't even in the spotlight until Cal dragged her into it."

"I don't know who, but the why is Ezra. It has to be. I just don't understand what we're missing there."

Maverick pulls his hair in frustration. "Ezra was a normal twenty-year-old college student. He wasn't mixed up in anything. It doesn't make any sense."

I'm about to agree with him, but just then, my phone starts ringing, and a name I didn't think I would see again appears on the screen.

"Dad?" I answer.

"You need to stop looking into Ezra." My dad's voice shocks me so much it takes me a moment to process what he just said.

"What? Why? Why would I do that?" My temper is escalating quickly. I haven't heard from this man in years, and he calls me just to tell me to stop looking for my brother.

"You need to stop, Malikai. You don't understand. Ezra is gone. Leave it."

"What the fuck, Dad?"

"Leave it!" he shouts before hanging up.

I immediately go to call him back, but I get a robotic message saying that the line is out of service.

"What the fuck?" I shout. Everyone is staring at me, waiting for an explanation. The girls must have made their way into the kitchen looking for us.

"My dad doesn't want me to look into Ezra," I explain, since that's all the information I have anyway.

"He's probably why Kelly just quit," Belle says, coming up to me and taking my hand in hers.

"Fucking probably," I sigh. All the outside forces trying to stop me from finding out what happened to my brother aren't having the effect they're hoping it would. If anything, I'm more determined now than I ever was.

"What now?" Belle asks, looking up at me with her bruised and swollen face.

"Right now, we head over to Cal's and figure out what's going on with him. Tomorrow, we work on everything else."

forty-five

BELLE

WE ALL PILED into Maverick's small sporty car. Willa and I are crammed in the back. I don't know what the point of putting seats back here was if someone as short as Willa is still cramped. Thankfully, the drive to my brother's house is quick.

"His fucking lights are on! And that's his car!" Maverick yells as we pull into the driveway. Clearly, I'm not the only one pissed off at Cal's disappearing act. By the time I'm able to get myself out of the car, Mav's already pounding on the door.

"We know you're here Cal!" He yells. I've never seen Maverick angry before and it's scary.

"Do you hear that?" Willa says. "Mav shut up for a second."

The moment silence falls on us, I hear it. Crying.

"Is that a fucking baby?" Kai says. His eyes are wide.

Cal swings the door open. He looks exhausted. "You woke my daughter up you assholes!" he yells before quickly moving away from the door.

294

"Excuse me? Your what?" I ask, running after him.

"My daughter," he says, sounding both awed and terrified.

"Dad?" I say as I round the corner and see my dad holding a crying baby girl wrapped in a soft pink blanket.

"Hi my beauty," my dad says happily, even with the screaming infant in his arms. "Come to meet your niece?" Then my dad looks up and his smile drops. The current state of my face would do that to most people. It's a testament to how tired and frazzled Cal is that he didn't even notice.

"I was coming to check to make sure Cal was still alive after he fell off the grid. Imagine my surprise to hear a baby screaming."

"What happened to your face?" my dad asks, ignoring everything I just said and coming over to me. The baby girl is still screaming between us.

That gets Cal's attention, and his tired demeanor quickly changes to anger. "Who did this? I'll fucking kill them!"

The baby starts screaming louder and Cal flinches. "I'm sorry, baby girl. Daddy didn't mean to raise his voice. Your Auntie Belle just has a scary booboo."

I stare at my brother, more confused than I've ever been in my life. "Daddy?" I ask.

"Uh, yeah," Cal says, rubbing the back of his neck. "This is Cora. She's my daughter." I look down at the sweet, red face of the angry little girl in my dad's arms.

"Oh, for fuck's sake," Willa blurts before pushing past everyone and snagging the baby from my dad. "Formula. Where is it? When was the last time you changed her?"

"Kitchen and just before you banged on the door," my dad answers easily. His eyes bounce between his children. I notice the concern when he looks at me and the annoyance when he looks at Cal. So not much different from normal.

Willa takes the baby to the kitchen, probably to make a bottle. My dad gestures to the couch and chairs for the rest of us to take a seat.

"You didn't tell anyone about this, Callahan?" my dad asks, sounding exasperated. "And you," he points at me. "What the hell happened?"

"Belle goes first," Cal shouts, sounding like a twelve-year-old version of himself. I roll my eyes.

"Brad," I answer and wait for the shock of that to set in. Is it mean? Yes, but he scared the shit out of me only to turn up with a baby who is apparently my niece. The dumbass deserves it.

Kai is next to me on the couch, with Cal sitting in the armchair across from us. I can feel his gaze swing back and forth from a tense and shocked Cal to an overly smug me. He sighs.

"Just put the man out of his misery, mo chridhe," he whispers and then kisses my hair.

"Fine." I tell my dad and brother everything that transpired earlier. I can see the guilt written across Cal's face when he realizes the reason I was at that house was because I thought he was there and probably hurt. My dad's hands are in fists, and they only loosen when Kai explains that Brad is now in police custody.

"You heard from your dad?" Cal asks Kai.

Kai nods, but it's my dad's face I'm watching. He seems more surprised that Gavin Irons bothered to call his son than he is about the reason.

"What do you know, Dad?" I ask, surprising everyone.

His eyebrows shoot up. "Nothing."

Cal is looking at him now too. My dad was never a good liar so it only takes a few seconds under the scrutiny of both his kids for him to break.

"I don't know anything. I just know that Gavin went to find Ezra. I honestly don't know anything else. He cut off contact with everyone, and I haven't heard from him since."

"He must have found something if he wants us to back off so badly," Maverick says, and the hope in his voice tears my heart to shreds.

"Alright. Explain this perfect baby," Willa says, sitting on my other side with a content Cora drinking from her bottle. I lean over to look closely at my niece. She has a shock of red hair on her head and cute rosy cheeks to match. Her face is shaped so similarly to mine and her nose is definitely from Cal that I'm stunned for a moment.

"I got a call early this morning that I needed to come pick up my daughter from a hospital in Boston. As you can imagine, I thought it was a prank," Cal says, looking at his feet and rubbing his hands on his jeans. "I ended up calling Frank to look into it. Sure enough, there was a baby there with my name on her birth certificate and my number as her contact. I drove down there as quickly as I could. Took a DNA test that they expedited because of the strange circumstances."

"He called me once he got the test results, confirming what's pretty obvious when you look at her," my dad adds while Cal regains his composure.

"Where's her mom?" I ask as gently as possible.

"She died. Postpartum hemorrhage. It was in the middle of the night and by the time they noticed, they couldn't stop it. Her name was Bailey. I gave Cora her name as a middle name. I didn't even really know her. She was just a fling. I —" Cal chokes up, and I throw myself into his arms.

"Does Bailey have any family?" Kai asks.

Cal shrugs, his arms still tight around me. "Frank is looking into it, but so far, the answer is no."

"You're a dad," I whisper.

"I'm a dad," Cal agrees, but he sounds exhausted. "I don't know how to do this, Belle. I barely know how to be an adult. Now I'm responsible for a whole person, and we're moving and writing an album and going on tour, and I don't know if I can do this."

I take my brother by the shoulders and shake him. "Yes, you can. Every single person in this room is here for you. We will help you. I still think moving is the best plan, especially since Dad lives near Boston. We'll figure out everything else as we go."

Cal nods and takes a deep breath.

"We've got you, man," Mav says, coming up next to him and hugging us both. Kai joins from the other side.

"I have the baby, but I'm hugging you in spirit!" Willa calls, causing all of us to laugh and the tension to break.

"What now?" Kai asks.

"We raise a baby, find Ezra, produce a best-selling album and sell out stadiums," I say.

"Easy," Kai responds.

BELLE

MOVING WITH AN INFANT IS STRESSFUL. Moving with an infant and your brother, who is somehow more dramatic than the baby, is something I wouldn't wish on anyone. I'm not sure how any of us survived it, but we did.

We all officially moved into our new homes yesterday. We were able to purchase new builds in a gated community that just popped up twenty miles outside of Boston. Our houses are all in a row, which I wouldn't have been excited about before Cora. But now? That fiery little girl has captured my heart, and I don't want to be more than a house away from her.

My dad is staying with Cal while we interview nannies. It's not going well. Willa has sat with him for over thirty-eight interviews, and he's hated every single one.

"I can't believe word got out about what happened with you and Brad," Mav says. He's been in a much better head-space since the move.

"I'm honestly surprised it took this long," Kai says, reading the headline of the article Mav just showed him.

"Rockstar Sweetheart Assaulted by Blond Ex-Beau," I read out loud. "I guess that's straight to the point."

"Weird that they have his hair color in there," Willa says.

"I think we've established that titles aren't their strong suit."

"Or the truth," Cal chips in.

"Where's Cora?" I ask him, not bothering to greet him. We're all sitting in Kai and my backyard. It connects to Cal's on one side and Mav's on the other. Willa is on the other side of Cal. We fenced in our yards all together instead of separating them.

"Napping. Dad is in the house with the monitor." Cal used to complain that I didn't even care that he was here anymore and only cared about Cora. He's only partially correct. Cora is now a month old and the sweetest baby. She has Cal wrapped around her finger.

"It's weird that you're a dad," Mav says.

"You say that every day," I point out, laughing. He's not wrong, but Cal is thriving as a dad. It's like he was born just to be Cora's.

With everything that went down with Brad and then the new baby, the studio gave us more time to work on the album. It doesn't hurt that the guy who owns it is married to and obsessed with my cousin.

We all relax and joke with each other until my dad texts Cal that Cora is up from her nap. He bolts back to his house, and we all laugh at him. He's convinced she's going to forget him if she doesn't see his face immediately after she wakes up.

I look over at Kai to see him frowning at his phone.

"What is it?" I ask him.

"Harrison Ray started on Ezra's case last week," he says. I nod. Kai has been good about keeping everyone up to date on that front. Plus, I live with the man and am with him all the time. Now I'm worried the frown is because we lost another PI.

"Did he quit too?" Willa asks, mirroring my thoughts.

"No. He found something."

Patrice Ashley is an author of romantic suspense. She loves writing and reading more than she likes leaving the house. If she isn't doing that, she's playing with her daughter and spending time with her husband. Patrice lives in New England and loves doing basic things like looking at the leaves change while drinking a pumpkin spice latte and wearing brown boots.

also by patrice ashley

Stay Series

Stay

Threshold

Retribution